TANDEM

Lees

Alibi for a Corpse

The trail was cold, to start with. The man had
been dead between nine and fifteen months.
Now there was nothing to go on but the
more or less bare skeleton and hair, and
never had there been a more uncommunicative
set of bones. No dental work, no old
fractures or abnormalities. All anyone could
tell was that the chap was between nineteen
and twenty-two, and between five foot four
and five foot four and a half inches, lightly
built, with long mousey-brown hair.

Detective-Superintendent Tom Pollard felt
none of his usual excitement at the beginning
of a case, just an uncomfortable sense of
frustration and anxiety. In his previous murder
cases the victim had been a recognisable
human being, quickly assuming an identity
and forming a launching pad for the enquiry.
One at least knew whose death one was
investigating. Here it wasn't going to be a
question of just finding out 'whodunnit',
but to whom?

Also by Elizabeth Lemarchand in a Tandem edition

DEATH OF AN OLD GIRL
THE AFFACOMBE AFFAIR

Alibi for a Corpse

Elizabeth Lemarchand

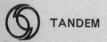

TANDEM

First published in Great Britain by
Rupert Hart-Davis Ltd, 1969

Published by Universal-Tandem Publishing Co Ltd, 1971
Reprinted November 1973
Reprinted March 1976

To Joanna

Tandem Books are published by Tandem Publishing Ltd,
14 Gloucester Road, London SW7
A Howard & Wyndham Company

Made and printed in Great Britain by
Hunt Barnard Printing Ltd, Aylesbury, Bucks.

ONE

THE SMALL boy navigating from the back seat of the car wrestled with the concertina folds of an Ordnance map.

'Don't joggle so,' he said impatiently to his twin sister. 'I can't see a thing. We'll be at the turning in a sec.'

Clare Wainwright hastily steadied her side of the map, and focused on Philip's grubby pointing finger.

'Straight on over the bridge, Dad,' he ordered.

The new A40 sailed up the steep hill beyond the bridge. Derek Wainwright glanced round and grinned at his wife Rachel, who responded by snuggling into the unaccustomed comfort of the passenger seat. Anyway, she thought, he enjoys driving the car . . . They swept up over the crest, and she gave an exclamation, echoed by the children. Appearing with dramatic suddenness the moor swept to the distant horizon, a tumbling sea of muted colours.

A sharp right turn sent Philip sprawling against Clare. Realizing that he had missed his supreme navigational moment he squirmed round to look out of the back window.

'I'd like to know how a person can be expected to see a grotty little signpost like that?' he demanded indignantly. 'It's half-buried in the hedge, anyway.'

'Daddy saw it,' Clare remarked pointedly.

'This is only a farm road, old chap,' Derek told him. 'I expect the farmer put it up himself. He—'

'Do let's stop just a minute and look at the view,' Rachel broke in. 'There's a gate coming.'

They drew up at a gateway on the left. A field of gorse, bracken and heather sloped steeply to a stream. Further down the valley this curved away to the right, round a cluster of farm buildings. In front of these, a low bridge carried the lane over the water to become a track, which rose past a cottage and vanished between two tors into the open moor beyond. Apart from some sheep grazing in the distance there was no sign of life, and the silence was almost audible.

'Can you go absolutely anywhere you like?' Philip asked.

'Anywhere, as long as you keep clear of the mires,' his father told him, 'I can hear larks—shut up a minute.'

Soon, bored with listening, the twins got out of the car and went to the gate. Rachel stretched and let out a contented sigh, resting her head against the window frame, her attractive pale fairness accentuated by signs of tiredness about her eyes. Becoming aware of her husband's silence she turned to look at him, and saw that the *élan* of driving the new car had evaporated. He was sitting abstracted with his hands resting idly on the steering wheel. He glanced up quickly, and met her gaze with a slightly guilty expression.

'I was thinking about this time last year,' he said.

Rachel nodded without speaking. The sickening impact of the car crash, the bright enclosed world of the hospital ward and her grief at her miscarriage, came back with astonishing vividness. The prospect of another child in their very straitened circumstances had been daunting, but its loss heartbreaking, all the same.

'Remember two years ago?' she asked, trying to break out of the memory. 'In that ghastly cheap holiday flat?'

'And now all this.' Derek Wainwright made a vague comprehensive gesture which took in the car and the middle distance. 'Of course I'm grateful to the late Bertha, but I can't help it making me feel more inept than ever. All I've been able to provide is a shoestring.'

'Our only shoestring's been financial, as you know as well as I do. And she was *your* cousin, anyway. Think how much worse you'd be feeling if she'd been mine!'

He laughed and kissed the top of her head.

'True enough, darling. But honestly, I could murder the old girl if she were still above the ground. Why the hell couldn't she have got in touch before, if she was going to leave me the money and the house? Think what a spot of lolly would have meant over our bad patches. When you were ill, for instance.'

'Fantastic to carry on a family feud into the third generation,' Rachel agreed. 'Like an improbable Victorian novel. You know, I still simply can't get over her leaving instructions that you weren't to be contacted until the funeral was over. No sense of proportion. Hallo?'

Two faces had appeared at the window.

'Can't we go on now?'

'We're absolutely starving.'

'You'd better hop in, then,' said Derek, pressing the self-starter. 'Let's hope Nora Pearce, Miss, has laid on a decent tea for us.'

The children giggled as they scrambled into the car. The signature of the late Miss Bertha Wainwright's house-keeper amused them immoderately.

Almost at once a small bungalow appeared on the right of the lane.

'Watchers Way,' Clare read aloud from a board on the gate. 'What a funny name. Oh, look, here's another house coming. P'raps this one's ours.' She bounced up and down on the seat in excitement.

Derek braked sharply.

'Moor View,' he said. 'This is it.'

There was silence as they sat and stared.

'Lavatory brick in a place like this!' Rachel exclaimed in horror. 'How *could* anyone?'

Moor View had been built at the turn of the century by the late Bertha Wainwright's father, a prosperous dealer in animal feedstuffs and other agricultural requirements. Unfortunately his preference for country life had not included appreciation of the rural domestic architecture of the district. Moor View was a late Victorian terrace house in yellow brick, with bulging bay windows. It stood in incongruous isolation, its two sharp gables adorned with terracotta mouldings. A path bisected the rectangular garden with precision, and led to the front door. This was standing open, disclosing an inner glass door with panels of coloured glass.

'Well, we're here,' said Derek, getting out of the car and going round to help Rachel. As she extracted herself, a short, plump woman came out of the house and hurried down the path. Her hands, tightly clasped to her breast, suggested a state of nervous tension.

Leaving Derek to marshal the twins Rachel went forward smiling.

'Miss Pearce? We've got here at last! My husband and I are so awfully grateful to you for holding the fort.'

Nora Pearce was somewhere in her fifties with a kindly, if anxious, face. Her large white teeth were much in evidence as she talked volubly, her sentences running into each other. Rachel noticed that her hazel eyes protruded slightly. As she listened to the flood of statements, she became aware of a muffled altercation in the background, and realized that Philip was having one of his bouts of obstinate shyness. Looking round she intercepted an SOS from her husband, but missed the expression of startled surprise which came over Nora Pearce's face, quickly giving way to one of guardedness.

A very substantial tea had been laid on the dining-room table. Eyeing it, Philip and Clare slid into their places and devoted themselves to steady eating. Flushed with gratification, Nora Pearce plied them with food, while maintaining disjointed general conversation with their parents. At long last they were replete, and began to fidget and look imploring.

'All right,' Rachel said. 'You can go off and explore now, but don't stray too far till you've got the hang of the place.'

'I'll come along soon,' added Derek. 'I'll meet you somewhere around those two tors.'

'They're called Buttertwist and Skiddlebag,' Philip informed him. 'It says so on the map. OK, Dad. Be seeing you.'

The door shut noisily, and a moment later there came the sound of running feet and the slamming of the front gate.

'Such dear little people!' Nora Pearce combined a sigh and a smile.

'I hope you won't find them too much of a good thing,' remarked Derek. 'They do crash about, although we try to keep the row within bounds.'

He held out his cigarette case, but she drew back awkwardly.

'Oh—no, no thank you. I don't smoke. I wonder,' she broke off, and moved her plate the fraction of an inch, 'I wonder if, perhaps, it would be a suitable moment to discuss just one or two matters?'

'Why, of course,' he said. 'I hope you haven't had anything tiresome to cope with?'

'Oh, dear me no! At least...' She flushed deeply, glanced away, and then plunged into rapid speech. 'Of course, it's never very pleasant being in a position of responsibility for a house full of other people's property. Things can be said... Of course, there's an inventory of Miss Wainwright's jewellery and the silver for the insurance company. But there's so much else. Not really valuable things, but such a great quantity, as you'll see presently. So I thought it best to make lists of everything, room by room, and sign them. I have them here for you.'

She fumbled in a holdall on the floor beside her, and extracted two folders which she presented to Derek.

'My dear Miss Pearce,' he said, accepting them with some embarrassment, 'it really wasn't in the least necessary to give yourself all this trouble. My cousin obviously had the greatest confidence in you, and so has her solicitor, I can assure you.'

'Mr Greenwood's said several times in his letters how lucky we've been to have you here to look after things till we could get down,' put in Rachel.

'You are both so kind...' To their discomfiture Nora Pearce produced a handkerchief, wiped her eyes and blew her nose vigorously. 'Do forgive me. If you are quite sure that you have finished your tea, perhaps you would care to have a look round the house now?'

The kitchen premises were north-facing and dreary, their cavernous cupboards stacked with household equipment, china and glass. The Wainwrights exchanged appalled glances.

'Now the little breakfast-room is very bright and cosy,' Nora Pearce told them, 'especially in the mornings with the east sun.'

They inspected it and moved on. The drawing-room felt chilly and unused, in spite of its south aspect and open windows. It was heavily overfurnished, and every available space was crowded with silver and china ornaments. Watercolours in gilt frames and faded photographs almost completely covered the walls.

'Having all this stuff about must have made a frightful lot of work,' Rachel ventured.

'Ah, yes, but you see Miss Wainwright dearly loved to see all her family treasures around her. Right up to her last illness she used to spend hours in cleaning the silver and washing the ornaments. The house was her life. We lived very quietly.'

'And they say we moderns are materialists.'

Nora Pearce looked in a baffled way at Derek, who was standing on the hearth with his hands in his trousers pockets.

'Yes,' she said uncomprehendingly. 'Would you like to go up to the first floor now, Mrs Wainwright?'

They followed her through the bedrooms, each one furnished with a kind of heavy comfort and a total absence of taste. Finally she opened the door of a cupboard on the landing and switched on a light.

'This is the linen cupboard.'

They peered in at shelves laden with stacks of house linen and blankets, all in impeccable order.

'Miss Wainwright always kept up good stocks and bought the very best. She said it was an economy.'

Catching sight of Derek's wry smile Rachel hastily interposed a question about laundry collection and delivery.

'Well, I imagine you've no doubts now about selling the place?' Derek asked when they were alone in their bedroom.

'Heavens no!' Rachel sank on to the end of the bed. 'It's the most gorgeous part of the world, and if the house had been half the size and not utterly hideous, I suppose we might have kept it on for holidays, and faced the distance. But as things are the sooner we get rid of it the better, don't you think?'

'I certainly do, and most of the horrific contents with it. We can pick out anything we want and arrange for it to be packed and taken home at the end of the holiday. Do you think we can persuade the Pearce to stay on and see the furniture sale through, or shall we have to come down again?'

'We could try. Mr Greenwood will probably have some helpful ideas when you see him tomorrow. I say, what about the children?'

'Good Lord! I'd completely forgotten them! Have you any idea where you packed my Marks and Sparks bags?'

Dashing out of the house, the twins had plunged into an ocean of delicious warm air, tangy with the scent of bracken and heather. They were nine years old, fair, blue-eyed, and bursting with life and energy. They pelted down the lane towards the farm, stopping just short of it in unspoken accord. From this point they advanced more cautiously towards the gate.

Across a cobbled yard they saw a long low house of grey granite, with a big porch and massive chimneys. On the left of the yard was an immense ancient barn, facing new and functional buildings on the right. The front door of the house was open, and a broad passage ran straight through to a garden at the back of the house. The figure of a woman flashed across it.

'Let's go down to the stream,' Philip suggested.

They found a line of stepping stones beside the bridge, and made several crossings before running on again. Passing the cottage they breasted the rise between the tors, and finally collapsed panting on the heather at the side of the track. Clare recovered her breath first and sat up to take stock. With a squeak of excitement she grabbed her brother's arm.

'Phil! Look!'

A group of mares and foals drifted into sight from behind Skiddlebag.

'Keep quiet!' he hissed. 'You'll scare them off.'

They rolled over on to their stomachs and lay watching, so absorbed that they failed to hear the rider coming off the moor until he was almost level with them. As they sat up quickly he reined in his pony and gave them a keen look.

'You from Moor View?' he asked brusquely.

He was a powerfully built man with springy black hair, sharp dark eyes and a formidable jaw. Clare drew back a little, but Philip met his stare squarely.

'Yes, we are,' he said. 'It belongs to my father now, and we're staying there for a holiday.'

'Young Wainwrights, are you? That's a different story. Fine old lady, Miss Wainwright was. Enjoyin' yourselves?'

Realizing that they were now identified and accepted they nodded vigorously.

'Please, are those your ponies?' Clare ventured.

'That's right, love. Some o' the Twiggadon ponies, those. You passed the farm backalong.' He jerked his head in the direction of the tors. 'Reg Bickley's my name. Well, be seein' you, I don't doubt.'

He raised his whip in salute, and trotted off, two lithe sheep dogs rising soundlessly from the bracken and bringing up the rear, noses close to the ground. The children watched him disappear over the rise.

'I say, d'you think he might have some ponies we could ride?' breathed Clare.

They began to retrace their steps, discussing this enthralling possibility as they went. There was no sign of their father, and they paused to inspect the cottage. It was built of the same sturdy granite as the farm, and had a small walled garden in front. Philip gave a sudden exclamation.

'Great galloping horses! That's the hugest cat I've ever seen.'

The black and white monster sunning itself on the wall contemplated them appraisingly. Philip had a passion for cats, and advanced with ingratiating noises. It responded by rolling over and purring loudly.

'Puddy-wuddy-woozle,' he crooned, massaging its stomach, while Clare tickled it gently behind the ears.

A harsh shout sent them both springing back in alarm. An extraordinary figure was coming through the gap between Buttertwist and Skiddlebag and striding towards them. Immensely tall, long-limbed and crowned with a wild shock of grey hair it resurrected fairytales of the grimmer sort, and they stood paralysed.

'What the devil d'you mean by teasing my cat?'

It was, after all, only a very tall man, but he was furiously angry, and kept jabbing the ground with the tall staff he carried. Stung by the sheer injustice of the accusation, Philip reacted indignantly.

'We weren't teasing it. We were only stroking it.'

'Well, whatever you were doing, keep your hands off it in future—d'you hear? You're the brats from Moor View, I suppose? Don't let me catch you hanging about round my cottage again.'

He slammed the gate in their faces and went up the path with the cat in his arms. Scarlet with rage Philip snatched up a stone.

'We don't want to come near your beastly cottage!' he shouted.

'What on earth's going on?' Derek Wainwright ran up from the direction of the farm, followed by Reg Bickley and the dogs. As Clare flung herself into his arms and burst into tears Philip unobtrusively dropped the stone again.

On hearing their garbled story the farmer was surprisingly adroit.

'Why, no one takes no notice of old Blow-'is-top Stobart,' he told them. "E don't mean nothin'. Fond o' cats, are you? There's a pack of 'em in the barn, an' kittens, too. Take a look, shall we?'

Returning, he was reassuring to Derek.

'Not to worry, Mr Wainwright. The old boy won't do the kiddies no 'arm. A bit cranky from livin' on 'is own that's all 'tis.'

'How in the world does he come to be living out here?' asked Derek. 'I should have thought you'd need that cottage for a farm hand.'

'So I do, but old Daggs, the chap I bought the farm from twelve years back 'ad sold'n the place, so I can't do nothin' about it, see? 'Twas this way. Daggs was a proper old soak, an' let the farm go right to pieces. Then 'e started sellin' bits an' pieces. Why, the land that bungalow Watchers Way's on, is Twiggadon land b'rights. An' 'e even let off a field for an ole car dump up yonder. Still, 'tis an ill wind as they says. If the place 'adn't bin to pieces twouldn't've bin in my price range, an' that's a fac'. An' Stobart ain't no trouble. 'As 'is milk an' eggs off the missis, an' pays on the nail. 'Alf the time 'e's out on the moor birdwatchin' an' roamin' around, lookin' for all the world like a bleedin' great daddy-long-legs, 'e's that tall an' spindly.'

Derek laughed, and held out his cigarette case.

'The farm looks in pretty good shape now.'

Gratified, Reg Bickley expanded this theme with some complacency.

'How did you get on in that awful winter?' Derek asked him. 'It must have been grim out here.'

'Didn't lose a beast. I'd stocked up well with feed, and got 'em into the yards and home fields, in good time, same as anyone else could've done. We didn't need no 'elicopters droppin' supplies, an' sendin' in bills after as long as yer arm.'

'You must be a good weather prophet. I should have thought most of you hill farmers were.'

For some reason Bickley seemed discomfited by the turn of the conversation.

'There's some as are,' he replied briefly, and glanced round as the twins came out of the barn. 'There won't be no trouble with Stobart, Mr Wainwright, see, so long as the kiddies keeps clear of the cottage an' the bloody old cat. 'E's mazed about it. Anyone care to come along an' lend a 'and with the 'ay in the mornin'?' he asked the children. 'Baler's due afore dark.'

They accepted with enthusiasm, the encounter with Henry Stobart already almost forgotten. That night, however, he troubled Clare's dreams, symbolized by confused shapes of terrifying height and length. She tossed and turned in her sleep, and once cried out.

TWO

The following morning was fine and still, promising a perfect August day. Sounds of the hay baler at work came floating up from Twiggadon Farm, and the moment breakfast was over Philip and Clare melted away. Derek Wainwright, reluctantly putting on a collar and tie, collected a file of correspondence and set off in the car for the solicitor's office in Bridgeford, twenty miles distant. Rachel had agreed that nothing was to be gained by sorting the contents of the house at this stage, and having ascertained that Nora Pearce's helper had arrived, made for the garden and the rare luxury of an undisturbed and absolutely free morning.

She found a pleasant spot and installed herself in a deck-chair with a newspaper. In the intervals of glancing through it she gazed across at the moor, which was already quivering in a heat haze. Derek was beginning to accept the situation more easily, she thought with satisfaction. What an incredibly marvellous difference a reasonable amount of money made to one's life. Her thoughts drifted happily from the improvements to be made to their house at Wrilburn, to the question of schools for the twins, and on to the alluring prospect of a completely new autumn outfit for herself ...

2

It was with dismay that she suddenly heard the clink of china, and turned to see Nora Pearce approaching with a laden tray. There were two cups on it, and she roused herself to be welcoming.

'How lovely,' she said untruthfully. 'Do bring another chair for yourself.'

As they sat drinking coffee Rachel wondered if it were a good opportunity to enquire into Nora Pearce's future plans, with a view to asking her to stay on, at any rate until the sale of the furniture had taken place. She decided on some tentative probing.

'It seems so extraordinary that neither my husband nor myself ever saw Miss Wainwright,' she remarked. 'I expect you know that there was a frightful feud between the two branches of the family. And now she has simply transformed our life through her will.'

Nora Pearce set down her half-empty coffee cup on the tray with meticulous care.

'I, too, owe her more than I can ever say,' she replied at last. 'All these years in this dear place . . .' She broke off, her voice uncertain, and sat gazing down the valley. 'And now this wonderful legacy. I do hope that neither you nor Mr Wainwright think . . .'

Rachel hastened to reassure her. They were both delighted about it.

'Money isn't everything,' she went on, 'but it does make a difference, let's face it. Derek and I haven't had too easy a time, you know. He's the Curator of the Wrilburn Museum, quite a good job as they go, but curatorships aren't very well paid on modern standards. I worked, too, when we were first married, but then the twins came along and put a stop to that. And we've had a lot of bad luck one way and another, especially over illness. Last year I was pregnant again, and had a very bad miscarriage. To crown it all, just before I came out of hospital we found dry rot in the house we were struggling to buy through a mortgage. It's been a terribly difficult year—at least, until we heard what Miss Wainwright had done for us.'

Nora Pearce's eyes were moist with sympathy.

'Oh, Mrs Wainwright, what a terrible struggle you both have had! And to think that you can put it all behind you now! Of course, your health is the very first consideration. You must have a complete rest ... the moor air is such a wonderful restorative ... and not concern yourself with the housekeeping at all. I really think this is the moment for me to put my little plan to you. For the future, you know, in case you are worrying about how to manage when you can't be down here.'

With dismay Rachel realized what was probably coming, but before she could speak Nora Pearce had hurried on.

'Well,' she said, clasping her hands so tightly that the knuckles were whitened, 'it's like this, you know. One can't leave these moor houses empty for long—certainly not in the winter months. It's most unwise. They soon get very damp without fires and regular airing. Now, I should be so happy—so very happy—to become your resident caretaker. You are such dear, kind people. Without salary, of course. I shouldn't think of taking a penny. Just in return for light and fuel, and you can rest assured that I should be most economical. And with part of my legacy I should buy a little secondhand car, and take a part-time post in Bridgeford. And you would be able to run down for a visit whenever you could manage it, and find everything in apple-pie order!'

She raised her clasped hands, let them fall back on her lap and smiled at Rachel like an excited child.

While listening to the spate of words Rachel had hurriedly searched for the kindest way of breaking unwelcome news.

'It's most awfully good of you, Miss Pearce,' she said,

when at last it came to an end, 'and I know Derek will appreciate it as much as I do, but the fact is we've come to the conclusion that it really wouldn't be sensible for us to keep on the house, and we're going to put it up for sale.'

An unbecoming deep red spread over Nora Pearce's face, slowly ebbing to leave a startling pallor. Dreading an emotional scene Rachel plunged into speech once more.

'You see,' she hurried on, 'it's so far from home for the twins' half-terms and any odd week-ends Derek can take. The traffic's really frightful in summer, too. We think a much smaller place nearer home would be more practical, although this is an absolutely lovely part of the world, of course. But please don't think there's any hurry at all for you to make plans. We're hoping you'll be able to help us for some months ahead, if you feel you can.'

She suddenly realized that Nora Pearce had not heard a word, but was completely absorbed in mentally contemplating a situation which she found quite shattering. Acting on impulse she touched her gently on the knee.

'We're most anxious to help you in every possible way when the time comes to make a change. We wondered if, perhaps, you'd care for some of the furniture for a little flat?'

The professional mask of a housekeeper-companion dropped over Nora Pearce's face with an almost audible click.

'It's so kind of you to take such an interest,' she said brightly. 'I shall have to put on my thinking cap, shan't I? Stupidly it had never occurred to me that you wouldn't be keeping on the house. Now, I must be running along to see how Mrs Steer is managing in the kitchen.'

She gave a quick nervous smile, gathered up the tray and hurried off.

Finding herself unable to recapture her pleasantly

relaxed state of mind, Rachel presently set off for a stroll. Turning left on leaving the garden she wandered up the lane, considering possible ways of helping Nora Pearce to launch out on a new life. She had forgotten the existence of the bungalow called Watchers Way, and started on being spoken to by someone standing at the gate.

'Oh, good morning,' she said, feeling foolish. 'Such a beautiful one, isn't it?'

The speaker had been an unkempt-looking woman with faded blonde hair and strange, lifeless grey eyes. She could have been any age between thirty and fifty-five.

'I'm Sybil Pendine,' she said abruptly. 'No doubt you've been well primed about me by the housekeeper.'

There was no mistaking the malice in the last sentence. Rachel had a flash-back to Nora Pearce's remark at the tea table, that 'things could be said'.

'Actually, I haven't heard her mention you,' she replied coolly.

There was a silence, and she was on the point of walking away when the woman spoke again.

'I've got·a message for you—or rather for your husband. From Bertha Wainwright.'

'From Bertha Wainwright?' Rachel echoed in bewilderment.

'The fact that people have passed over is only a barrier to the earth-bound,' Sybil Pendine said contemptuously. 'I and my circle are in constant contact with the Beyond. The message I have to give your husband is that all is forgiven. Henry is there, too, and someone whose name was difficult to make out; the spirit writing often becomes illegible if there are hostile influences at work. It looked like Virtue. That's all I have to tell you.'

She turned abruptly on her heel and went up the path into the bungalow.

Rachel stood staring after her for several moments. Then, feeling that she had had more than enough of eccentricity and odd behaviour for one morning, she retraced her steps and made for the farm in search of the twins.

Derek was all but late for lunch, and Rachel could only warn him hastily not to mention the sale of the house. To her relief Nora Pearce seemed quite normal, apart from being rather less talkative than usual. Any shortfall on her part was more than made up by the twins, who chattered endlessly about their morning on the farm, and the exciting discovery that there were two young Bickleys, at present on a visit to an aunt, but due home in a few days' time. They each had a pony, and Mr Bickley had said that he was sure some riding could be fixed up if Mr Wainwright was willing. From this the conversation passed naturally to possible expeditions on the moor.

After lunch the family went into the garden. Philip and Clare rested under protest for half an hour, and then hurried off again, announcing that they were going to explore the stream. As the gate clicked behind them Derek looked enquiringly at Rachel.

'Did Nora Pearce go through the roof when you told her we were selling the place?' he asked. 'Sorry you got landed with breaking it.'

'No, she didn't blow up, or anything like that. She was just appallingly upset, as if life had suddenly ceased to have any meaning for her. She looked about twenty years older. And when I tried to be sympathetic the bright professional façade descended, and I was quite definitely warned off.'

'Perhaps she'll be a bit more expansive about what she wants to do when she gets to know us better.'

'I only hope she will : it's so difficult to know how we can help her. Then, after she'd gone off, I went for a stroll up the lane and met a woman who lives in that bungalow we passed. She seems most peculiar, too. She obviously loathes N.P.—there's no love lost either way. She went on to say she was in touch with Bertha Wainwright in the Beyond, and had a message for you.'

'Good God ! I suppose she's a spiritualist crank of some sort. What was this message ?'

'That everything is forgiven on the Other Side. And there were greetings from someone called Henry, and somebody else whose name she couldn't quite get, but seemed like Virtue.'

'That's damned odd,' said Derek thoughtfully. 'The family feud started between Bertha's father, Henry Wainwright, and a cousin of his who was my great-grandfather, and called Vercherre Wainwright. It was an old family name. I wonder how she could have got on to that ?'

'I didn't like her at all. Actually, I thought she was a bit spooky, and she was really spiteful about poor old N.P. . . . Much more important, though, how did you get on with the solicitor ?'

Derek reported a satisfactory morning. Mr Greenwood had been most pleasant and helpful. He had agreed that the house had better be sold, and a telephone call to a firm of estate agents had resulted in an arrangement being made for one of the partners to come out and inspect the place on the following day.

'Greenwood seems quite optimistic that it'll sell, rather to my surprise. He thinks they may suggest an auction.'

It was a hot afternoon, and presently their conversation became desultory. Glancing at Derek, Rachel saw that he was asleep. She relaxed in her chair, watching a fuchsia alive with bees. Their comings and goings set up an endless unvarying humming note . . . She drifted imperceptibly into sleep herself.

The thudding of running feet began to penetrate Rachel's consciousness. She was at first aware of rhythmic beats, which linked in her drowsy mind with the image of someone in a hurry. Then the urgency behind the beats came through to her disturbingly. She woke, and sprang to her feet as the twins began struggling with the unfamiliar gate. Before she could reach it herself it burst open, and they tore towards her, their faces ashen. As Derek came dashing up, Clare grabbed her wildly.

'Mummy! Mummy!' she screamed. 'Those awful, awful long fingers!'

She was suddenly and violently sick.

Derek dropped on to his knees and took Philip by the shoulders.

'Just tell us what's frightened you, old man,' he said quietly.

The boy's eyes were unnaturally bright, and his breath was coming in great gasps.

'It's—it's a skelerton,' he gulped. 'We found some old cars in a field, an' looked in one of the boots. Its—its arm fell out.'

THREE

'FAG?' ASKED Dr Alan Pulman of the Wintlebury Forensic Laboratory, holding out a crumpled packet. 'I thought you Yard blokes would be along. It's leaked out that Bridgeford can't match up the remains with any of their disappearances.'

He broke off and stared hard at Detective-Superintendent Tom Pollard of the CID. 'Hey, wait a bit ... I've got it! About a month ago in the chattier Press. Youngest Super at the Yard, wasn't it? On the strength of some of those headline-hitting cases of yours, I take it?'

'I wouldn't know.' Pollard flicked his cigarette lighter and held it out. He decided that he liked Alan Pulman, a large red-faced extrovert. 'Anyway, time's on my side. This is my sergeant, by the way. Sergeant Toye.'

The pathologist nodded to Toye. Expelling a mouthful of smoke he slapped the file in front of him.

'It's all here. You'll find a duplicate at Bridgeford. Nothing more we can tell you, I'm afraid.'

'I realize that,' said Pollard, 'but somehow it's more satisfactory to hear it straight from the horse's mouth, if I may put it that way. So I thought I'd drop in for a few minutes on the way down, if it isn't wasting your time too outrageously.'

'Not a bit. Pleased to meet you. Besides, it's a damned intriguing case. And it's not as though you're dashing down to salvage perishable clues : the trail's stone cold after all this time.'

'Between nine and fifteen months, you say?'

'Yea. Within those limits I'm prepared to be definite.' Alan Pulman opened the file and turned over some pages of typescript. 'The boot cover fitted badly, but I've allowed for that. Establishing identity's another matter, though, and I hope you enjoy the job. We'd nothing to go on but the more or less bare skeleton and the hair, and I've never struck a more uncommunicative set of bones. No dental work, no old fractures or abnormalities. Not a clue as to how the chap was done.'

'I suppose he was done, and not run down accidentally by a car, and then dumped by someone who'd panicked?'

'I'd thought of that one myself, but unless the chap died from shock without receiving fatal injuries there'd have been a fractured skull or stoved-in ribs, or some definite evidence. Besides, surely it's highly improbable that if it had been an ordinary road accident no enquiries would have been made by friends or relatives?'

'What about the smashed face?'

'Only superficial damage : by itself it wouldn't have caused death. A panic measure afterwards, I imagine, to conceal identity in case some nosey-parker opened the boot too soon. All we can tell you is that the chap was between nineteen and twenty-two, and between five foot four and five foot four and a half inches. He was lightly built, and had long mousey brown hair. All details in here, and endless photographs. Take a look.'

Pollard contemplated a series of macabre studies of a skeleton. It lay on its right side, with knees drawn up. The left arm hung down out of the car boot as if groping for the ground.

'Bloodstains?' he asked, examining a close-up of the face.

'Divil a one. We removed the car bodily on a lorry, you know, and brought it up here, and our chaps pretty well took it to pieces. Not a trace of blood or anything else but the usual sort of muck in the boot—dried mud, and what-have-you. Maggots, of course. All nicely analysed and docketed for you, but I doubt whether it's in the least relevant. No fibres or threads. Looks as though the body was put in stark naked.'

'After rigor had gone off, and the face had stopped bleeding,' Pollard said thoughtfully. 'I'm afraid you're only too right about the car itself being irrelevant. I gather the dump's been discontinued for ages?'

'About fifteen years, Bridgeford says. Chap who started it went smash almost at once. There are only a handful of cars there.'

'Are they obvious?'

'You can't see them from the main road, if that's what you mean. Personally, I'd put my money on one of the locals. It would be a nice handy place for dumping a stiff, one dark night, and people go to bed early in the country. And talking of locals there's a decent one round the corner. I usually go along for an early snack at lunch-time. What about it, before you push on?'

As Sergeant Toye manoeuvred the police car through Wintlebury's heavy traffic, Pollard studied the large scale map which he had just bought. He saw at once that Twiggadon was by no means the isolated hamlet which he had at first imagined. It was just off a good second-class road from Bridgeford, and only twenty miles distant from it, while Torcastle, a smaller town, was only ten miles away. Moreover it was in one of the leading holiday areas of the whole country. His lively imagination at once peopled the neighbouring moor with innumerable summer picnic parties, arriving by car and establishing themselves with folding tables and chairs and a wealth of gay plastic equipment. Presently, after eating, the more active members would wander off to explore. Even a few stranded cars would be quite a conspicuous feature of the landscape to anyone at the Twiggadon end. He saw, too, that the lane from the main road petered out at the farm, but a track went on out into the moor and eventually reached a stone circle called 'The Nine Watchers'. He had come across archaeological enthusiasts before, and it was safe to assume that a good many people had gone down the Twiggadon lane to inspect the circle over the years, presumably passing close to the car dump. Farms weren't the self-contained units they used to be, either. They were visited by tradesmen's vans, Ministry officials, lorries—the lot.

Pollard frowned, and shifted his long legs which always got cramped in a car. Obviously it was a waste of time to speculate about who, other than the locals, was likely to know of the dump's existence until he'd seen for himself just how visible and accessible it was. Anyway, people living on the spot were the obvious first line of investigation. He wondered how much ground Bridgeford would have covered.

Folding up the map and pushing it into the dashboard, he realized that the excitement which he always felt at the beginning of a case had mysteriously evaporated, leaving in its place an uncomfortable feeling of frustration and anxiety. It came to him that the frustration was linked with the stark anonymity of the photographs of the skeleton. In all his previous murder cases the victim had been a recognisable human being, quickly assuming an identity and forming a launching pad for the enquiry. Here it wasn't just finding out 'whodunit', but to whom?

If he knew anything at all about crime detection this was going to be one hell of a long, slow job. This was what was biting him, of course—in his first job after his promotion, blast it. He could see the whole thing fizzling out in dreary failure after endless protracted enquires... chaps who'd been passed over talking among themselves... Jane, on top of the world in their first house, with their first baby due at Christmas, having to share the humiliation.

A flash of insight revealed to him that prospective paternity was making him anxious to cut a dash for the benefit of the new arrival, and he grinned and promptly felt better.

'Main road to Bridgeford, sir?' asked Toye. 'We could turn right, and get on to that road that goes past Twiggadon, just to take a look in passing.'

'Better stick to the book. You can bet your bottom dollar that Bridgeford would get to hear we hadn't gone down to them direct for briefing. Here goes : Bridgeford straight ahead. Step on it when you can.'

Pollard sat considering possible variations on the usual procedures for establishing identity. Presently he glanced at Toye.

'What are your reactions to the job up-to-date?'

Toye skimmed dexterously round a couple of pantechnicons travelling much too close together.

'Funny thing,' he said unexpectedly. 'It puts me in mind of a game we played at home when I was a kid. You threw dice and moved little metal cars along a board. Like Snakes and Ladders, it was. Only you couldn't get started till you'd thrown a six. I used to get into a proper sweat waiting for one to come up.'

Pollard looked at him in astonishment.

'You're right on the beam. Sweat's going to be the

operative word until we find out whose murder we're investigating, and can get started.'

The atmosphere of taking over a case was never twice the same, Pollard reflected. There were five of them in the Super's office at Bridgeford's police station. Superintendent Puckeridge was massive and bull-necked, Major Preece-Rilby, silver-haired and clipped of utterance and moustache. Inspector Crake, who had been in charge of enquiries into the Twiggadon case up-to-date, gave the impression of keeping his thoughts to himself. The usual opening gambit, of overwork and undermanning having made it necessary to call in the Yard, had not been proffered. Instead, it was being made abundantly clear that the Super and the CC felt that the discovery of the skeleton had landed them with an unreasonable and virtually insoluble problem owing to the special character of their area, and that they were only too anxious to pass the buck to the Yard. Pollard sat listening to a duologue on the annual influx of summer visitors.

'Cool half-million of 'em last year, the Tourist Board says.'

'Come swarming in like lemmings . . . cars, coaches, caravans. Great unwashed louts cadging lifts.'

'Roads choked . . . nuisances on farm land, and gates left open . . . shoplifting.'

'Life absolutely intolerable for residents. Blaring transistors . . . filthy litter.'

'Force double the size of ours couldn't cope with 'em around here. A dozen murders could've been committed end of July and beginning of August last year, when we'd Dincombe on our hands into the bargain.'

'Good God!' interrupted Pollard, suddenly alerted. 'Dincombe! It must have been sheer hell with that to cope with as well.'

Major Preece-Rilby unconsciously assumed the bearing of a man being decorated by his Sovereign.

'Magnificent work . . . disaster area . . . whole rescue operation co-ordinated . . . Force personally congratulated by the Home Secretary.' He waved a hand in the direction of a framed letter on the wall.

Pollard hastened to add his own congratulations.

'I take it,' he went on, tactfully steering the conversation back to the matter in hand, 'that you don't think this is a local crime?'

'Put it this way,' replied Superintendent Puckeridge. 'First and foremost, as you'll see in the report from the Forensic at Wintlebury, there's not a clue as to who the chap was, and no proof that he was murdered, come to that. Inquest was adjourned, as you know, pending enquiries. Then the remains aren't related to any reported disappearance in these parts. I'll grant you there are plenty of unreported ones among young people these days, but this isn't London.' He eyed Pollard and Toye with disapproval. 'No big cities down here, and folk know each other's business only too well. Nobody's come forward with information, not even with something made up to get themselves into the papers. So it seems to me it stands to reason that if the remains aren't local, the chap who bunged 'em into the car wasn't either.'

Pollard agreed that it amounted to a strong probability.

'All the same,' he went on, 'somebody smashed up the young man's face, kept the body hidden somewhere, and finally got it into the boot without being spotted. Quite a job at a time of year when there are so many people about. To my mind it calls for a long hard look at the Twiggadon locals.'

'Inspector Crake's carried out preliminary enquiries up there, and taken statements,' Major Preece-Rilby interposed. 'Spent a lot of time on it, too. Got your report here, Crake?'

'Yes, sir,' replied the inspector, speaking almost for the first time, and producing a folder.

At Pollard's suggestion that he and Toye should digest the report before deciding on their next step, the CC broke up the conference with alacrity, while assuring him that any assistance required would instantly be forthcoming, however inconvenient this might be at the height of the tourist season.

When they had migrated to the small room allotted to the Yard men as an office, Pollard asked Crake about the Dincombe tragedy in order to break the ice.

'Didn't a landslide dam up a valley during the night?'

The inspector produced a large-scape map and indicated the long narrow gorge known as Dincombe Cleave, immediately above the village. An abnormally wet July, he explained, had culminated in four days of torrential rain with hardly a let-up. Then, late in the evening of July 29, a violent thunderstorm started up, and went on for most of the night.

'That's how it was nobody at Dincombe recognized the noise of the landslide, and raised the alarm. They just took it for thunder. The stream was in flood, and it didn't take long for a whacking great lake to get ponded back behind the rocks and stuff that'd come down. Then, about three o'clock in the morning it bust through, and millions o' tons o' water came down on the village.'

'What was the final death roll?' asked Toye.

'Nineteen.'

'Didn't you have some trouble over identification, if I remember?' Pollard said.

'There was one chap who'd only come into the place the evening before, and put up in a cottage that was clean swept away, and the whole family drowned as well. A

32

young fellow who'd been hiking along the coast, he'd told somebody. The papers and the telly were a help, putting out a description, though, and you'd be surprised at the parents who came chasing down, saying they hadn't a clue where their kids had got to. In the end he turned out to be the half-brother of a gentleman over to Torcastle, on the other side of the county.'

'I only wish we'd got a recognizable description of our chap for them to put out,' Pollard said with feeling. 'Were you the first to go out to Twiggadon on Tuesday afternoon, when the call came through?'

'That's right, sir. With Dr Mead, who's the police surgeon, and Constable Brown. Soon as we saw it wasn't a recent job, I rang back to the Super, and he got on to Wintlebury right away, for the experts to come down. They got started that same evening. I'd rung from Moor View, the house belonging to the gentleman whose kiddies had found the remains.'

'What I can't understand,' put in Toye, 'is why they hadn't found 'em long before, the way kids poke their noses into things.'

'The family'd only arrived the day before. The house'd just been left to this Mr Wainwright by an elderly relative who died about a month back.'

Pollard groaned.

'That's one possible witness gone.'

'Mr and Mrs Wainwright weren't too keen for me to question the kiddies,' pursued Inspector Crake. 'Twins of nine, they are, and the little girl had taken a nasty shock. But after a bit they agreed to me having a word with 'em, and it was clear as daylight they'd nothing useful to tell. They'd come paddling up the stream from the bridge, spotted the cars, and gone to have a look at 'em. They'd opened several other boots before they came on the remains. So it looks as though we can wash out the whole family, and I'd say the same for the housekeeper. She's a Miss Pearce, who'd been with the old lady ever since the war. Bit of a twitterer, but quite sensible. You can't see the dump from Moor View, and she was sure she'd never noticed any stranger coming out of the field.'

'Can you see the dump from the other houses?'

There was a pause, during which Crake seemed cagey again.

'Not that you can have had time to check up on all this,' Pollard added tactfully.

'I've had time enough, sir,' Crake said reluctantly. 'Trouble is, I haven't been able to get a statement from the people in two of 'em.'

'You mean, they refused to play?'

Crake, looking unhappy, produced a rough plan from the folder containing his report.

'The dump's in this field, on the left as you go down,' he said, marking the spot with a cross. 'This house nearly opposite is called Watchers Way. It's one of those bungalows with a room in the roof, and there's no doubt you'd get a good view of the cars from the window. A Mrs Pendine lives there on her own. She's a widow, about fifty, and I'd say she's pretty well round the bend. All I could get when I asked her if she'd ever seen any suspicious behaviour in the field, was a lot of boloney about a Road of Death running down the valley, and some rot about the past and the present being all the same. Constable Haycraft, who's stationed over to Wilkaton, says she's one of those spiritualists, and holds seances for calling up the departed. The country folk say she's a witch. You come on real pockets of backwardness in some of these places,' he added apologetically.

'Good Lord!' exclaimed Pollard, much intrigued. 'You can have first innings at Watchers Way, Toye. Carry on, Inspector.'

'Now this place here's called Farm Cottage sir. Gentleman known as Mr Henry Stobart lives there. He wouldn't come to the door, but asked me what I wanted through the window. When he heard, he said I could go to hell, and slammed it shut. Constable Haycraft says he's a "recloose". Came there soon after the war, and has lived there all on his own ever since. Even does for himself, washing and all. Watches birds—feathered ones, I mean—and writes about them. As the CC and the Super had started talking of calling you gentlemen in by then, no further steps have been taken in regard to Mr Stobart.'

Pollard and Toye exchanged fleeting winks.

'Very wise,' commented Pollard. 'Much better wait until there's more to go on before we start hinting at bringing him along here if he won't talk.'

'At the farm, now,' Crake continued, with signs of returning confidence, 'there might be just the hint of a lead. I won't say more than that. The farmer's Reg Bickley, a hefty aggressive sort of chap, with a jaw like a bulldog. He owns the place, and lives there with his wife and two kiddies. I didn't see them, as they're away staying with an auntie. The dump's on Bickley's land, started in the time o' the farmer Bickley bought from. This chap let the field to a fellow who wanted to start up in scrap metal dealing, but he went smash quite soon, and that was the end of the dump. You can't see it from the farm, although you can from the cottage, as I should have mentioned. Bickley and his missus had never seen any funny business—or so they said, but Bickley went on about the summer visitors, and said he wouldn't put murder past half o' them. Now, when I was getting the lowdown from Haycraft, he said there was talk in Wilkaton about this time last year that Bickley'd caught some young hooligan chasing his ponies on a scooter, and had beaten him up. But no complaint was made, so Haycraft took no steps, and didn't put in a report.'

'Any chance that it was a Bridgeford youth?' asked Pollard thoughtfully.

'I've started enquiries in likely parts of the town,' replied Crake, with a touch of self-congratulation. 'But as you know, sir, we've had no report of a disappearance, not in that age group. Much more likely to have been a summer visitor, I'd say.'

Considerably later that evening Pollard stretched, and looked across the paper-strewn table at Toye.

'A very small point,' he said, 'but it strikes me as just a bit curious. In his statement this Wainwright bloke says he's never been in Twiggadon before this week. You'd expect him to have been on visiting terms with a relative who was leaving him a house.'

Toye considered.

'Funny that he'd *never* been down,' he agreed, 'not even for the funeral.'

'She might have been buried somewhere else, I suppose. Or even cremated. Well, more seems to have come out of the bag than I expected. We've got a recluse, a reputed witch, and an alleged beater-up of a youth. Something to start on, anyway.'

'There's the summer visitors, too,' Toye said demurely.

'Too right. Let's join them, shall we? I feel just about ready for some grub. Got your transistor?'

FOUR

AFTER AN early breakfast on the following morning Pollard and Toye called in at the police station on their way to Twiggadon.

'Nothing doing,' Pollard said, as he came out again and got into the car. 'Not a cheep's come in from any other part of the country about a vanished youth of the right age and size.'

In spite of the lack of news and the depressingly grey day, he had recovered his usual zest. As they drove out of Bridgeford and made for the open country he once more ran over the case in his mind, reviewing the steps already taken. Passing on to immediate priorities he decided to call on the Wainwrights first, as their household had sparked off the inquiry. Then an attempt had better be made to get a statement out of Henry Stobart, unless he had vamoosed for the day to avoid a possible call by the police. The fact that the car dump was on Bickley's land was a useful pretext for a call at the farm : important not to put him on his guard until Crake had finished investigations about the alleged beating-up.

They left the main road after a few miles, and were soon on the outskirts of the moor. Toye pulled out to pass two cars packed with children, dogs and picnic gear. A little further on they passed a Dormobile and two caravans which were parked in a disused quarry.

I mustn't get a fixation on the Twiggadon locals, Pollard told himself. The place is anything but off the map.

The gradient began to flatten out. Toye, a driver who always did his homework before starting out, remarked that they'd be at the Twiggadon turning any time now. The road made a slight curve to the left, and half-way up the final rise they nearly overshot the inconspicuous signpost which had aroused the indignation of Philip Wainwright.

'Let's park here,' said Pollard, pointing to a level stretch of rough grass between the road and the low banked-up hedge. 'We'll be less obvious on our feet, and I want to spy out the land a bit first.'

As Alan Pulman had said, the cars could not be seen from the road. The convex slope of the ground cut them off, together with the houses. On the left, beyond the stream, the moor was a vast sombre expanse under the sunless sky, the rocks crowning the tors black and menacing. Toye said that as far as he was concerned anybody could have it.

'Wait till the day brightens up a bit,' Pollard told him, turning and walking across the road to look in the opposite direction. There were signs of an old track continuing the line of the Twiggadon lane, which he pointed out to Toye.

'Wonder if that's the spook woman's Road of Death?' he said. 'It's one of the ancient trackways over the moor, and probably has some legend tied up with it. We'll try it as an opening gambit with her. Let's go along to the dump now. Crake said it was the first gate on the left.'

The field sloped down towards the houses as well as in the direction of the stream, and the huddle of derelict cars was on the former slope, near the hedge bordering the lane. There were not more than a dozen, together with a scatter of miscellaneous junk. Toye, a vintage car enthusiast, bore down on them eagerly.

'Coupla bull-nosed Morrises,' he announced. 'Here's the body and wheel of a Model T Ford. Engine and chassis went for scrap, I expect. Why, here's a Bean Tower radiator and—'

'Come off it,' said Pollard, amused. 'We aren't at Lord Montagu's place at Beaulieu. Look, this must be where the car was. The Wintlebury chaps must have borrowed a tractor to drag it clear. An old Austin Sixteen . . . Can you see any other which would have done as well from the murderer's point of view?'

'None of this lot has outsize boots,' replied Toye, running a critical eye over the battered assembly. 'That Vauxhall Twenty's would have been about the same size, but the car's much harder to get at behind all that stuff. I reckon the Austin was the obvious choice.'

Pollard nodded, and began to consider to what extent the dump was an obvious feature of the landscape. Anyone on the far side of the stream could not fail to see it, and could easily come over and investigate. Hikers crossing the bridge and following the track out into the moor could see it, too, although the hedge screened it from the lane. Of the four Twiggadon houses, the farm and Moor View were out of sight, but the cottage had an unobstructed view up the valley, and Watchers Way was only a short distance down the lane. Pollard went to the spot formerly occupied by the Austin Sixteen, and looked up at the dormer window in the roof of the bungalow. As he did so, he thought he detected a swift movement of withdrawal.

'Come away from the hedge,' he said to Toye. 'You never know whose ears are flapping on the other side.'

Standing in the middle of the field they discussed the technical problems involved in getting the body into the boot.

'I'm quite certain it was done by night,' Pollard insisted. 'I can't believe anyone would risk it in daylight, in what's almost a public place. The simplest thing would be to bring a car to the gate, but could this have been done without attracting attention at Watchers Way or even at Moor View, which isn't much further on?'

'If the car'd come from the top it could coast down in neutral, but you'd either have to leave the engine running, or start up again, and I don't think anyone in Watchers Way could help hearing. Quite small sounds wake you if they're out of the ordinary, as a car would be in this lane in the middle of the night. Coming up from the farm you'd have to pass both houses, and the engine'd make more noise anyway.'

'Let's suppose Bickley did the job. This is his field. Couldn't he have driven up here with the body hidden under some sacks, without anyone paying any attention? He could have taken a look round, and then heaved it into a ditch if there is one, and come up on foot during the night to finish the job.'

They made a careful search, but found no ditch or other possible hiding-place. Out in the lane once more they paused to look back towards the road.

'An outsider could have done it, you know,' said Pollard. 'I can visualize some sort of invalid's chair with wheels, which would fold and go in the back of a car. It's a thousand to one against anything coming along this road in the middle of the night, just when you were yanking the corpse out of your own boot and tying it into the chair. You'd have oiled the wheels, and arrive down at this gate without making a sound.'

Toye considered.

'You'd have to have a torch. Else you'd risk tripping over some of the junk in there, and making the whale of a clatter. Still, a light'd be much less of a risk than a car.

40

All the same, sir, I'd put my money on its being a local job.'

'You're probably right,' Pollard agreed, 'but I maintain it could have been a physical possibility for someone from outside, provided he'd reconnoitred the cars first, of course. Come on, let's go and meet the Wainwright family.'

A beach bag bulging with towels and swim suits, and a large basket of food lay on the grass inside the gate of Moor View and children's excited voices were coming from the house. The next moment two small fair-haired figures in shorts appeared in the doorway and came dashing out, only to stop short in surprise.

'Hallo!' said Pollard. 'You must be the Wainwright twins. Is your father anywhere about?'

For a second they stared at the detectives, interested but a little wary, like a pair of young animals.

'We'll go and tell him,' said the boy. 'C'm on, Clare.'

They vanished into the house. Perhaps a boy like that, thought Pollard with sudden excitement, with a fantastic potential for life and action . . . Or a girl . . . She was utterly different, although the physical resemblance was so strong. A bit withdrawn already. Absorbing to watch a woman develop from scratch . . .

He hastily slammed down on his private life as Derek Wainwright arrived.

'Good morning, sir,' he said, producing his official card. 'Are you just off for the day? Or could you spare me a few minutes first?'

'By all means, Superintendent. We can't start till my wife comes back from Wilkaton with the car. Won't you come in?'

He led the way into the drawing-room, indicated chairs and offered cigarettes.

'I don't wonder you feel staggered,' he said, smiling.

'Incredible, isn't it? I've just inherited the house and its entire contents from an elderly cousin, who'd lived in it for nearly seventy years.'

Responding easily in the same vein Pollard studied Derek Wainwright with interest, noting the intelligent brow, strong chin and sensitive eyes and mouth. Which strain comes uppermost in his character, he wondered? As the conversation progressed his trained observation registered a slight wariness. Is it chronic, he speculated, or specific in relation to me or the present situation? He decided to put out a feeler.

'I expect you know this part of the world well, as you've had a relative living here for so many years?' he remarked casually.

'You'll hardly believe it,' Derek Wainwright replied, 'but last Monday was the first time I set foot in this house. My late cousin—she was a very distant one, incidentally—carried on a long-standing family feud to the bitter end. Her solicitor tells me that she had a frightful tussle with herself about leaving me the place and her money, but I'm the only surviving Wainwright, and I suppose the Victorian sense of property triumphed. Have you ever seen a more shatteringly hideous house? We've already put it up for sale.'

All true, and my question skilfully sidetracked, thought Pollard with mounting interest.

'It does rather hit you between the eyes,' he agreed, 'and your visit has got off to a most unpleasant start, I'm afraid. Are the children badly upset?'

'Clare certainly was. After the first shock scientific curiosity got the upper hand with Philip. The odd thing is that they don't seem in the least bothered at the thought of a murder having happened just up the lane. They're quite excited at the thought of Scotland Yard detectives turning up. If you could possibly just speak to them they'd be thrilled to bits.'

'We certainly will,' Pollard promised. 'Of course, there's no actual proof that a murder has been committed, you know. Not up to the present. All we can say definitely is that the skeleton belonged to a young man of about twenty, but we haven't established his identity yet. There are absolutely no distinguishing marks, like dental work or old fractures.'

'How can you even begin to track him down, if that's the case? Surely it must have happened years ago for the poor chap to have been reduced to bare bones?'

'Not all that long ago,' Pollard replied. 'We know pretty well when it happened. Death occurred sometime between May and November of last year. If we take the half-way mark, it could have been round about this time last year. So we've got something to work on. We're starting an intensive enquiry about any strangers seen around here then.'

With a small thrill of excitement he saw Derek Wainwright's hand stop dead in the act of returning his cigarette to his mouth. There was a pause, slightly too long to be normal, before he spoke.

'That's going to be a bit of a problem for you,' he said, without looking at Pollard. 'You'd be surprised at the number of hikers who come along here.'

'I was rather afraid of that,' Pollard answered. 'However, it's quite astonishing what you can unearth if you stick at it long enough. By the way, I understand that your late cousin's housekeeper is still here. We might begin our enquiries by having a chat with her, if she's available.'

As he spoke a car drew up at the gate with a couple of toots, and the children could be heard running through the hall.

'Oh, there's my wife!' There was recognizable relief in

43

Derek Wainwright's voice. 'You'd like to meet her, I expect, although she can't help you any more than I can.' He turned to the door as it opened, and Rachel came into the room. 'This is Superintendent Pollard and Sergeant Toye of Scotland Yard, darling. I've just been telling them that we're new to the place, and can't tell them anything, beyond what happened on Tuesday afternoon.'

Rachel impressed Pollard favourably. No wariness here, he thought, meeting her frank interested gaze as they talked. He formed the opinion that if her husband were involved in something illicit, she almost certainly knew nothing about it.

Nora Pearce was nervous at first but soon responded to Pollard's conversational technique, pouring out a stream of information about her post with Bertha Wainwright.

'Yes,' she told him, with a quick smile and a flash of teeth, 'I've been here nearly twenty years. Such a long time, but it doesn't feel like it! I came to dear Miss Wainwright just after the war, so very thankful to leave my wartime work. I cooked for a Land Girls' hostel, you know, and I'm afraid I did find it rather uncongenial. Not the hard work, though hard it certainly was. I was glad to play my little part under dear Mr Churchill's leadership— or should I say Sir Winston's? But some of the Land Girls were, well, a little rough, although on the whole a splendid set of young women, you know. But of course this dreadful thing must have happened before I came to Miss Wainwright, surely? A very long time ago, if—er—what was found was as the police say.'

'On the contrary,' Pollard said, deciding to play the same card again, 'it happened quite recently. Probably about this time last year, or a bit earlier or later. So you may be able to help me, Miss Pearce. I want you to think back to the middle part of last year. Try to remember if you ever saw anyone acting at all suspiciously around here, especially during the night.'

He watched a whole sequence of expressions pass over her face. Initial incredulity was quickly followed by illumination, dismay, and finally sheer terror. She went very white, and nervously moistened her lips with the tip of her tongue.

'Oh, no,' she said hoarsely, after an appreciable pause. 'Nothing at all. Of course, there are a lot of visitors about during the summer. In the daytime, that is.'

'Take your time, Miss Pearce,' Pollard said reassuringly. 'There may have been some small incident which you didn't give a second thought to at the time. Do you keep a diary, by any chance?'

She reacted so violently that he was quite startled.

'I couldn't show you my diary,' she almost sobbed, colour flooding into her face again. 'It's private. You—you haven't any right.'

'Miss Pearce, I shouldn't think of asking to see it. I should be grossly exceeding my duty. It simply occurred to me that if you did keep one, looking through it might bring something which you noticed last summer to your mind. Will you do this for us, just on chance?'

She nodded dumbly.

'Thank you. We shall be very grateful. Let us know if you come on anything that might possibly have a bearing on this case: we shall be around for the next day or two. And now we'll be off. Don't bother to see us out.'

In the lane Toye turned a puzzled face to Pollard.

'She'd have cracked in another minute, sir. Why did you lay off her? It's plain enough she knows something.'

'She wouldn't have cracked. Not today, anyway. She'd have taken refuge in hysterics. Believe me, middle-aged women with principles are about the toughest nuts of the lot. Besides, who is it that she knows something about?. Surely the maidenly blushes over the diary can't be anything to do with Derek Wainwright? The plot thickens.'

Toye whistled.

'December love?' he suggested.

'Well, say October. She can cook, presumably, and sew, too, I expect. Not all that ineligible from the point of view of an elderly male. She's got a nice little nest-egg tucked away, I bet.'

'Could she be sweet on Bickley or Stobart, sir? Not much choice round here, is there?'

'It could be someone a bit further afield. I think we'll call on Constable Haycraft presently, when we nip over to Wilkaton for some bread and cheese and beer. What did you make of Derek Wainwright?'

'It put the wind up him when you mentioned this time last year, didn't it? He's been here before, and unless there was something fishy about the visit, why lie about it?'

'The odd part is,' Pollard said thoughtfully, 'that he lied about it from the start, in his statement to Crake. Unless he committed the murder, which frankly doesn't seem very probable from what we know at the moment, he wouldn't have known that last summer was a suspicious time for anyone to have hung around Twiggadon. I watched him very closely this morning, and I think he genuinely believed that the skeleton had been in the boot for years. Most people are very vague about the rate of post-mortem decomposition, and think it's much slower than it actually is. Anyway, we can't do anything more about him until the report from the Wrilburn police comes in.'

They stopped at the gate of the farm, and Pollard ran an appreciative eye over the house and the great barn.

'Bickley will be out on the farm at this hour,' he said. 'You go in and ask his wife when it's convenient for us to see him. Ingratiate yourself, and she may offer you a glass of cider. It's important not to step off on the wrong foot with Bickley; we shan't get a word out of him if we do. I'll go on and have a bash at Henry Stobart—if he's there.'

As he walked on it struck him that the cottage had the look of a frontier post in mountainous country. The track narrowed between the two tors, the one on the right rising sheer, a fantastic pile of huge granite blocks from which shattered turrets projected skywards. A bit overpowering as a near neighbour, Pollard thought.

The cottage was uncompromisingly shut up, with a curtain drawn across the lower window. He knocked and listened, his ear against the door. No sound came from within. He knocked and listened again. Then, satisfied that the place was empty, he took an official card from his wallet. Under his name he wrote 'I wish to interview you, and shall call again later today. Kindly remain at home when you return.' He added the date and time, and as there was no letter box pushed the card under the door.

Looking about him he decided that although the cottage was small and would certainly lack mod. cons, it had an air of snugness. The small front garden was neat. An outsize sleek cat slept in a corner of a well-tilled vegetable patch at the side. A wooden shed was padlocked, but through the window he could see a tidy array of tools, logs and a big drum of paraffin. Obviously the chap's got something to live on, he thought as he retraced his steps. If there's a bank account it ought to be possible to find out where he came from.

Rounding the corner he came face to face with Toye, and made a gesture of empty-handedness.

'Out,' he said, 'and the place bolted and barred, but somehow I don't think he's done a bunk. I've left a note to say we'll be back. How did you get on?'

47

'Lumme,' said Toye with feeling, 'she rattles away like a machine-gun. You can hardly take in what she's saying. One of those women who streak around at such a rate that they raise a draught. Bickley's up on the moor, but he'll be bringing his hay in from the fields behind the farm this afternoon, so I said we'd look in then. You were right about the cider, sir. Smashing it was: the real stuff out of a cask.'

'I suppose you know that sort's highly intoxicating,' Pollard told him. 'I think I'd better drive into Wilkaton. It might look bad if you rammed the war memorial. The Wainwrights' car gone. What's the betting that Nora Pearce is hard at it burning her diary to save it from our sacrilegious hands?'

As they approached Watchers Way a curious little scene took place. A young girl came furtively out of the gate, and gave a start on catching sight of them. She was pale and adenoidal, with lank hair hanging over her shoulders, and wore a navy blue anorak, almost as long as her mini skirt. She hurried off up the hill clutching a small parcel wrapped in newspaper, and was joined by another girl who darted out from the cover of a gateway. As they made for the main road they conferred anxiously with heads close together, giving a glance over their shoulders from time to time.

'What do you make of that?' asked Pollard.

'Nicked something while the lady's out?' suggested Toye doubtfully. 'Hardly have stopped to parcel it up, though, would she?'

Pollard frowned as he stood watching the two scurrying figures vanish round a corner.

'I've just remembered something,' he said. 'In Crake's report. He said the Pendine woman sold homemade herbal remedies and beauty aids. Aids for village maidens in a spot of bother, do you think? That kid seemed a bit edgy

48

for anyone just buying a pot of face cream. Having seen her may come in useful.'

They went quietly up the path and knocked at the door. It was ajar, and badly in need of a coat of paint.

'You back again, Myra?' a woman's voice called impatiently. 'Can't you read? The directions are on the label.'

'Excellent,' said Pollard loudly. 'Just as they should be. May we come in?'

There was silence, and then a quick step.

'Who are you, and what do you want?'

Sybil Pendine confronted them in the doorway of a room on the left. Pollard's first reaction was that she had taken a sharp jolt, and his second that she was an extremely odd-looking woman. Her faded blonde hair, streaked with grey, was dragged back into a loose knot, accentuating the narrowness of her face. Her deep grey eyes were opaque to the point of muddiness, the pupils narrowed defensively to the merest slits as she stared at him. A really curious face, Pollard thought, with its beaky nose and small mouth turned down at the corners. A fastidious man, he noted with distaste her crumpled cotton frock, none too clean, bare hairy legs and cracked white sandals. At the same time he recognized instantly that behind this unpromising exterior there was a personality to be reckoned with.

'Not customers this time, I'm afraid,' he said, with a slight emphasis on the word, watching a faint flicker in the strange eyes. 'Detective-Superintendent Pollard and Detective-Sergeant Toye of New Scotland Yard. Here is my card. We want your help in our enquiry into the finding of a young man's skeleton in the field opposite.'

Sybil Pendine relaxed imperceptibly, but made no attempt to move.

'I've already told one policeman that I know nothing whatever about it.'

4

'All the same,' Pollard told her, insinuating himself skilfully into the doorway, 'we of the Yard like first hand statements, so I'm sure you won't mind going over the ground once again. We shan't keep you very long.'

She hesitated, and then turned abruptly into the room. Pollard followed, giving a quick glance round which registered its shabbiness and makeshift appearance. He sat down cautiously on a chair with badly sagging springs. Toye took a seat in the background.

'I was interested to see in your statement to Inspector Crake, Mrs Pendine, that you were not at all surprised that human remains have been found in the field across the lane,' Pollard started off conversationally. 'An unusual reaction, in my experience.'

She looked taken aback, and also, he thought, distinctly gratified.

'But then I am an unusual person,' she told him. 'There are very few surprises for people like myself who dwell in the Now.'

'The now, Mrs Pendine?'

'I am referring to the timeless Now, in which past, present and future are one. You won't have heard of it, naturally.'

'I imagine,' Pollard went on smoothly, 'that your normal physical perception of the present is combined with extra-sensory perception of the past and the future?'

'I'd no idea,' she replied, obviously, if unwillingly impressed, 'that the police had ever heard of ESP.'

'Is this lane,' Pollard pursued, feeling his way, 'which I believe is known traditionally as the Road of Death, particularly favourable to ESP?'

Sybil Pendine looked at him sharply, and smiled secretively to herself.

'Do you know where this lane will take you?' she asked, with a dramatic emphasis.

'As far as I can judge from the Ordnance Survey, across the moor to a group of Bronze Age burial mounds on a tor called Lordsbarrow,' Pollard replied in matter-of-fact tones.

'The processions of the Great Ones to the pyres on Lordsbarrow were very long ... many went to the fires with them ... it was terrible and splendid ... the route smells of death ... it will for ever.'

She spoke with the unconscious confidence of an actual spectator, and for a moment Pollard found it uncannily convincing. He moved sharply, and glanced at Toye who was writing diligently, his expression inscrutable.

'I suppose, Mrs Pendine, that you find some times and seasons more propitious to ESP than others? Midsummer Eve, for instance?' he asked.

She nodded slowly, several times.

'Where do you keep watch at these times?'

'Why, with The Nine. They saw too much, once long ago, but one has to take risks.' Surely the weather must come into it, Pollard thought prosaically.

'From here, too?' he suggested. 'One would have expected—er—manifestations where the skeleton was found.'

'Last Lammas Eve,' she said dreamily. 'A fearful time, with the waters trying to cover the whole world. It happened at midnight. I saw it from the Gateway of the Tors.'

'What did you see, Mrs Pendine?'

'I saw the torchbearers leading the procession through the field. I fell to the ground.'

'And when it came?'

'It never came,' she said abruptly, in her normal voice. 'Some earthbound influence interrupted the manifestation.'

'Have you any idea what this disturbing influence was?' Pollard struggled to keep any suggestion of urgency out of his voice.

He realized that she had not heard him, and was staring in surprise at some point behind and above him.

'Why,' she exclaimed, 'I see a woman so clearly, high up from the ground. Red-gold on her head, and a river of gold flowing from her hands. She's laughing. And she's pregnant.'

Pollard's spine went ice-cold. Then sheer fury welled up in him that this distasteful creature could somehow make contact with his unconscious, and share a memory of Jane looking down at him and making some absurd remark, as she hung curtains of soft gold brocade in the sitting-room of the new house. For a moment his hands ached to seize her by the throat . . .

There was a slight sound, and he became aware that Toye was staring at him with a puzzled expression.

'Mrs Pendine,' he said harshly, 'kindly answer my question. I'm asking you what brought this manifestation you speak of to a sudden end.'

'What on earth does it matter to you?' she said impatiently. 'It was last Lammas Eve, and that skeleton must have been there for years and years.'

Am I going to pull off a hat trick, he wondered.

'On the contrary,' he said, watching her intently, 'we know that the human body of which it was a part was put into the boot of the car sometime between May and November of last year. So possibly on Lammas Eve.'

He expected a furious outburst at this possible interpretation of her experience, but it did not come. Instead, alarm, shrewd calculation and finally a mulish obstinacy passed over her face.

'I haven't the remotest idea what interrupted the manifestation. One seldom has.'

At the gate of Watchers Way, Pollard, who was abstracted, nearly collided with a woman carrying a well-filled basket. As he stepped aside with an apology she gave a start, coloured up, and almost pushed past him, exchanging a hurried greeting with Toye as she did so.

'Mrs Bickley,' Toye murmured.

The door of the bungalow slammed shut behind the visitor.

'Chicken, eggs and a nice jar of cream,' observed Toye. 'A bit lush on the housekeeping for that set-up in there.'

'Decidedly lush. You know, I'm beginning to be interested in Mrs Pendine, quite apart from her extra-sensory activities. Could it be a little something for keeping her mouth shut about Bickley's assault and battery, I wonder?'

'Could she have seen him coming away from the field that night she was out spook-hunting?'

'Even if she did,' said Pollard thoughtfully, 'I don't believe she's making him pay up on that score. I'm certain she was as staggered as Derek Wainwright and Nora Pearce to hear that the corpse was only parked in the boot about a year ago. And I'm equally certain that the idea of cashing in on someone flashed into her mind immediately.'

'I wonder if it was that same night that Nora Pearce saw whatever it is she won't let on about, sir? Then there's Mr Wainwright. When was he around, if that's what he's trying to cover up?'

'For a small hamlet there seems to have been a surprising amount going on, doesn't there? Let's make for Wilkaton and consult the chap stationed there, as soon as we've had something to eat at the pub.'

FIVE

CONSTABLE HAYCRAFT of Wilkaton was fourteen stone, with a round moon of a face which might have been drawn by a child. His eyes, sunk in creases of fat, were exceedingly shrewd. A slow smile crept upwards towards his ears as he explained that it wouldn't have been no manner of use to delve into the rumours about Reg Bickley walloping a Ted. Why, there wasn't a man, woman or child who'd give evidence against a man protecting his own beasts.

'I see what you mean,' Pollard said, amused by this rationalization of a policy of *laissez-faire*, 'but could it be the Ted's skeleton in the boot, do you think?'

The idea had obviously occurred to Haycraft himself, but he had come down heavily against it. If Reg Bickley had landed himself with a corpse inadvertent like, he'd've found a better place to stow it than a car dump on his own land, hardly a stone's throw from his house. Plenty of old mine workings up over, and no one knew the moor better than Reg.

. 'What about a sort of double bluff,' suggested Pollard, 'to make people say he'd never put it there because he'd have too much sense?'

'No, sir, I don't see Reg Bickley doin' that. Bull at a

54

gate, yes, but 'e ain't subtle and serpent-like to go thinkin' that out.'

It transpired that Haycraft had nothing against Henry Stobart, whose eccentricities seemed to be taken for granted locally, and even applauded, especially his reactions to callers from the Rural District Council.

'You wouldn't know where he came from, I suppose?' Pollard asked, not very hopefully.

Haycraft's smile became broader than ever.

'Happen I does, sir. Epsom, 'twas, wur they runs the Durby. Leastways, that's what the chaps as brought 'is stuff in one o' they moving vans told Tom Pugsley over to the Cat an' Fiddle. Before my time, 'twas, but it bein' Epsom it stuck, the missus an' I 'avin' a bit on annual.'

'That's a most valuable piece of information,' Pollard told him, highly gratified by this short circuiting of what had threatened to be an interminable search into the obstructive Henry Stobart's antecedents. 'Now, I don't suppose you had many dealings with the late Miss Bertha Wainwright of Moor View, but has her housekeeper, Miss Nora Pearce, many friends in the neighbourhood?'

Haycraft shook his head. The two ladies had kept very much to themselves, especially these last years with Miss Wainwright failing.

'No suitors?' Pollard enquired with a grin, 'There was a nice little bit of money involved.'

Haycraft gave a fat chuckle.

'That old maiden, sir? Bit long in the tooth, I'd say. Still, 'tis wunnerful what a bit o' money'll bring about.'

'Now for Mrs Pendine, and then I've done,' Pollard said. 'You told Inspector Crake that she had the reputation of being a witch, and that local people were scared of her. Can you add a bit to that? We're rather interested in her.'

Haycraft shifted his monumental rear to a more comfortable position on the hard upright chair.

'Put it this way, sir. Backalong 'twas called witchcraft, an' they burnt 'em at the stake. Now 'tis on the telly, all scientific, with a great long name to it that I can't get me tongue round. Seein' things other folk can't see an' knowin' what they doesn't know. I reckon there's allus bin a few o' that sort around, and Mrs Pendine, she's one for sure.'

'After our interview with her this morning I'm quite ready to go that far with you,' Pollard said with complete sincerity. 'But at the moment I'd like to know if you've ever suspected that she makes use of anything she happens to know to get things out of people. Chickens and eggs, for instance, or possibly money.'

He went on to describe the encounter with Mrs Bickley, noting with interest that Haycraft's good-humoured face had become somewhat impassive.

"'Tis well-known folks gives 'er presents,' he said noncommittally. 'Pot o' honey, butter an' such. Maybe they thinks it's a sorter insurance. But I've never 'ad no complaints. Not ever.'

'Why don't you make enquiries?' Toye, an ultra-conscientious officer, could contain himself no longer.

Haycraft looked at him pityingly.

'All complaints is investigated fast enough, same as up to Lunnon. But 'ereabouts the more you pokes an' pries into folks' doings the less they tells 'ee, an' that's 'ow 'tis. Eyes an' ears open, an' trap shut's my motto.'

'What about this herbal muck the woman sells?' interposed Pollard. 'We saw a young girl come slinking out with something in a parcel, and Pendine called out after her that the directions were on it. A pale leggy girl, with mousey hair, wearing one of those navy blue anoraks. Had she been to buy a herbal remedy for being in the family way, do you think?'

'There ain't never been no complaints o' that sort,' Haycraft asserted emphatically. "Twould've bin Myra Durdle,

56

over to Boddacott, after summat to dab over 'er face, silly maiden. 'Er Mum'd skin 'er if she knew. Mighty in the MU, Mrs Durdle, an' can't abide Mrs Pendine. An' as to it's bein' muck as Mrs Pendine sells, beggin' pardon, sir, 'tis better'n any chemist's stuff for coughs and stummicks an' the rheumatics.'

'I wonder if he gets a bottle of something for his out-size stummick now and again, for letting sleeping dogs lie?' Pollard said when they came out of the cottage.

'Lazy hulking bastard,' exploded Toye.

'His technique probably works very well, you know. He doesn't miss a thing and everybody knows it, and keeps within reasonable limits. Here's the telephone kiosk. I'll get on to the Yard about enquiries at Epsom, and then we'll resume our labours at Twiggadon.'

Toye studied the village street disapprovingly as he waited, and then strolled across to the shop in search of cigarettes. His eye was caught by a miscellaneous array of bottles on a shelf, all neatly labelled in a clear script. The elderly woman behind the counter noticed his interest, and broke into a eulogy of the local lady's wonderful herb medicines.

'Got anything for indigestion?' he said, with a vague thought of possible proceedings for fraud.

Assured that it would put him right in no time at all he left the shop with a small bottle labelled NATURE'S STOMACH SOOTHER: *A teaspoonful as needed*. Back in the car he withdrew the cork and sniffed cautiously, before putting the bottle into the dashboard.

'Well, that's under way,' said Pollard, reappearing and getting into the car. 'It was a tremendous stroke of luck getting on to the Epsom link. And it's obvious, of course, that the Pendine manages to exact tribute from some of the locals. You saw that ready reckoner expression this morning when she suddenly grasped the significance of whatever she saw that night? If only we could intercept her next attempt at a spot of blackmail we'd be quite a bit further on.'

He lapsed into thought as Toye pressed the self-starter. At precisely the same moment, in her bedroom at Moor View, Nora Pearce was putting down a pair of field glasses and hastily getting up from a chair in the window.

She went quickly downstairs and out into the garden, pausing at the gate to glance in either direction before setting off down the hill at a brisk pace. Her hands were clasped against her breast in a characteristic attitude of agitation, and her lips moved soundlessly from time to time. She halted just short of the gate of the farm, listened, and satisfied that the yard was empty, hurried on again towards Farm Cottage. As she approached it she faltered, half-noticing in a puzzled way a litter of torn scraps of white paper outside the gate. She saw that the cottage door was ajar and the door of the shed open, but there was no sign of Henry Stobart. Still hesitating she heard the sound of a car coming down the lane from the direction of the main road. Panic-stricken, in case the detectives were returning, she ran round and dived into the shed. Above the thudding of her heart she could hear the car come over the bridge and up the track. It stopped outside the cottage. Too frightened to peep out she started violently as its doors slammed twice. There was an interminable pause, broken by an inaudible remark, and the gate clicked.

'What the hell do you want?'

Over the years Nora Pearce had so often heard Henry Stobart's voice in her daydreams. Now, harsh and grating as if rusty from disuse, the reality was shatteringly unreal. She listened to Pollard's voice with its authoritative undertone introducing himself and Sergeant Toye.

'I can read. I'm asking you what you want, barging in like this?'

'We are conducting the police enquiry into the finding of the skeleton of a young man in one of the cars in that dump up there. We are particularly interested in the summer of last year. Have you at any time seen anyone examining the cars or behaving suspiciously in or near the field?'

'No. So you can clear off.'

Nora Pearce, huddled uncomfortably on a heap of logs, was trembling uncontrollably. The possibility that physical violence could break out only a few yards away terrified her. Already shaken by her own interview with Pollard, she had spent the entire morning watching for Henry Stobart's return, observing comings and goings which had filled her with apprehension. She had not dared to leave her observation post in search of lunch for fear of missing his return. Now her head was swimming with hunger and exhaustion, and she realized with dismay that she had lost the thread of the conversation.

'Bloody Gestapo!' Henry Stobart was shouting.

She bit her lip in dismay at this unseemly language. She had always thought of him as such a gentleman behind the iron mask of some terrible secret sorrow. Now the Superintendent was asking him about lights in the field where the poor young man had been found.

'Do you ever take these long walks of yours at night, Mr Stobart?'

'No business of yours if I do. A man's free to walk, isn't he?'

'Suppose I were to suggest to you that shortly before midnight on July 31 last year, you were seen near that car dump?'

There was a brief silence. Then Henry Stobart gave a hoarse laugh which had an oddly triumphant note.

'Ask that crazy Pendine woman what else she's seen round here. You'll be entertained. Or did you get it from that little fool of a housekeeper at Moor View who's got chronic verbal diarrhoea?'

Tears ran silently down Nora Pearce's burning cheeks. After a time it was borne in on her that Henry Stobart was signing some paper amid a good deal of abuse. Superintendent Pollard, unmoved as ever, was saying that it might be necessary to see him again. Then at last the gate clicked, and the car started up and drove slowly away. But she could not bring herself to move, and sat on in a kind of fatalistic stupor waiting to be discovered. After a timeless interval it happened. The shed door was flung wide open, and Henry Stobart loomed fantastically tall and gaunt against the light.

'God in heaven!' he shouted, in tones of exasperation and outrage.

Tearstained and dishevelled, Nora Pearce got to her feet, suddenly invested with the dignity of faded gentility. 'I came to warn you, Mr Stobart,' she told him, 'that I saw you coming down the lane late on the night the police were talking about. I—I happened to be looking out of the window. Please believe me when I say that I did not tell them. But the Superintendent is a very clever man, and I'm afraid he may come back and ask me more questions. This was the reason for my visit, which I realize is unwelcome. I came in here because I heard the police car. To wait until they went away.'

She made to leave the shed, and he moved back to let her pass. As she went down the track, almost incapable of further thought, she heard the cottage door slam and a key turn. She walked on blindly, hardly noticing the empty police car outside the farm. Arriving at Moor View she stared up at the house, realizing that it no longer mattered to her if it were sold. Her secret, timid hope, cherished over the years, of one day bringing companion-ship and happiness to Henry Stobart had been brutally annihilated.

She went automatically to her bedroom. Here she re-sorted to tried remedies for signs of grief which must be concealed from employers, bathing her face first in warm water, and then in cold, and dabbing lavender water on her aching forehead. Then she started downstairs to make herself a good hot cup of tea, but stopped abruptly as she recalled the nagging problem which had been eclipsed by the stresses of the past few hours.

Pollard and Toye had driven from Henry Stobart's cottage to the farm, and drawn up short of the gate. They sat piecing together the torn scraps of paper which they had collected from the track.

'These bits are my card,' Pollard said, pushing them aside. 'Now, what else so enraged the chap that he tore it up and chucked it out, contravening anti-litter by-laws? It might just be worth finding out.'

Carefully smoothing out the crumpled fragments they finally assembled a brief note in block capitals.

I DON'T SUPPOSE YOU'RE TOO KEEN ON THE POLICE KNOW-ING THAT YOU WERE WALKING DOWN THE LANE JUST BEFORE MIDNIGHT ON JULY 31 LAST YEAR? it enquired.

'Blimey,' remarked Pollard, 'I thought this sort of thing only happened in detective novels.'

Without comment, but with a touch of complacency, Toye extracted the bottle of 'Nature's Stomach Soother' from the dashboard and passed it over. Pollard whistled, and compared the block capitals and script through a pocket lens.

'The inspired forethought of the fictional detective, too,' he said. 'Can anything really be wrong with your stomach, after the meals you've been getting through lately? No, I

61

thought not. This effort's an opening gambit, I suppose. There's not much doubt that the same person's written both. Look how the script curve keeps creeping into the block letters. Easy enough to establish Pendine as the writer, too. I'd like to whisk her off for questioning at Bridgeford, out of her spooky context, and get this Stobart business cleared up, but we'd better see the Bickleys, having made the date with them.'

'Stobart would tie up with Miss Pearce's diary better than Bickley, don't you think, sir? No accounting for taste, I suppose.'

'It's a projection of her romantic fancy she's been cherishing, not the real chap. Rather pathetic. Re Stobart, though, it's one thing to prove that he was prowling about on a night when lights were seen in the car dump field, and quite another to link him up to the murder. A good deal depends on what the Yard unearths at Epsom. One thing's certain : he didn't show the faintest sign of being rattled just now. In fact, I thought he seemed remarkably confident.'

They got out of the car and walked across the cobbled yard to the door, knocked and waited. Pollard looked with interest at the massive thickness of the granite walls, and the cross-passage running through to the garden behind the house. After a pause a woman's quick light steps came from a room on the right, and Mrs Bickley appeared in a flowered apron.

'You're wanting my husband,' she said hurriedly, as if to preclude further conversation. 'If you'll step inside and take a seat I'll whistle 'im up from the fields.'

'Just a minute, Mrs Bickley,' Pollard called after her. She paused on her way to the garden door, and turned back with obvious unwillingness.

'We're asking every local resident this question,' he told her. 'Have you at any time seen anybody in the field where the old cars are who had no reason to be there, or any suspicious behaviour around here?'

'No,' she said, emphatically, 'nobody and nothing, as I told the Inspector, Wednesday. You can't see the cars from 'ere, nor from the lane. Not that I've time to go gaddin' about, what with the meals and the washin', not to mention the poultry an' the bit o' dairy work.'

'I'm sure you haven't,' Pollard said tactfully. 'You must be on the go from morning till night. And I expect you supply the local households with the sort of first-rate home-produced stuff we saw in your basket this morning?'

'Not regular,' she said hastily. 'That was just a bite for Mrs Pendine, friendly-like. She's put to it to make ends meet now her husband's gone. Now I'll call up Reg, if you'll excuse me.'

She vanished. Pollard and Toye went into the kitchen, a big, stone-flagged room with immense oak beams, black with age. It was spotless and comfortable, its modern equipment an indication of the farm's prosperity. Pollard walked over to examine a splendid grandfather clock. In the distance came a prolonged blast on a referee's whistle.

'Perhaps the husband doesn't know about grub going up to Pendine,' Toye suggested. 'Suppose she saw the dust-up with the youth and let Mrs B. know she had, and that it needn't go any further if the larder was stocked up now and again?'

Reappearing, Mrs Bickley announced that her husband was on his way.

'Maybe you could all do with a cuppa,' she added, and busied herself noisily with crockery.

A heavy tread in the passage announced the arrival of Reg Bickley, who came in wiping the sweat from his face with a coloured handkerchief.

'Afternoon,' he said tersely. 'Inspector was along Wednesday, an' we told 'im what we know, which was nothin' at all. I'm a busy man, I am.'

'Anyone can see that from crossing your yard out there,' Pollard replied, 'and a first-rate farmer, too, from the look of the place. We won't waste your time. Just a quick run-through of what happened last Tuesday, first.'

'Reckon we may as well sit down,' Bickley said, somewhat mollified. 'Let's 'ave a cuppa, Ruby.'

'Just drawin',' she said, vigorously stirring the contents of the teapot.

As Reg Bickley described how Derek Wainwright had rung him urgently after the discovery of the skeleton, Pollard studied his powerful build and aggressive jaw. A formidable chap, and quick on the draw, he thought, but if he was unlucky and hit that hooligan too hard, I don't see him being subtle enough to cache the body in one of his own fields.

Ruby Bickley interrupted the story of how a guard had been kept on the field, by whisking three enormous cups of strong tea on to the kitchen table.

'Plenty more in the pot,' she remarked, and retreated to an ironing board in the background.

In reply to Pollard's questions Bickley was emphatic that he had never seen anyone messing around in the car dump, and if he had they'd've been out of it on the toe of his boot in less than no time.

'Mind you,' he said, 'it's easy enough to come across the stream, summertime anyway. Some kids did, year or two back, and one of 'em cut 'is leg on a rusty bit of iron. Real nasty letter I got from 'is dad, sayin' the cars was a public danger, an' that 'e was consultin' a solicitor. But it didn't come to nothin'. Turned out the manager from the Galaxy Insurance over to Torcastle looked in that mornin', come about extra cover when us put up the new sheds. So I showed'n the letter. Why, 'e says, dump's on your land, innit? You come an' take a look, I says. So us went up, an'

I showed'n the cars, an' that the stream's my lawful boundary. Don't you answer that letter, Mr Bickley, 'e says. A try-on, that's what 'tis. So I didn't, an' never 'eard no more of it.'

Alternating swishes and thumps indicated that Ruby Bickley was ironing with energy. She made no attempt to join in the conversation, but Pollard got the impression that she was following it closely.

'Have you ever thought of having the dump cleared up?' he asked. 'It must be annoying to have to take on a mess like that.'

The question sent Reg Bickley off in full cry against scrap dealers who said it wasn't worth their while to come out for what wasn't a full load, and the iniquities of his drunken predecessor who had been responsible for the dump's existence, and for Henry Stobart's ownership of the cottage.

'Yes, I should think you could do with a farm hand over there to help keep an eye on things,' Pollard remarked casually. 'Do you have much trouble with visitors doing damage and interfering with your animals? It seems a popular place for picnics round here.'

There was silence, dominated by the remorseless ticking of the grandfather clock. Ruby Bickley suddenly burst into a spate of words.

'Litter louts, that's what they are. The nerve they've got parkin' cars on our land this side o' the stream and scatterin' their nasty rubbish all over. Moves 'em off, I does. Private property, this is, I tells'n. Go up over an' park on t'other side if park you must, an' make the place filthy with the stuff you brings and won't be bothered to take back. Moor's free to all, but our land ain't, I says.'

A neat bridging operation, Pollard thought, watching her husband take a great gulp of tea and regain his equilibrium.

5

'Broken glass is the worst,' he declared. 'Sets up the bottles they've brought their booze in, an' chucks stones at 'em, some of 'em does. Why last summer I 'ad to call out the vet to one o' the Galloways—'

The raucous note of a telephone bell interrupted the narrative. Ruby Bickley streaked across the room and seized the receiver. She stood frowning as she listened. 'That's right,' she said. 'Twiggadon Farm. Name of Bickley. 'Oo? Yes, I'll tell 'im ... It's for you,' she told Pollard.

Inspector Crake's voice came quacking over the line in guarded sentences.

'OK,' Pollard said at last. 'We'll be along.'

'Crake says some important information has come in,' he told Toye when they reached the car. 'He suggested we came back to Bridgeford.'

'Not Epsom already about Stobart, sir?'

'No. They've got on to the boy beaten up by Bickley. Indirectly that is. Apparently he turned up in the town about Easter last year, got a job of sorts and picked up with a youth of his own age and went to lodge with the family. Crake was much too correct to mention any names over the blower. The said youth owned a scooter, and has admitted letting the lodger have a go out here, in the course of which ponies were chased and Bickley suddenly appeared like an avenging angel.'

'But where's this chap now, sir? The pony chaser, I mean.'

'This is it. He'd taken such a bashing that he had to lie up for a day or two, and passed the time by saying what he was going to do to Bickley when he'd recovered. Then one morning he took his belongings and slipped off without a word to anyone—or paying his landlady—and was never seen again. According to the owner of the scooter who came and gave the information, he was a small chap,

66

about five foot four, with mousey sort of hair which he wore long.'

SIX

'ANYTHING KNOWN about this chap who owned the scooter?'
Pollard asked Inspector Crake.

'He was up in the juvenile court when he was ten for
damage to an empty house. Apart from that he's got a
clean sheet. He's called Trevor Cupple, aged twenty, an
unskilled labourer in a building firm. Lives in a roughish
part downtown, and went around with a rowdy teenage
gang till recently, but seems to have steadied lately, according to our people. Not much in the top storey, I'd say.
Shall I bring them along, sir?'

'Them?'

'He brought his bird. Or she brought him, more like.
Pert little piece, but a lot more sense than him.'

A few minutes later Pollard was studying the pair with
interest. The girl, Moyra Fox, sat fashionably slanted, her
head inclined at an angle. Her hair flowed over her
shoulders, and her mini-shift was abbreviated to a degree
which made Pollard hope she was wearing tights. Her
sharp-featured little face was alert and slightly sardonic.
It was clear that Trevor Cupple had been firmly annexed
and reorientated, probably without being conscious of his
fate. He wore a bright orange shirt over scarlet jeans, but
was clean in his person and only moderately long-haired.

His expression was uneasy and defensive, his mouth slightly open.

'Ran into 'im in the bar o' the Red Lion,' he told Pollard. 'Us got talkin'—y'know.'

It emerged that the beaten-up boy's name had been Steve Mullins, or so he had given out. He said he had thumbed lifts down from London, and thought he'd pick up a job for a week or two before moving on. Asked if he knew of a cheap bed which wasn't lousy, Cupple, whose mother sometimes took in a lodger, had taken him home, and board and lodge terms had been agreed upon.

Moyra Fox caught Pollard's eye and gave a half-amused, half-contemptuous shrug. 'Barmy,' she remarked succinctly, indicating Cupple. 'See where 'e's landed 'imself.'

Pollard pointed out that there was no proof whatever that the skeleton in the car was that of Steve Mullins, merely a remote possibility. By dint of skilled and patient questioning he succeeded in building up a fairly detailed description of Mullins, wishing heartily that Cupple's acquaintance with the shrew-eyed Moyra Fox dated back to the previous summer. Asked to stand up, Cupple gave his own height as five foot ten, and after a prodigious mental effort opined that Mullins had come up to about the level of his nostrils.

'Somewhere round five-four,' Toye said, after measuring.

Mullins had been small but the wiry sort. When Pollard enquired if he had ever mentioned breaking any bones in an accident, Cupple looked baffled, and shook his head. He hadn't noticed anything about the lodger's teeth, but Mullins had worn his hair longer than most. An enquiry about its colour led Cupple to gaze round the room, as if in search of inspiration.

'Bit lighter'n 'ers,' he said at last, with a jerk of his head in Moyra's direction, at which she rolled her eyes at

Pollard.

A certain caginess came over the interview when the subject of the trip to Twiggadon with the scooter was introduced. It was quickly obvious that on the appearance of the irate farmer, Cupple had gone to ground to save his own skin, and was therefore unable to give much of a description of him, beyond the fact that he was a bruiser and had black hair. To cover his embarrassment he repeatedly asserted that if he'd any idea that Mullins would go after the gees, he'd never have let him have a go on the Honda. He, Trevor Cupple, didn't hold with tormenting animals.

"'E wouldn't 'urt a fly, 'cept when 'e's a bit boozed-up,' contributed Moyra Fox, giving him a fond, if cynical glance.

Mullins had been no match for his assailant, and had emerged with a black eye and split lip. When the two youths eventually got home Mrs Cupple administered first aid, and advised Mullins to lie up for a day or two to stop the neighbours talking. He fair raved against the farmer chap, and how he was going out there again to get his own back. Then, on the Monday, he'd cleared out while the house was empty, taking his bits of things, and leaving half a week owing.

'Did he ever say anything about being on the run?' asked Pollard.

'Nix.'

'Sticks out a mile!' broke in Moyra Fox impatiently. 'Nice thing, too. Jus' see what 'appens if you brings chaps 'ome orf the street when us is married.'

'Shan't be bringing no one back then, ducks,' he told her with an amorous wink.

Attempts to fix the date of the Twiggadon expedition were unsuccessful. The best Cupple could do was that it had been summertime, and before the Bank Holiday. More likely a Saturday in June than in July, but he really couldn't say, not all that time back. Surprisingly, however, he remembered the name of the man who had taken on Mullins to help with a milk round.

'We shall want to see this chap,' Pollard said, making a note of it, 'and Mrs Cupple, too. Who else lives in the house? Your father?'

'Dad's up the cemetery. There's only me an' me Mum, when we've no lodger.'

'Right. Well now, Mr Cupple, when we've typed out what you've been able to tell us we shall ask you to read it over, and to put your name to it if you think it's a true statement. But I want you to think once more if there's anything else you can remember about Mullins. Anything which might help us to trace him and count him out of the enquiry we're making.'

Trevor Cupple scowled in the throes of unaccustomed mental effort, and scratched his head.

''Ere,' said Moyra Fox suddenly, 'didn't 'e say, 'e'd bin to the Grammar? Fat lot o' good it did 'im!'

She spoke with such bitterness that Pollard spared a fleeting thought for the advantages of comprehensive schooling.

'That's right,' Cupple replied. 'So 'e did.'

'Thank you, Miss Fox,' Pollard said, turning to the girl. 'That may be a useful bit of information.'

She covered her self-consciousness at being thus addressed with a toss of her head.

When Sergeant Toye returned from dealing with the Cupple statement he found Pollard scribbling furiously. 'Time to get a few facts down on paper,' he said, looking up and pushing some blank sheets across the table. 'Let's assume for the moment that Cupple was speaking the truth, and start off with Mullins.'

They settled down, at first working independently, then pooling and summarizing their ideas. Finally Pollard wrote the last words of a final version, and they sat reading it through.

STEVE MULLINS

Height, build and hair colour appear to correspond with those of the skeleton. He was beaten-up, almost certainly by Bickley, and announced his intention of getting even with the latter.

Shortly after being beaten-up he vanished.

He claimed to have been to a grammar school.

REG BICKLEY

Physically powerful and hot-tempered.

Almost certainly attacked Steve Mullins.

Owns the land on which the car dump is situated, which is very near his home. Ill at ease when questioned about hooligans molesting his stock. So was his wife.

Constable Haycraft discounts him as the corpse-dumper on psychological grounds. Sybil Pendine may have some hold over the Bickleys.

HENRY STOBART

Sybil Pendine claims to have seen him in the lane on the night of July 31 last year, shortly after seeing moving lights in the car dump field. When taxed with having been there he did not deny it. His way of life is eccentric, and he reacts violently to any invasion of his privacy.

(Further information about him awaited.)

DEREK WAINWRIGHT

From his reactions and those of Nora Pearce it seems possible that he is lying about never having been to Twiggadon before.

Seemed genuinely astonished to learn that the dead youth had only been put into the car boot last year. These points suggested :
(*a*) that he was in Twiggadon last summer, but
(*b*) was not involved in the dumping of the corpse.
Query: What is he lying for, then?

SYBIL PENDINE

Her activities are eccentric, and some of them may be illegal.
She admits to being out and about on the night of July 31 last year (a date and time with traditionally sinister associations : Lammas Eve).
Claims to have seen moving lights in the car dump field, and Henry Stobart in the lane shortly afterwards, and has sent him what may fairly be called a threatening letter on the subject, probably the first step in a blackmailing attempt.
The reactions of Haycraft and the Bickleys suggest that she may exact tribute elsewhere.
Query: Could she have been an accessory to Stobart? Bickley? A.N.Other? She has not got the physique to have killed and dumped the youth on her own.

NORA PEARCE

Her reactions when questioned suggest :
(*a*) that she saw Derek Wainwright in Twiggadon last summer, and does not want to give him away.
(*b*) that she is concealing information about someone about whom she has emotional feelings. This could be Wainwright in theory, or Bickley or Stobart. Or A.N.Other again.

'Difficult to think of anyone of her sort falling for Bickley or Stobart, wouldn't you think, sir?' Toye asked presently.

'Imagination boggles at what some women can fall for. No, I don't think either of them can be ruled out on that score. She must have had a lonely, restricted sort of life with old Miss Wainwright, and might have invested one of them with a totally false glamour as a form of escapism, you know. Where do we go from here, I wonder? On the whole I think you had better work this end : Ma Cupple, and the trail of Mullins when he left Bridgeford. I suppose he did leave it? Perhaps you'd better take a look under the Cupple floor : they might have discovered that he had some natty loot on board. Then there's the chap he worked for. It may be impossible to track him down on a Sunday, of course. I'll go over to Twiggadon again, and follow up some of these queries. There's just the chance we might get something about Stobart by the evening.'

Pollard started well ahead of the Sunday morning traffic, and was able to mull over the case as he drove out to Twiggadon. He finally decided to begin with a call on Sybil Pendine. The torn fragments of the note had proved informative. Henry Stobart's prints were on them, super-imposed on others. These latter were identical with two clear prints on the bottle of 'Stomach Soother' bought by Toye. After being fingerprinted the scraps of paper had been put together again and mounted. He would confront her with the finished product, and in the course of questioning her about Stobart suddenly switch to the subject of Reg Bickley, to see how she reacted.

As he slowed down to take the turning two small figures emerged from the hedge, and with expressions of portentous secrecy signalled to him to stop.

'Hiya, helpers!' he said. 'Got anything for me?'

'We've come to report, sir,' Philip told him with eager formality. 'It's top secret. Could be big stuff.'

'You'd better get in,' Pollard said, slewing round and

74

opening the rear door. 'It's more private in the car.'

They nodded vigorously, perched bright-eyed on the edge of the back seat. The sun had brought out a crop of freckles on their faces. Philip had a scratch on his nose, and Clare had grazed her knee. With an effort Pollard brought back his attention to the matter in hand.

'Go ahead,' he invited.

'We've watched out for anything funny-peculiar, the way you asked us to,' Philip told him. 'It was Clare noticed it,' he added, struggling to play fair. 'Go on, you tell.'

Clare gave Pollard a shy glance, blushed slightly and finally plunged.

'It's Miss Pearce,' she confided. 'We think she's a— Secret Agent.'

'You're doing it all wrong,' Philip interrupted impatiently. 'You're hopeless, isn't she, sir? When you're making a report things ought to be in order, oughtn't they?'

'You find out much more if you let people tell you things in their own way,' Pollard said. 'You'll soon find that out if you join the CID when you grow up. Carry on, Clare.'

'Well, she sits up in her bedroom window with a pair of b'noculars, watching the path out on to the moor, and that cottage where the horrid tall man lives. So p'raps he's a Russian spy, and traitors go there with secret plans. It's Phil's idea, really,' she concluded magnanimously.

In spite of the absurdity Pollard felt his interest quicken sharply.

'When did you see her doing this?' he asked

'Lots of times,' they replied in chorus. 'First morning we were here,' Philip went on, 'we got up t'rrifically early, didn't we, Clare? Hours before everybody else. We went out to explore, and saw her then, and we've seen her every day since. I asked her if she was a bird-watcher, but she said she wasn't specially.'

'We haven't told anyone,' Clare assured Pollard.

'That's jolly good,' he replied. 'You've both done very well. Most people come unstuck because they can't keep quiet.'

They went pink with pleasure.

'I say, sir,' burst out Philip, 'd'you think it's true? About N.P. being a secret agent?'

'I mustn't say what I think, you know. The CID has to be very very cagey. But just go on keeping your eyes open —without letting anyone see you're doing it, of course.'

'We can be on duty all day today,' Philip assured him. 'Daddy's gone off for a terrific hike. He said it was much too far for us, so we're having a day at home with Mummy and N.P.'

'Is your mother at home now?'

They nodded, and Clare volunteered the information that she was sorting things for the sale.

Pollard made a lightning decision, and offered them a lift home. On the way they chattered about Nora Pearce, whose stock had risen sharply with them.

'She's a fab cook, too,' Philip said. 'Meals are smashing.'

Rachel Wainwright greeted Pollard with a complete absence of constraint, and led him to the drawing-room, but he sensed at once that she was worried and pre-occupied. The twins hesitated for a moment on the threshold, and then removed themselves after giving him looks full of significance.

'Do sit down,' she said, dropping into a chair and indicating another. 'I hope the children aren't being a nuisance. It's so good of you to let them think they're helping you. They're so excited about it that they seem to have forgotten the shock they had.'

'Not a nuisance in the least,' Pollard assured her, as he

rapidly improvised a question on a wholly fictitious issue. 'They're a most taking pair. Actually I looked in on the chance of a word with your husband, but as I gather he's out perhaps you can tell me what I want to know? Did old Miss Wainwright ever own the field where the cars are?'

Rachel shook her head.

'I'm afraid I haven't a clue. I should think Derek would have said so if he knew she had. I can't tell you when he'll be back, either. He felt like a long walk, and has gone off to climb Lordsbarrow, isn't it called? The highest tor. He thought he'd make a round, and took some sandwiches.'

Her voice trailed off slightly.

She's uneasy about him, Pollard thought. Can he have gone off because they'd had a row? Somehow it doesn't seem in character—her character, I mean. Behind that pale gold fragility of hers there's a sort of maternal stoicism and staying-power.

'I must say I envy him,' he remarked pleasantly, beginning to work the conversation round to the real purpose of his visit. 'It's a marvellous part of the world. I gather it's a first visit for all of you?'

'Well, actually Derek did dash down to Bridgeford for one night last summer, for a Curators' Conference. But unfortunately I was in hospital at the time, so he cut the trip as short as he could. It's all entirely new to me and the twins, and we think it's super.'

Pollard made a sympathetic enquiry about the hospital. Rather to his surprise she began to talk freely, almost with relief. He learnt about the motor accident, and the loss of her baby, and the transformation of the family fortunes by Bertha Wainwright's bequest. It struck him that she showed a curious lack of jubilation about the latter development, and he wondered what snag there could be.

Finally he rose to go, apologizing once more for taking up her time, and saying he would look in again to see if her husband could clear up the point about the field.

Scrapping his original programme he turned the car and drove to Wilkaton. Calling at the police cottage he found Constable Haycraft off duty, gardening in his shirt-sleeves, and asked for the use of his telephone. He rang Bridgeford, and was put through to Superintendent Puckeridge. After listening, the latter pointed out in a resigned tone that Sunday wasn't the day you'd choose for making enquiries about conferences held a year back, but undertook to get the information wanted through a private source. In a surprisingly short time he rang back. No Museum Curators' Conference had been held in Bridgeford during the previous year, or in fact, at any time during the past five years.

Pollard thanked him warmly, told Haycraft that he was following up a useful lead, and drove off again leaving the latter looking unmistakably relieved. Once clear of the village he stopped and studied his large-scale map of the area. Assuming that Derek Wainwright had gone on to the moor by way of the Nine Watchers' track, it seemed reasonable to suppose that he would take as direct a route as he could to Lordsbarrow, and reach its summit at a suitable hour for his picnic lunch. On the far side of the moor a convenient B road skirted the lower slopes of the tor. Pollard looked at his watch, and debated with himself for a few moments. Then he started up again, and made for the road in question. It's a chance, he thought, to take him completely by surprise. Admittedly, I can't see him committing a murder and then heaving the body into a car boot, but why the hell did he fake this conference if it wasn't to get himself down to this part of the world for some reason. Another woman? Suppose he had some per-

78

fectly legitimate reason which he didn't want to worry his wife about, as she was ill? Could he have run a chap down on the road who died of shock, as Pulman had said was possible, and then panicked and dumped the body? But then, if there hadn't been a still earlier visit to Twiggadon also unknown to his wife, how would he have known about the car dump?

Half an hour later, still speculating, he was following a rough track through waist-high bracken, devoutly wishing that he were more appropriately dressed for moor walking. He took off his coat and rolled up his sleeves, only to be bitten by a horse-fly. Improvising a fly-whisk he plodded up and up, pausing at intervals to admire the panoramic view unrolling below him. Far away on the eastern horizon was the gleam of the sea, and he suddenly yearned for a cool, refreshing swim. Hot and sweaty, he arrived at last at the lower slopes of one of the impressive barrows from which the tor took its name, but there was still no sign of Derek Wainwright. It was not until he reached its top that he saw him lying on his back in the heather, so still for a moment Pollard's heart missed a beat. Then, hearing approaching footsteps, the figure suddenly came alive, sat up, and looked round.

Pollard raised a hand in greeting, but there was no response. Surely, he thought, he isn't going to cut and run . . .

'How on earth did you know I was up here?' Derek Wainwright demanded, looking white and strained.

'I called in at your house to ask if you could give me a piece of information,' Pollard replied easily, dropping onto the heather beside him, 'and your wife said you were making for this place, so I thought I'd cut round with the car on the chance of finding you.'

There was a short pause.

'What is it you want to know?'

Pollard emerged from the handkerchief with which he was mopping his face.

'It's about the field where the cars are. Did your late cousin own it at one time?'

'Good Lord, I've absolutely no idea! It might have been, I suppose. The solicitor in Bridgeford'—He broke off abruptly, and stared warily at Pollard.

'Look here, I just don't believe that you've sweated up here to ask me a footling question like that? What are you hounding me for like this? Why don't you come out with it?'

'Hounding strikes me as a bit of an overstatement,' said Pollard mildly. 'But you're perfectly right. What I've really come for is to give you an opportunity—in decent privacy —to reconsider the statement you made to Inspector Crake last Tuesday. In it you said categorically that you'd never been in Twiggadon before.'

'Oh, I see. You're trying to pin the murder of that chap in the car on me.'

Pollard lit a cigarette, and puffed smoke at the flies circling round his head.

'An outrageous remark, really, Mr Wainwright. Stupid, too. At the lowest level I've got my reputation and career to think about.'

In the silence which followed he watched a passing breeze set up a ripple in the bracken. It swept past them, and moved swiftly and silently into the distance.

'I apologize,' Derek Wainwright said unexpectedly. 'I take it back. The fact is that through sheer bad luck I've landed myself in a ghastly spot—I can see that. It's the sort of thing that would happen to a mutt like me. I'd better tell you the whole thing, I suppose ... Aren't you going to caution me?'

'We only caution people when we're going to make a charge. I'm merely asking you if you'd like to amend your original statement.'

'All right, then. I can't imagine how you've got on to it, but I did come down last summer. I meant to have a go at touching my cousin. We were absolutely on the rocks...'

Pollard listened once again to the story of the family's misfortunes, and of the long-standing feud between the two branches. The prospect of making a successful appeal to Bertha Wainwright had seemed so forlorn that Derek had decided to keep his plan from Rachel. Hence the need to invent a conference at Bridgeford, to account for his visit to the area. The Wrilburn Museum authorities had been very ready to give him leave of absence to attend to urgent family business, and a friend had lent him a car, his own having been smashed beyond repair in the accident.

At this point in his narrative Derek broke off.

'What was the date of this visit?' Pollard asked, to get him moving again.

'July 31.'

Either a damn clever bit of bluff, or an almost incredible coincidence Pollard thought.

'What time did you get to Twiggadon?' he asked.

The problem had been filling in time without spending money. He had driven down in a leisurely way, and arrived at Twiggadon just before five, feeling that this was the most propitious hour for an uninvited call on an old lady. He had parked at the turning, and walked down to find the house, having previously looked up its name in a telephone directory.

'And then, Mr Wainwright?'

'And then, the plain truth is that I hadn't the guts to put my pride in my pocket and go in.' Derek stared at him with a kind of hopeless bitterness. 'A successful chap like you just wouldn't know what it feels like not to be able to provide decently for your wife and family, especially with your wife in hospital only just getting over a miscarriage.

6

It's a peculiarly degrading sort of hell, take it from me. And I knew that I'd make a bish of seeing Bertha, anyway. I always do. I muffed my Oxbridge interviews, and had to go to Redbrick. I'd never have got my present job if the chap they'd appointed hadn't ratted on them at the last minute, and they were in a hurry to find someone. And I've applied for bigger jobs dozens of times, knowing perfectly well that I could make a success of the work, but they've only got to see me to turn me down. Of course, I rationalized not going in to see my cousin. I stood outside that ghastly house telling myself that she might leave me something after all, but that if I tried to cadge now, I'd risk any chance I had of a legacy, and that I'd be a fool to do it. But I knew perfectly well that I was being gutless, of course.'

'How long did you stay in Twiggadon?' Pollard asked without comment.

'I don't know exactly. I seemed to lose count of time. I walked down past the farm and the cottage, and sat on a rock for a bit, thinking things over. Then I went back to the car, and sat there.'

Questioned closely as to whether he had seen anyone about, Derek was emphatic that the place had seemed completely deserted. He'd thought it surprising. Then he had decided to start driving homewards, looking out for a lay-by where he could spend the night, to save the price of a bed. Later, being badly in need of something to eat, he stopped at a village about sixty miles on the Bridgeford side of Wintlebury, at a cottage offering bed, breakfast and supper.

'A nice old girl said she'd do me some bacon and eggs and a pot of tea, although it was late : getting on for ten.'

'What time did you push on again?'

'Not until the next morning after all, as things turned out. I was just finishing the grub when a hullabaloo broke out in the street : someone had spotted smoke coming out of the roof of the cottage opposite. So of course I dashed across to help the locals get the people and furniture out, and do what we could till the fire brigade turned up. Then I helped hump the stuff we'd salvaged to a barn. By the time everything had calmed down again it was getting on for two. The old girl insisted on my staying the night, and gave me a whacking good breakfast the next morning, and refused to take a penny. I got back to Wrilburn in the afternoon.'

Psychologically convincing, thought Pollard, and what looks like a genuine alibi. Moreover, there seems to be absolutely nothing to connect him with the corpse ...

'Were you away from home on other occasions between the spring and autumn of last year?' he asked.

Derek Wainwright shook his head.

'Only when I was in hospital after the accident. We hadn't the cash for a holiday last summer. Ask my wife. And my sister-in-law who came to look after the children while Rachel was ill ... Oh, of course, a wife can't be forced to give evidence against her husband, can she?' He stared at Pollard with a kind of incredulity. 'Do you really think I'm a murderer? A chap like me? It's crazy.'

'Frankly I don't,' replied Pollard, 'but what a policeman thinks is neither here nor there. One has to have verifiable facts. Could you find the cottage where you stayed again?'

'Good Lord, yes. It's on the main road. I had to look out for it on the way down last Monday, although I knew it would bring the whole blasted trip back.'

'Let's go, then, and try to get confirmation of all this.'

Old Mrs Hunt of Wisteria Cottage, Clysthead St John, recognized Derek Wainwright at once, saying several times over how real nice it was of him to call in and bring his friend. My, what a night it had been, to be sure, with Mr

Hodge's cottage going on fire... She insisted on producing tea and homemade cake, and without prompting plunged into an account of the fire which bore out Derek's account in every particular. She also stated that she hadn't been able to close her eyes for the rest of the night, she'd been that upset, and had got up and gone down twice to make sure she'd turned off the electric.

Eventually they managed to get away.

'Well?' asked Derek, as they drove out of the village.

Pollard was silent for a moment.

'In return for your frankness, however belated,' he said, 'I'm prepared to tell you confidentially that at present we're interested in the night of July 31 last year. You are now right out of the picture, thanks to that fire. If it turns out that we're barking up the wrong tree, we shall have to start all over again. In that case we might conceivably make routine enquiries to check up your statement about not having been away from home on any other occasion— bar going to hospital—last summer. But I think this is unlikely to happen.'

'Thank you for telling me : I realize it's a good deal more than I deserve. You must think me a poor type.'

'We've got to live with our temperaments.' Pollard was deliberately robust. 'Besides, there are the obverse sides of people's qualities and defects. A chap with a lot of punch and drive can go through life like a bulldozer. And circumstances can and do alter cases. Money's a great giver of confidence.'

'The trouble is that the wretched money seems to stick in my throat, after that trip to Twiggadon, and never having managed to provide enough off my own bat.'

'Isn't that a bit hard on your wife?' remarked Pollard, with a sudden illuminating memory of Rachel's lack of enthusiasm on the subject. 'By the way, do you want a lift back, or would you rather cut across the moor on foot?'

Derek Wainwright decided to walk, saying that he wanted to think things out. Pollard dropped him at a suitable spot without regrets, as he wanted some time for reflection himself before deciding on his next step. There was no proof that the man's motive in coming down to Twiggadon the first time had been to visit his cousin, he thought. But was this matter really relevant to the case as it stood at the moment? He decided that it was not. The important thing was that it had been established beyond doubt that Derek had not been in Twiggadon during the night of July 31, and it was inconceivable that anyone of his type would have risked putting a dead body into a car boot in broad daylight. Still, to round things off, it would be satisfactory to find a witness of his visit. Nora Pearce was obviously the most hopeful line to follow up. As well as her alleged activities with binoculars there was her agitation when questioned about seeing anything unusual in the lane. Could she have seen Wainwright as well as someone for whom she cherished a secret passion? Pollard resolutely stifled his pangs of hunger, and decided to make another call at Moor View.

His luck was in. Rachel had taken the children out for a picnic, and Nora Pearce was alone. She was looking older and very tired, he thought, but greeted him with a new composure and resolution. Wondering what was coming, he began by asking the now well-worn question about the original ownership of the field containing the car dump. She discounted the idea that it had ever formed part of Bertha Wainwright's property. She would certainly have mentioned it: she disliked the dump, and not infrequently complained about it.

Pollard thanked her, and there was a pause...

'I—er—have been looking back over my diary as you requested,' she said, without looking at him. 'I find that on one occasion I did notice something rather unusual. Just a little out of the common, shall we say? Although I cannot believe for a moment that the person in question could possibly have anything to do with the—er—unhappy business in the field over there. No, not for a moment. Now, I must explain to you that my bedroom has a very beautiful view right down the valley. I often sit and enjoy it in my free time. Also I am not a very good sleeper.' She hesitated, and then went on. 'In the country one notices such little things, you know. They stand out. So it happened that rather late on the night of July 31 last year I noticed that the friendly little light in the window of Farm Cottage— the only light I can see in this very rural neighbourhood— never went on. This was most unusual. Mr Stobart is a great reader, and always stays up very late. Then, just after midnight, I heard footsteps in the lane. That, too, was so unusual that I looked out. It was bright moonlight : quite a beautiful night after the terrible rain we had before the disaster at Dincombe. So I saw him clearly.'

'Who, Miss Pearce?'

'Why, Mr Stobart, Superintendent. Then not long afterwards the light went on in his cottage, and almost at the same time I heard more steps, and Mrs Pendine of Watchers Way came up the lane. But that was not really remarkable. I have known her roam about the moor at night on quite a number of occasions.'

'Miss Pearce,' Pollard said, 'I don't for one moment question your reliability as a person, but can you be absolutely sure that the two people you saw were Mr Stobart and Mrs Pendine? It was, after all, the middle of the night.'

He watched her colour up and struggle with herself.

'Quite sure,' she said firmly, regaining her composure. 'I have a pair of binoculars. Quite good ones, which belonged to my dear father. It is really wonderful how near they seem to bring things. I enjoy watching the moor ponies through them.'

'You mean that you would be prepared to swear in a court of law that you saw those two persons?' he persisted.

She nodded, without speaking.

'Thank you,' he said, wondering if anything specific had happened to bring about the change in her attitude. For some reason the strong emotion she had shown the day before had given place to a much more characteristic sense of responsibility and public duty. 'As you say,' he went on, 'what you have told me may very well turn out to have nothing to do with my case, but you are absolutely right to report it.'

Nora Pearce bowed her head slightly.

'Perhaps your diary for that day mentioned Mr Derek Wainwright's visit, too?' he asked.

Completely taken by surprise she gave a violent start, and stared at him in undisguised horror.

'You know, Miss Pearce, it's far wiser to be frank with the police,' he told her, not unkindly. 'Anything else simply draws our attention to the person you're hoping to shield. Now, for my part, I'm going to break every rule in the book, and take you into my confidence, because I've complete faith in your discretion and loyalty, and also because I want every bit of help you can give me. I have had a talk with Mr Wainwright today, and he has told me that he came down here on July 31 last year.'

Towards the end of Pollard's narrative Nora Pearce unashamedly wiped her eyes.

'Oh, dear,' she said, 'so sad, and so unnecessary. A great deal of unhappiness is, in my experience. Miss Wainwright was such a good woman, but so much in the grip of the past. And poor Mr Wainwright is so very sensitive... Really, it's wonderful to meet someone in these days who isn't—well—ruthless, and ready to trample over others in order to get on in the world. Of course, it was wrong of

87

him not to be truthful—not that I am in a position to say so—but it was very understandable. I am quite sure that he has what I think is now called an inferiority complex about success. All on account of his wife and children, you know.'

'You actually saw him then?' Pollard asked her.

'Oh, yes.' She coloured up again. 'I happened to be sitting in my window on this occasion, too, and using my binoculars. I noticed a man sitting on the rocks at the bottom of Buttertwist, that's the tor on the left of the track down here. I remember thinking it was rather unwise— from the health point of view, I mean, after the heavy rain of the past few days—'

'Can you remember what time this was?' Pollard interrupted.

'It must have been about six o'clock, during my free time after washing up the tea things. Then, when I ran up to my room to tidy myself for supper, just before half past seven, I glanced out again, and saw him coming up the lane. He stopped and gazed up at the house so long that I should have been a little uneasy if he hadn't had such a nice face. I took a good look at him, and of course I recognized Mr Wainwright the moment I saw him last Monday. Naturally, I made no remark, although I thought it rather strange that he did not mention the visit. Then, from something Mrs Wainwright said to me, I realized that he hadn't told her either. That was the day the dreadful discovery was made, and when the Inspector from Bridgeford said that he understood Mr and Mrs Wainwright had never been to Twiggadon before, I'm afraid I—I let it pass. I knew he couldn't have had anything to do with it, although it was all so terribly puzzling,' she concluded rather incoherently.

No one who was trying to dump a body would conceivably draw attention to himself by hanging around like that.

Pollard thought. Another important outcome of the day's work was Nora Pearce's confirmation of Henry Stobart's and Sybil Pendine's presence in the lane that night. He decided that this cut out any urgent need to question Sybil Pendine before returning to Bridgeford: her attempted blackmail could wait. With a clear conscience he tactfully extricated himself, and headed for somewhere to eat.

SEVEN

SERGEANT TOYE'S approach to his work was less pragmatic than his superior officer's. Unlike Pollard, who had left for Twiggadon after breakfast on Sunday morning with his plan of campaign relatively fluid, he had drawn up a carefully-planned programme for himself.

He surmised that Mrs Cupple would be enjoying a long Sunday lie-in, and an early call on her was, therefore, out. The milkman who had taken on Steve Mullins as an assistant was a much more suitable proposition, probably being anxious to get his round over and done with as soon as possible. After checking up on the address of the dairy, Toye accordingly borrowed a bicycle from a gratified constable, and pedalled through pleasantly quiet and empty streets towards the poorer quarter of the town.

He found the shop without difficulty, surmounted by a sign announcing A. H. STENTIFORD. *Prop*. It was small and old-fashioned, but had somehow managed to avoid being swallowed up by one of the milk distributing giants. A brass churn polished to a dazzling brilliance occupied a central position in the window, flanked with glass jars which had been forcibly crammed with asters. The churn was a collector's piece, engraved with a design of buttercups and the entwined initials of its original owner. Under cover of admiring it Toye took stock of the situation inside the shop, which was open. A steady stream of customers was coming and going, most of them in varying degrees of dishabille, carrying bottles of milk or small basins of cream. A brisk trade in miscellaneous groceries was also in progress. A white-haired woman in a print overall presided at the counter. She seemed personally acquainted with everyone, and there was a cheerful babble of chat and backchat.

As Toye was estimating the sensation which his entry and enquiry for Mr Stentiford would cause, an urchin in grubby khaki shorts squeezed his way out of the shop, a bottle of milk in one hand, and a bilious-green lolly in the other. He eyed Toye curiously, and was just going his way when the latter called him back.

'Hi!' he said, jingling the loose coins in his trouser pocket. 'Know where I can find Mr Stentiford?'

The boy's eyes brightened hopefully.

"'E's on 'is round. You comerlongerme, mister. I knows where 'e'll be, near 'nuff.'

He set off up the road, looking back from time to time to make sure that Toye was following, his tongue exploring the surface of the lolly. At a street corner he stopped and listened. From a distance came the unmistakable clink of bottles.

'Down the bottom, an' turn left, mister. Yer can't miss 'is float. Me Mum's waitin' fer the ruddy milk, see?'

Toye produced a sixpence, and coasting down the street as instructed came in sight of a milk float lumbering slowly and asthmatically towards him. It drew up with a rattling shudder, and an elderly man leapt nimbly out, seized a carrier of full bottles and dived into a succession of doorways.

'Mr Stentiford?' enquired Toye, arriving on his bicycle in time to intercept him before he re-embarked.

The milkman had a slightly pugnacious expression and grey bristling hair. He looked Toye up and down before replying.

'That's my name. What's the big idea? I take it you're not chasin' after me to pick up a pinta.'

Toye presented his official card, and briefly stated his business, watching gratification spread slowly over Mr Stentiford's rosy face as he visualized himself in an important role in a police investigation.

'That's right,' he said. 'Worked for me four weeks, Mullins did. Then 'opped it without a blessed word. That's what you get these days. Look, I've gotta finish the round, see? You cut round to the yard back o' the shop, an' I'll be along inside ten minnits. Don't you go through the shop : 'tis full o' clackin' wimmin.'

Toye complied, and duly found himself in the Stentiford kitchen, a haven of solid old-fashioned comfort, smelling appetizingly of fried bacon. Within a few moments there came the sound of the milk float's arrival in the yard, and Mr Stentiford entered with a pressing invitation to sit down and have a bit of breakfast with him.

The meal was served by Mrs Stentiford, who made a succession of brief darts into the kitchen during temporary lulls in the shop. Her determined efforts to contribute to the conversation led to some confusion, and Toye was thankful when she finally drew up to the table herself, announcing that she had dropped the blind, and latecomers could take themselves somewhere else.

In his usual painstaking way Toye took the Stentifords over the whole period of Steve Mullins's employment. No, he hadn't got the job through the Labour Exchange. Mr Stentiford didn't hold with the place : they'd send along any riff-raff. When he wanted someone he always put a notice in the shop window. So Mullins must have seen it, or been told there was a job going. No, he hadn't been able to produce any references, but you had to take what you could get these days, and count yourself lucky. Yes, they'd wondered between themselves if the chap was on the run, and kept a sharp look-out for the stores and cash, but there hadn't been anything amiss, not the whole four weeks he'd been on the round.

Toye turned next to the subject of what Mullins had looked like. The two Stentifords confirmed Trevor Cupple's description of his height, build and long lightish hair, and after some argument agreed that his eyes had been a sort of blue grey. Toye conscientiously refrained from prompting, and was rewarded by a spontaneous remark from Mrs Stentiford.

'Mullins 'ad a nice set o' teeth,' she declared. ''Is own, that is. Mouth on the big side, I'd say.'

Asked about the shape of the face, they were undecided : not round so as you'd notice it, nor yet lantern-jawed. No, he'd never said anything about having had an accident or breaking any bones, nor mentioned hospitals or operations. He'd been very close about what family he had, and where he'd come from. A bit surly with customers, too. Mr Stentiford had told him of it, and that a man in business on his own couldn't afford not to be obliging, but he'd no interest in his work, like all the young chaps these days. Life was a lot too easy for them, that was the trouble.

'All the same, 'e'd got the 'ang of retail tradin',' remarked the dairyman. 'Maybe 'is folk was retailers.'

Toye was interested, and followed up his statement, but soon realized that the Stentifords could tell him nothing more on the subject. He turned to the question of dates.

'You say the last time Mullins worked here was the morning of Saturday, July 28?' he asked.

The ledger was produced in evidence. It recorded that Mullins had been given his week's pay on that day, and had his card stamped up-to-date. He had said nothing whatever about not turning up again on Monday. Toye asked about the insurance card. He learnt that Mullins said he had lost his on the way down from London, and the local office had issued him with another, pending enquiries. Later, a man came round saying that they were unable to trace the issue of this lost card, but by that time Mullins had gone off and taken the new one with him.

A possibly useful lead gone west, Toye thought regretfully.

'Now, this is very important,' he told them. 'I want you both to think very carefully before you answer. During the week before Mullins went off, did you notice anything different about him? For instance, did he seem worried or excited?'

The Stentifords admitted reluctantly that they could not remember anything of the kind. Everyone had been properly browned off that week with the rain. It had been something terrible, ending up with that awful flood at Dincombe, and all those people drowned. The things that happened these days, and now the skeleton up to Twigga-don. Did Sergeant Toye really think it was Mullins, poor chap?

Toye sidestepped the question, emphasizing that there was no evidence that this was the case, but naturally the police were enquiring into unexplained disappearances from the area. He wondered how long it would be before the story of the pony-chasing and the assault on Mullins got round. Assuring the Stentifords that they had been most helpful, and thanking them for the meal, he took his leave.

He felt that it was still on the early side for a visit to Mrs Cupple, and bicycled to a nearby park. There were very few people about, and sitting down on an empty seat he made notes on his interview with the Stentifords. Then he took out a map and began to consider the various routes by which Mullins could have left Bridgeford.

What had been his purpose in leaving Bridgeford? The only clue to his plans was his alleged statement that he was going to get even with the farmer who had beaten him up. There seemed no reason why Trevor Cupple should have made this up, even if he had the imagination to do so. Was Mullins simply talking big, to cover a sense of humiliation, or was he the sort to nurse a grievance to explosion point? Not that this really mattered at the moment. There were some definite resemblances between Mullins and the skeleton, and the possibility of his having returned to Twiggadon must be investigated thoroughly. To get there he would have to go out on the London road, and branch off. Bus services must be looked into, but surely it was much more likely that he would have thumbed a lift: a depressing thought. It had been in the middle of the holiday season, and passing motorists might have come from anywhere between Land's End and John o' Groats. An enquiry on a gigantic scale seemed to be looming ahead. If he had not gone to Twiggadon he might have returned to London, or taken the Wintlebury fork, or left the town in the opposite direction, heading west. Or, of course, struck out across country by one of the innumerable by-roads shown on the map. Then there was the railway.

Unless the chap just couldn't wait to get at the farmer— almost certainly Bickley—it was decidedly odd that he went off so suddenly, when he must still have been feeling a bit of a mess. If only we knew why, Toye thought, it would be comparatively easy to work out where he went, and either find him alive and kicking somewhere, or identify the skeleton as his. However, speculation got you nowhere. The next step was to see Mrs Cupple, and get every possible bit of information about Mullins out of her.

Mrs Cupple opened the door of number twelve Hobbett

Street so promptly that Toye wondered if she had been watching hopefully from behind the curtain of her front room. He placed her at once as a good-natured type in process of going to seed. She had let her figure go, her arches had dropped in protest, and he detected a whiff of spirits.

The cramped little terraced house was congested to suffocation point with the characteristic products of the Affluent Society. Invited to enter, Toye squeezed with difficulty past the Honda in the narrow passage, and followed her to the kitchen.

It was not a large room, and as well as an electric cooker, a table, some chairs and a dresser, it contained an outsize television set which was blaring powerfully, and a refrigerator. Every available surface was crowded with cooking utensils, crockery, tins and general odds and ends. It was hot, and the air was thick with the savoury smell of a roasting joint, the sizzling of which could be heard in the brief pauses in the television broadcast. In response to a gesture from Toye, Mrs Cupple turned off the sound, leaving the picture flickering industriously away on the screen.

'Bit warm,' she remarked conversationally, clearing a space on the table with a sweep of a large bare arm. ' 'Ow about a nice cuppa? You'm 'uman, even if you'm a rozzer, I says.'

Toye was feeling decidedly replete after two breakfasts, but felt it expedient to accept. Mrs Cupple switched on an electric kettle which quickly roared up to the boil, and within a few minutes he was sipping a potent brew of tea.

Rather to his surprise he found himself liking Mrs Cupple. There was something disarming about her, and he found it impossible to visualize her as a murderer or an accessory. Moreover, the house was so crammed with furniture and other objects that there seemed to be little space available for the concealment of a body. He had already noted that the diminutive lean-to scullery and the kitchen were both stone-floored. However, he'd manage to look over the place later...

'Loored to 'is doom, pore young fella,' pronounced Mrs Cupple with dramatic relish, clattering down her cup. 'Follered down 'ere by one o' them Lunnon gangs.'

'Did Mullins ever tell you he'd been mixed up with a gang?' Toye asked her.

'Not 'im. Close as the grave. 'Ad to be, on the run from a gang. But they got 'im. Yer sees it ev'ry day on the Noos.'

Behind her ghoulish enjoyment Toye sensed a higher IQ than her son's, and began to question her carefully. Her description of Mullins included all the items already supplied by Trevor and the Stentifords, and when asked about the shape of his face she replied at once that it was a bit weaselly-like. As a lodger he'd fitted in well, taking them as he found them, and paying on the nail. He'd given no trouble, unless you'd call patching him up a bit after he'd taken that bashing giving trouble. She, Ena Cupple, never grudged lending folk a hand when they were down on their luck.

Toye's thoughts returned to the topic of Steve Mullins's sudden departure.

'All the same,' he said, 'I understood from your son that Mullins went off owing you half a week's money. A bit shabby, surely, after all you'd done for him?'

Mrs Cupple's enjoyment of drama, however, prevented her from seeing it in this light. If a gang was on your heels you could hardly be expected to think of trifles like a few days owing. He'd probably got a tip-off somehow, and hoped that if he went fast enough he'd shake them off. Why, Trevor'd seen it that way at first. It was the snooty little bitch he'd taken up with as was grabbing after every penny.

'But did he get a tip-off?' asked Toye. 'Now this is very

7

important, and I want you to think carefully. Did you notice anything in the least different about Mullins during the week before he cleared out so suddenly? Did he strike you as frightened or worried, for instance?'

''E come in different on the Friday afternoon,' she replied without any hesitation. 'Where 'e'd bin, I can't say, but 'e 'adn't come direck from work, not by an 'our or more. 'E wasn't what you'd call excited, but so as 'e'd made up 'is mind to summat.'

Toye pounced, but all his skill and experience in questioning failed to extract a shred of evidence to support this statement. It was apparently based solely on feminine intuition. Pressing on with his enquiries he learnt that after Trevor had come in, they had had a meal round about quarter to six. Then Trevor had gone out again, and Steve Mullins had sat reading the evening paper while Mrs Cupple did the dishes. Then he'd offered to stand treat at the Spotted Dog, round the corner.

''E weren't mean, that girl can say anythink she likes,' Mrs Cupple reiterated with warmth. ' "Come on, Ma," 'e said. "Let's go an' 'ave a nice booze-up. Treat's on me. It's pay-day termorrer." Mind yew, 'e was puttin' on an ack.'

'What do you mean by that?'

'Why, talkin' that way, 'Twasn't nacheral to 'im, see? Times 'e'd come out quite clarse, when 'e were off 'is guard. Not real clarse, like the Juke, but 'e'd 'ad a lot better schoolin' than most folk round this way. Bears out 'e was on the run, don't it?'

'About those threats of his to go back to Twiggadon and get even with the chap who'd lammed into him. Do you think that was what he meant to do, and he thought it would be healthier to clear out of the neighbourhood altogether when he'd done it?'

Mrs Cupple shook her head so vigorously that her double chins wobbled.

' 'E never,' she said decisively. ' 'E'd take the easy way, Steve Mullins, sooner than stick out 'is neck. Just shootin' 'is mouth, 'e was.'

'I suppose he didn't have any letters or callers while he was here?'

'Not a one. Lyin' low, 'e were, but they got 'im, an' put'un in that car up to Twiggadon. I 'opes the perlice gets 'em, that's all.'

Toye pointed out once more that there was no definite evidence to support this theory, at which she sniffed and tossed her head. Much to his relief she took it for granted that he would want to look over the house, and he reflected that there was something to be said for crime plays on television and even for detective novels. An unexpected stroke of luck was a resounding crash from the kitchen, just as they reached the top of the stairs. Mrs Cupple descended again with surprising speed, luridly apostrophizing her neighbour's cat, and he had time to open cupboards and look under beds. The room which Mullins had occupied was a slit over the front door, just able to take a bed and an upright chair. Mrs Cupple informed him that two other lodgers had rented it since. No one ever stayed long as it was a bit cramped : only while they were looking around. Not that she bothered. What with her office cleaning job, and the widow's pension and Trevor's money things weren't so dusty. And when he married that Moyra, God help him, she'd do up his room nice, and get a permanent.

Toye was amused at her detailed knowledge of Steve Mullins's wardrobe, and other scanty possessions, and made a note of what he must have been wearing when he left.

'I want to narrow down the time when he went off as far as we can,' he told her. 'Can you remember roughly when you and your son were both out that day?'

To his satisfaction Mrs Cupple was quite clear on this point. Normally both Trevor and herself went off to work soon after half past seven, but she didn't go on Mondays, having cleaned the office on Saturday morning. She always stayed at home Mondays, did the bit of washing, tidied round and then went out to the shops. That would have been round half past ten. How long was she out on her shopping? Well, say about an hour. The shops were only just round the corner, but you met your friends, and everyone had a crack after the weekend.

Feeling that he had for the moment exhausted her as a source of information, Toye thanked Mrs Cupple for her help, managed to avoid having another cup of her tea without giving offence, and took his leave.

Back at the police station after a snack at a pub. Toye found that no message had come through from either Pollard or Scotland Yard, and settled down to consider the facts which he had collected in the course of the morning.

It was obviously a matter of urgency to find Steve Mullins if he were still alive. If he could only be tracked down, the possible case against Bickley would cease to exist. Of course, Bickley wouldn't be out of the running altogether, but at present nothing else was known about him which was a potential link with a skeleton found on his land.

The only hope of finding Mullins was to get out the fullest available description of him. Perhaps there were enough particulars now for the back room boys to build up an Identikit portrait. Slowly and meticulously Toye listed every scrap of information about Mullins's appearance and personality provided by the Stentifords and Cupples. Then he re-read Alan Pulman's detailed description of the skeleton, and felt impressed by the indisputable points of resemblance. Still, the search for Mullins had got to go ahead, and as quickly as possible. He sat pondering on the best use to which he could put his time until Pollard reappeared.

The post office would be shut, so enquiries about possible letters sent to Mullins *poste restante* must wait until the next day. Enquiries at the railway and bus stations were almost certain to turn out a waste of time on a Sunday afternoon : there would be no one who could look up records of duty rosters for July 30 last year, even if these had been kept, which did not seem very hopeful. But the prospect of merely hanging around waiting for the return of Pollard, was a waste of time which Toye's zealous and conscientious soul deplored. As he cast about for some alternative programme there came steps in the corridor, and a knock heralded the appearance of Inspector Crake, less inhibited in Pollard's absence, and obviously bursting with curiosity about progress in the case.

Toye welcomed him with relief, and plunged into a *résumé* which brought him up-to-date, not forgetting to be congratulatory about the local enquiries which had resulted in Trevor Cupple's coming forward. Crake agreed that nothing worthwhile could be done with the public transport authorities until the following morning.

'It'll be a waste of time anyway, if you want my opinion,' he said frankly. 'Chaps like this Mullins—and God knows we get enough of 'em in these parts—'d rather lie down and die in a ditch than fork out a fare. If he left Bridge-ford, it was on somebody else's four wheels, you can bet your bottom dollar.'

'That's just about the length of it,' Toye replied gloomily. 'The place must've been stiff with visitors from anywhere you like. I suppose there's a chance something might come in if we put out a broadcast appeal, but it's over a year ago.'

'When was it he vamoosed from the Cupples?'

'Monday, July the thirtieth.'

'Time of day?'

'Between half past ten and half past eleven, roughly. There doesn't seem any doubt about that.'

Inspector Crake looked thoughtful.

'It's just on the cards that being a Monday morning might make it a bit easier,' he said cautiously. 'A lot of the local people from the villages all round come in to do their shopping Monday mornings. There'd more likely be a spare seat with one of them than in a car bung full of summer visitors.'

At the prospect of a lead, however slight, Toye showed keen interest.

'That would mean, then, that anyone thumbing a lift from one of these locals would soon get slung out, and have to pick up another car if he wanted to push ahead?'

'That's right,' Crake agreed.

'Well, then,' Toye went on, visited by a promising idea, 'let's say Mullins cleared out of the Cupples by eleven. He wouldn't have wanted to hang around once he'd heard Mrs C. go out, especially as he owed her money. The chances are that he went on one of the main roads. Say half an hour to get out of the town and strike lucky with a car. It isn't everyone'll give a lift these days, and small wonder. So he wouldn't have landed up anywhere much before twelve : more likely after. If he found himself in a village, what's the betting he made for the pub?'

Crake looked impressed.

'You could be on to something there,' he admitted. 'If the chap got a lift from someone local, that is. It's a sporting chance, anyway. Our men out in the villages could start on enquiries. Shall we put it to the Super? Let's have a look at the map.'

With Crake's help, a list of likely villages within roughly a twelve-mile radius of Bridgeford was drawn up. There were an awful lot of them, Toye thought.

'Any chance of my borrowing one of your cars?' he

asked. 'I might try a few of the nearer ones myself. There's not much else I can do till Superintendent Pollard comes back.'

'Sure,' Crake told him. 'Help yourself when you're ready to go. Nice thought, a pub crawl.'

Left alone Toye thought long and hard about the departure of Steve Mullins and the motive behind it. Whether he'd returned to Twiggadon or not, he'd probably have been quite keen to cover his tracks, and the best place for this was a large town. He might have been making his way back to London, but was this very likely, since by his own account he'd only recently left it? Mightn't he have branched off from the London road and headed towards Wintlebury? Just the sort of place where you could vanish without trace, and pick up a job of sorts, too.

The more he considered it, the more tenable the Wintlebury theory became. Anyway, if Pollard hadn't returned by five he'd start off, and look in at some of the nearer pubs.

The enquiries took longer that Toye had expected. The first likely pub he came to had recently changed hands, and the former landlord, one Sam Jeffreys, was now living in Bridgeford. This involved doubling back again, and tracking him down in a small bungalow on the far side of the town. Both he and his wife were flattered by the visit of a Scotland Yard detective, and anxious to be helpful, but had no recollection whatever of a youth like Steve Mullins coming in with a black eye over twelve months ago. Mr Jeffreys pointed out the all too obvious truth that youths of that sort who'd been in a dust-up weren't all that out of the ordinary these days, and you couldn't hardly be expected to call to mind every chap coming into your bar, could you?

Toye agreed, thanked them both, and set off once again on the road leading out of the town.

At his next port of call the landlord was keenly interested and inclined to be garrulous. Some elderly regulars were already installed, and he suggested asking them if they remembered a lad like the one the sergeant was asking after. A lively but time-consuming discussion developed, but it produced nothing of value. Refusing a drink, Toye pushed on once more.

The Cross Keys at Kennaford, the next village, had expanded into a modern road house. A number of cars were already parked outside, business was brisk and Toye's visit unpopular. He was obliged to exert his official authority to get co-operation from the landlord.

'This isn't a one-eyed village inn,' the latter said aggressively. 'How the hell d'you think we can remember who came in on July 30 last year? Why, chaps are coming and going all the bloody time in the summer when the visitors are around.'

Toye, imperturbable, stood his ground. He declined to leave until he had satisfied himself that none of the bar or café staff had any recollection of a youth resembling his description of Steve Mullins. On coming out of the Cross Keys he paused, crossed it methodically off his list, and after looking at his watch went into a telephone kiosk and rang the police station at Bridgeford.

He was told that Superintendent Pollard had just come in . . .

'Hullo! Crake tells me you're doing a pub crawl,' came Pollard's voice a few moments later. 'Nice work if you can get it. Are you on the point of solving the case, by any chance? No? Well, I should think you'd better come back here, and I'll report on the meagre results of my own day.'

EIGHT

'Superintendent Pollard's on the line to Scotland Yard,' the duty sergeant told Toye, as the latter came into Bridgeford police station. 'Call came through five minutes ago.'

Toye waited and speculated. They could hardly have got on to much yet. Come to that, Stobart had been living on his own down at Twiggadon for the past fifteen years, so there couldn't possibly be any personal link with the dead youth going all that way back—he'd only have been a small kid. Still, by unearthing Stobart's past some indirect connection might be brought to light.

His musings were interrupted by the return of Pollard, with some sheets of shorthand notes in his hand.

'Hullo,' he said. 'That was Evers, with what they've managed to dig up so far. It was a bit slow at first, because it turned out that Stobart didn't live in Epsom after all, although he employed a removal firm from there. He lived in Sallowbourne. Know it? It's one of those ghastly outer suburban no-man's-lands, with all the roads exactly alike. The gist of what they've discovered is that Stobart came out of the army at the end of the war, and went back to his old job—or got a new one—in London, commuting from Sallowbourne, where he somehow managed to get a small house. About 1950 his wife left him, taking the child, a boy of about six. Nothing's known of where they went, or where they are now. Stobart presumably gave up his job, sold up the house and went off, too. They're getting on to the removal firm tomorrow, if it still exists. Sallowbourne's one of those places with a high turnover of population, and so far no one has been found who remembers the Stobarts at all clearly. Of course there was a tremendous lot of coming and going in the post-war period. But it's interesting about the boy, isn't it?'

'You mean that he'd be about twenty now, sir?'

'Yes. Youths of about twenty are getting a bit thick on the ground. There's our skeleton, to start with. Then there's Steve Mullins, and now a possible young Stobart.'

'Funny if all three of them were really one and the same,' remarked Toye with interest.

'You sound like the Athanasian Creed. Not meaning to be blasphemous,' Pollard added hurriedly, remembering that Toye was a sidesman at his parish church. 'Have you had anything to eat on your pub safari, by the way?'

On hearing that Toye had not, he sent him off to get a meal and settled down to type out the report which he had just received over the telephone. On re-reading it he decided that it did not amount to very much. It was, of course, useful to have got a lead of a sort on what had precipitated Stobart into his hermit existence at Twiggadon, but was this very likely to be relevant to the case? Unless the man was a maniac as distinct from an eccentric, was it imaginable that he would have murdered his own son if the latter had turned up at the cottage? In spite of the fact that Stobart was popularly believed to have no visitors in the usual sense of the word, had the two been in touch? Suppose Steve Mullins was really young Stobart, and had been killed in a second dust-up with Bickley? Fantastic coincidences did happen...

Firmly putting aside further speculation on this score,

Pollard filled in time until Toye came back by amending the case summary which they had drawn up. He added a note on Derek Wainwright, to the effect that he had admitted a visit to Twiggadon on July 31 of the previous year, given a credible reason for it, and produced an unshakable alibi for the whole of the following night. In default of any known link between him and a youth of about twenty, there was no reasonable ground for considering him as a suspect in the case.

Anyway, Pollard thought, it's been a worthwhile bit of thinning out, even if it's taken the best part of a day. Now for Bickley and Stobart. Not forgetting, of course, that there's no proof that the whole job wasn't done by a complete outsider, and we haven't even got started yet.

This idea was so discouraging that he decided to give himself a bracer by ringing Jane . . .

'Not much traffic, but what there is is a bit impeding, all the same,' he told her in their private code. 'I did manage to cover a bit of ground today, though . . . No, I don't see any prospect of getting back at the moment . . . Tell me what you've been doing all day. Not hanging curtains, have you?'

'Hanging curtains?' Jane Pollard sounded mystified. 'What on earth made you think of that? I got the last lot up days ago.'

'Good,' he said, half-ashamed of himself. 'I don't think expectant Mums ought to shin up step-ladders on their own.'

Jane hooted derisively.

'Have you been chatting to the local Sairey Gamp?' she asked.

'Well, not exactly. All right—laugh! There go the blasted pips again.'

'On the whole,' Pollard said, after he and Toye had

pooled their day's findings and discussed them at length, 'I'm inclined to think it's odds on that the skeleton is Mullins. After all, the physical resemblances are quite marked, and Mrs Stentiford's remark about the nice set of teeth took them a good step further. If it is Mullins, Bickley seems more likely to be involved than Stobart, as things stand at present. It all underlines the fact that we can't try hard enough to pick up Mullins's trail, and we've far more chance of doing it in this part of the world than anywhere else. One of the few things we do know for certain is that the chap was around here right up to the time he disappeared. I'll see Puckeridge first thing tomorrow, and discuss getting out a description, and the possibility of his men making enquiries in the villages. I'm sure your pub idea is worth following up, but we can't spare the time to work on it ourselves. We can soon weigh in if someone thinks he's got a lead.'

Toye agreed.

'Did Evers say what other lines they were working on, sir?'

'Stobart's war record, his job, Somerset House to find out if the wife and boy are still alive—always assuming they stayed in the country—and any local gossip in Sallowbourne. It'll take a bit of time. Meanwhile, we're to let them have all particulars for an Identikit of Mullins. Another thing I want to do is to get Sybil Pendine to confirm that she saw Stobart in the lane that night. We'll confront her with the note, and go on to the evidence of her dabs if she digs her toes in. Then there's the important point about whether she's blackmailing the Bickleys, and if she is, on what score. It's just possible that we might get an admission out of her which would justify charging Bickley with murder—or anyway manslaughter, and the concealment of the body. But I'm not counting on it at all. I think it's more likely she saw Mullins being beaten up, or is cashing in on something which happened in the pre-Mullins era.'

'Are you going to tackle the Bickleys themselves to-morrow, sir?'

'It depends a lot on what we can get out of the Pendine. Anyway, we'll go out to Twiggadon as soon as I've seen the Super about the Mullins enquiries in the villages. He'll hate our guts, won't he, diverting his chaps from the summer visitors? Still, he gets things done.'

The following morning was wet and dismal. Far more cars were coming into Bridgeford than were leaving it, and Pollard and Toye noticed the high proportion of local numberplates and women drivers.

'Here come Crake's Monday shoppers,' Pollard remarked. 'The return flow would be in full swing by eleven-thirty, wouldn't you say, if they're going to be home in time to get the lunch?'

'That would be about it,' Toye agreed. 'Funny how Monday washday's gone out. It's the machines. You just chuck the stuff in anytime you feel like it.'

Pollard's thought reverted to Sybil Pendine. It was ridiculous to let her get under his skin, not to say deplorable for a Superintendent of the CID, whose job it was to carry out impartial investigations. Undeniably she'd got unusual powers—well, all right. As that old hulk Haycraft had said, there'd always been people like that . . .

He decided that a debunking line might cut out the 'wise woman' patter, and make it possible to get at some actual facts. Watchers Way looked more down-at-heel than ever under a smudgy grey sky. The front door stood open. As Pollard knocked he was greeted by a sour pungent smell of a culinary kind.

'Superintendent Pollard, Mrs Pendine,' he called. 'May we come in?'

Sybil Pendine was sitting at a table strewn with litter, in

the midst of which she was inscribing labels for her herbal preparations in her neat, clear script. She barely glanced up.

'You're wasting your time,' she remarked, in a voice devoid of interest.

'I don't think so,' Pollard replied, taking up a label bearing the legend HEDGEROW HAIR RESTORER. He scrutinized it carefully, and then took from his brief-case a thin piece of cardboard on which the reassembled fragments of the note found outside Henry Stobart's gate had been pasted. After comparing the two he held out the note to her.

'Look at this, please, Mrs Pendine,' he said. 'You admit having written it, I imagine?'

She did not make any denial or show surprise, taking refuge in a show of contempt.

'A scruffy sort of job, yours,' she commented, 'grubbing after people's letters and piecing them together.'

'So you know that Mr Stobart tore it up and threw it out?' Pollard sat down, indicating another chair to Toye. 'Perhaps you followed up the note with a personal call? It was just the opening gambit in a blackmailing game, wasn't it?'

'You can't prove a thing,' Sybil Pendine said coolly, taking up another label, and beginning to write. 'It could just as well be a friendly warning.'

'Unless Mr Stobart makes a complaint to the police, you probably won't hear any more of this matter,' Pollard agreed. He slightly stressed the penultimate word, and thought he detected a slight sign of uneasiness. 'But your hold over the Bickleys is another matter,' he said, with an abrupt change of tone. 'It was equally unfortunate for Bickley that you happened to see him, wasn't it?'

For the first time she seemed to him to react with complete spontaneity, looking up with an astonished expression.

'I didn't,' she said categorically. 'I didn't see anyone that night but Henry Stobart.'

'I'm not referring to that night,' Pollard cut in quickly, and saw her bite her lip. 'I'm talking about the occasion when you saw Bickley assault a youth who was chasing his ponies on a scooter. A violent assault, wasn't it? Quite a useful handle where Bickley was concerned. Not good enough for exacting big sums as the price of silence, but payment in kind can be very useful, can't it? Having one's larder stocked up is quite a thing these days, isn't it?'

Angry at having slipped up, and harassed by his staccato questions she attempted an inept defence.

'I never told him I'd seen him hit the boy. I've never said a word to him about it, so you can't prove it—he didn't notice I was up on Buttertwist. The little beast deserved all he got, anyway.'

'That's beside the point, Mrs Pendine. You may not have approached Mr Bickley personally, but you let his wife know what you'd seen, didn't you? Just mentioned it to her, and left it at that. No unpleasantness. Much wiser than confronting Mr Bickley himself. He could be quite a tough customer, don't you think? You knew that it would be quite easy for her to slip up here now and again with a few things off the farm.'

'They've been giving me that sort of thing for years,' she retorted with a return of confidence. 'You can ask them. And well they might, too. I've saved them hundreds of pounds by my warnings.'

'What do you mean, your warnings?' Pollard asked, deliberately provocative.

'What's the use of telling you? You wouldn't believe me. People like you think you know everything.'

'If I did, I should hardly be spending my time questioning you, should I?'

He watched her calculate swiftly, and assume a withdrawn expression, her strange dead eyes becoming remote as she stared at him. When she spoke her voice seemed to come from a distance, and was oddly compelling. He wondered if she had some natural hypnotic gift, and had studied ventriloquism as a useful asset.

'I knew the great cold in the Now, long before it struck ... I felt its cruel burning ... its whiteness blinded me. And the water comes ... so stealthy under the doors ... long curving fingers clawing its way into the house under the doors.'

'There's no point in turning on your professional techniques for our benefit,' Pollard said loudly and brutally. 'I'm quite prepared to accept that you have some extra-sensory powers, and may be able to issue long-term weather forecasts through them. If people find them useful and like to show their appreciation, that's quite in order. But, let me warn you: from now on the local police are going to take a keen interest in all your activities. You may think it's as well to discontinue some of them.'

Sybil Pendine seemed sunk in a sullen lethargy, and did not answer him, so he went on.

'My main purpose in coming here this morning is to ask you to sign a statement of what you saw taking place on the night of July 31 last year. We have brought with us a summary of what you told us last time. Are you prepared to read it over, and sign it if you find it correct? I may say that we already have a witness of Mr Stobart's presence in the lane at midnight.'

'That holier-than-thou little bitch Nora Pearce, I suppose? She'd enjoy being in with the police.'

The remark struck Pollard as strange as well as vindictive.

'We're here to ask questions, Mrs Pendine, not to answer them,' he told her.

'Oh, call it a day, can't you?' she said impatiently. 'I'll sign the thing if it's what I told you before.'

'Later on we may ask you for a statement about the

encounter between Mr Bickley and the youth. Can you remember the date when it took place?'

'No, I can't, but you can look it up for yourself if you want to. It was on the day before the Dincombe disaster : a Saturday afternoon during the awful rain and the floods. There was a let-up for an hour or two, and I'd gone down to see if the bridge had held.'

Pollard watched her reading through the typed statement with an air of shrewd attention. Finally she signed her name carefully. It struck him as pathetic that in spite of her unkempt appearance and scruffy surroundings she took pleasure in her good handwriting.

'Why don't you try to find more selling outlets for some of your herbal preparations?' he asked on a sudden impulse. 'There might be a shop in Bridgeford glad to sell them on a commission basis.'

A flicker of ironic amusement passed over her face.

'I might try,' she replied. 'As you say, some of them.'

As she handed him back the statement she looked at him squarely.

'That youth wasn't killed by Reg Bickley, if that's what you're thinking. I saw him get up afterwards and go off with another one who'd been hiding behind a rock.'

'Thank you,' said Pollard. 'That's useful confirmation of. a piece of information which we've already been given.'

Sybil Pendine made no move as he rose to leave, but went on staring at him.

'You're the first person who's tried to do me a good turn for a very long time,' she said. 'I'll do you one in return, although I'm out of practice. I was born under Aquarius— that's the water sign, you know. I've got something about water. Why, and how, I can't tell you, but water matters to you at the moment. And rain and wetness comes into it somehow.'

*　　*　　*

8　　　　　　　　113

As soon as they were out of earshot Toye snorted with disapproval.

'Slippery as they come behind all her blah. If that Haycraft wasn't in it, she'd've been laid by the heels long ago.'

Pollard brought his mind back from Jane, and possible hazards by water.

'She's certainly a very odd woman,' he said cautiously. 'Anyway, we've now got Nora Pearce's statement confirmed, and I'm sure Pendine was speaking the truth about seeing Bickley weighing into Mullins, and the two youths going off afterwards. And I'm satisfied that she knows nothing about a return visit by Mullins. Hullo, what's afoot here?'

Rachel and Derek Wainwright were seeing off a man and two women in a car, bright and slightly unnatural smiles on their faces. As it drove away they relaxed visibly, seized each other's hands and executed a lighthearted twirl round.

Marked easing up, thought Pollard. I do believe he's told her all about last summer.

Catching sight of Pollard and Toye, the Wainwrights hastily composed themselves. If Derek felt embarrassment at the encounter he did not show it.

'Prospective purchasers, come to inspect the house,' he explained. 'They seem to have swallowed the agent's blurb hook, line and sinker. Substantially-built period house in impeccable order, and all that.

'They seem to think it would make a good small guest house,' said Rachel. 'Of course, we plugged the idea as hard as we could.'

Pollard wished them luck over the deal.

'I'm sure you'd be thankful to sell the place before the winter,' he said. 'It'll be an upheaval for Miss Pearce, though.'

'Oh, she's agreed to come back with us,' Rachel told

him, 'as a part-time helper for me. Isn't it marvellous? I shan't know myself. Our house is big enough for her to have a flatlet of her own, so that she can be independent.'

'It's a relief that it's worked out so well,' said Derek. 'One felt a bit responsible for her. Fortunately she's gone down awfully well with the kids : they're absolute buddies. Aren't children unpredictable? We were afraid they might start playing her up when we first arrived.'

Pollard learnt that the twins were out on observation duty, Nora Pearce having presented them with an old pair of binoculars for which she said she had no further use.

'There's tremendous finality about that gesture,' Pollard remarked to Toye as they went on down the lane. 'I wonder where those two little tykes are spying from? We shall lose face if they see Bickley chasing us out of the farm on the end of a pitchfork. I've got a feeling that it's going to be a difficult interview.'

Ruby Bickley came out of the kitchen in response to Pollard's knock, and went very white.

'Good morning, Mrs Bickley,' he said. 'Are your children at home?'

'Why, watcher mean?' she demanded, taken aback. 'That they're not. They're stayin' down with their Auntie with all this unpleasantness up here.'

'In that case, we'd like a talk with you and your husband. Is he around?'

'He's out the back,' she admitted unwillingly.

'Well, perhaps you'd tell him we're here, and ask him to come in. May we come in ourselves?'

'Can't keep you out, can we?'

She turned on her heel and went along the passage to the back door. Pollard and Toye wiped their feet on the mat and went into the kitchen. It felt warm and cosy after the damp dreariness outside, and the table was already laid for the midday meal. After a pause they heard Reg Bickley's heavy tread and his wife's quick light one.

''Ere,' he said, advancing with squared shoulders. He was in shirtsleeves, his crisp dark hair damp from the rain, and smelt powerfully of sweat and animals. 'I've 'ad enough o' this badgering from you chaps. Us don't know nothin' about that dead chap up there in the car, see? So that's the end of it.'

'In point of fact,' Pollard told him, 'we're here to ask you about that youth you beat up on the afternoon of Saturday July 28 last year. There was a witness, you know.'

Bickley's jaw dropped, and he stared open-mouthed at Pollard. The silence was shrilly broken by his wife.

'That dirty double-crossin' bitch!'

He turned on her angrily.

'What the devil d'you mean?'

Ruby Bickley burst into tears.

'Mrs Pendine, 'twas. She came down one day when you were out . . . made it clear as daylight she'd seen it all, but wasn't goin' to say nothin' so long as I made it worth 'er while.'

'You bin givin' 'er money?' shouted Bickley.

'I never, Reg. Only summat to eat, week b'week. I didn't dare tell 'ee, I was that scared of what 'ee might do.' She dropped on to a chair, and sobbed convulsively, her head on her arms.

'I suggest we all sit down,' said Pollard, pulling out a chair from the table. 'Personally—and I'm speaking off the record, Mr Bickley—I should have felt like knocking the daylights out of the youth myself. But I want your personal account of what happened, please.'

Bickley slumped down on a chair next to his wife, and touched her clumsily on the shoulder.

'Lay off cryin', Rube girl,' he said, with unexpected gentleness.

Helped by questions from Pollard he gave an account of the incident which tallied in every respect with that of Trevor Cupple. He had been riding round checking his stock, and just by the Watchers had come on a young hooligan on a scooter charging a herd of mares and foals, scattering them right and left. He'd shouted at him, but the youth had shouted back, and gone on, so he, Bickley, had galloped up, had him off the scooter, and given him a bloody good hiding. He'd left him blubbering in the bracken, and as he rode off he'd seen another youth come out from behind the rock, help the first one up, and after a bit they'd made off towards the road, taking the scooter with them.

'OK,' said Pollard, 'that's all quite clear. But what happened when he came back the second time?'

Bickley stared at him blankly.

'Come back? Not 'im, not after the bellyful I'd given'n.'

'The youth's name was Steve Mullins.' Pollard's tone was cool and almost conversational. 'He had been lodging with a family in Bridgeford for the past four weeks. When he got home that Saturday night, considerably the worse for wear, his landlady patched him up, and advised him to take a day or two off work. On the following Monday morning, while she was out, Mullins cleared off with his belongings, and hasn't been seen or heard of since.'

The kitchen fell quiet, so quiet that the faint squeak of the little ship rocking to and fro in the dial of the grandfather clock was distinctly audible. A cinder tinkled into the ashpan of the Rayburn, and a spatter of rain slapped across the window.

Suddenly Ruby Bickley gave a frightened gasp, and her husband swore luridly.

'So that's the game, is it?' he demanded. 'Tryin' to make out as I killed the chap up yonder, an' put 'im in the car? Think I'd be such a bloody fool as to dump the body on me

117

own land?'

'I've made no accusation whatever,' Pollard said evenly. 'I am merely stating facts.'

Ruby Bickley, tears forgotten, turned on him blazing with fury.

'If that wicked woman Sybil Pendine's sayin' my Reg's a murderer and you believes one word she says, why, you're stark starin' mad. A real bad lot, she is. I'm not the only one she's 'ad under 'er thumb, that I'm not. There was Effie Steer workin' for 'er a day a week, an' not a penny piece, all along of 'er findin' out she'd took a bit o' summat of old Miss Wainwright's. She'd be up there now, if Miss Pearce 'adn't tumbled to it, an' told 'er she'd 'ave the lor on 'er. As to—'

'Steady, Mrs Bickley.' A small piece of the puzzle clicked into position in Pollard's mind as he broke in on her angry denunciation. 'As I said, I'm dealing with facts. Mrs Pendine hasn't accused your husband of murder, or even hinted at it.'

'She'd better not,' growled Reg Bickley. 'As to bein' under 'er thumb, that don't apply to me, whatever Ruby's been silly enough to do. If you get a tip that pays off 'andsome, what's wrong with passin' a fiver for'n?'

'I understand that Mrs Pendine has given you warnings of bad weather and floods, and so on, which have enabled you to protect your animals and farm buildings?'

'S'right. As to 'ow she knows, t'ain't my business. Those chaps at the weather office or whatever 'tis called don't know everythin'.'

'Fair enough, Mr Bickley, as long as any money which has passed between you and Mrs Pendine has been payment for services rendered, and not in return for keeping her mouth shut about your activities. I must tell you that there are definite points of resemblance between Steve Mullins, and the skeleton found in the car, which not unnaturally makes us wonder if we'd heard the second chapter of the story. I suggest that Mullins did come back, probably on July 30 last year. Unless he was a half-wit he wouldn't have risked matching up to you again. But there are plenty of ways of getting one's own back on a farmer: firing a rick, for instance. Perhaps you caught him at it, and without meaning to, hit him too hard this time, and found you'd killed him. But most unfortunately for you, Mrs Pendine was around again, either at the time, or when you were hiding the body in the car one night.'

The china on the dresser rattled as Reg Bickley brought his fist down on the table with a resounding crash.

'As God's my judge,' he said surprisingly, 'it's lies from start to finish. You chaps is paid to catch folk out any ways you can, but I'll swear on oath I never set eyes on that Mullins again after I left'n snivellin' down in the bracken.' He stared at Pollard, the freeborn Briton's awareness of his legal rights dawning in his eyes. 'Maybe you think you've got circumstantial evidence agin me, but you won't get no jury convictin' on that.'

'Why don't you take a look next door, or up to Watchers Way?' demanded Ruby Bickley shrilly. 'Why don't you try to find that Mullins? 'E must be somewhere. Rather pick on Reg, I s'pose, an' get it chalked up you've caught the murderer?'

'At this moment,' Pollard told her, 'a large number of the County Constabulary is trying to trace Mullins, and other enquiries are being carried on not only by us, but by Scotland Yard.'

Reg Bickley still stared at him.

'If that little rat ever showed up round 'ere again,' he said, 'I reckon 'e was brought. Feet first.'

Deep in discussion with Toye, Pollard did not notice the Wainwright twins hanging over the gate of Moor View until they greeted him excitedly.

'Does your sergeant know everything?' Philip asked in a stage whisper.

'Sure,' Pollard replied. 'He's in on it all.'

The binoculars were produced and admired. He explained that secret service agents were taken off jobs after a time, in case they were recognized.

'We've found an awfully good place on Skiddlebag for watching the path and the cottage,' Clare said, 'but the man's been out all the morning.'

'Nobody's called, either,' said Philip. 'I say, sir, Henry Stobart must be an—an alibi, mustn't it?'

'Don't you mean an alias?'

'Isn't it the same thing really?' Philip looked puzzled. 'I mean, if you call yourself something else, isn't it an alibi for the person who's really you? Help! there's Mummy calling us for lunch. Be seeing you, Super!'

' 'Bye,' called Clare as they ran up the path to the house.

Pollard and Toye exchanged an amused glance as they went on up the lane. The rain had stopped, and as they reached the main road the sun came out in a rapidly clearing sky, investing the distant view with hard bright colour. In the car Pollard gave an exclamation.

'See who's there,' he said, his eyes on the driving mirror. 'Henry Stobart coming down the hill. Been into Wilkaton for something, I suppose.'

'True enough he's more like a blooming great insect than a human being,' Toye commented.

They sat watching Henry Stobart's long loping strides helped on by a tall staff, his head thrusting forward as he walked.

'Push off,' said Pollard. 'I don't want to get involved with him till we've more to go on.'

Toye pressed the self-starter, and the car moved slowly off the rough ground on to the road.

NINE

AT THE request of the Chief Constable a conference took place during the afternoon, at which Pollard gave an account of his progress up-to-date. As an appreciable number of Major Preece-Rilby's men were now engaged in enquiries about Mullins, he was prepared for a chilly atmosphere, and was agreeably surprised to find a good deal more interest and readiness to co-operate than on his arrival in Bridgeford. He sensed that this was partly due to the fact that Mullins, now a strong candidate for identification with the skeleton, was non-local, almost a summer visitor, in fact, and that the whole business could be attributed to 'foreigners', for whom the county authorities had only incidental responsibility. He also noticed a marked tendency to cast Henry Stobart, rather than Reg Bickley, for the role of leading suspect.

'This Bickley theory just doesn't add up for me,' said Superintendent Puckeridge. 'I haven't met the chap myself, but it's clear enough from you and Crake that he's a hefty, hot-headed sort of a bloke who might well kill someone in a scrap without meaning to. But thinking out a bluff like parking the body on his own property, where it'd be bound to turn up sooner or later, doesn't match, somehow. Marvel is, it wasn't found a lot sooner, the way picnickers go messing about.'

Pollard agreed.

'I don't think myself that it would be in character, especially after we grilled Bickley this morning, and watched his reactions. And unless he's a damn good actor—again, not in character—I'm inclined to think he was speaking the truth when he swore he'd never set eyes on Mullins from the afternoon he walloped him. But on the other hand, one can't get away from the fact there are several quite striking points of resemblance between Mullins and the skeleton, and the only known link he has with Twiggadon is the dust-up with Bickley.'

'Can't build on the skeleton being Mullins, all the same,' the CC remarked reluctantly. 'Chap seems to have been a poor physical type, in spite of his teeth, and there are plenty of 'em around in spite of all this free milk and what-have-you. Stunted. Industrial Revolution, of course. Wonder the country had any decent breeding stock left.'

'We know all about Bickley,' Superintendent Puckeridge pursued, ignoring this incursion into social history. He paused, to get his newly-lighted pipe drawing properly. 'Comes of a decent local family who've been farming in the county for the Lord knows how long. Father's got a big farm outside Torcastle, to the north of the moor, but this Reg Bickley's a younger son, and had to strike out on his own. Nothing's known against any of 'em, and there's nothing mysterious about 'em, either. This Henry Stobart's a different kettle o' fish altogether. I don't say Scotland Yard hasn't got on to his past pretty smart,' he added magnanimously, 'but I hold there's something damn queer about a bloke who lives the way he does. What does he really do with himself out there? Haycraft says he goes off all day sometimes. How do we know what contacts he's got? Needn't be local ones. He could be picking up letters addressed to him at post offices, easy as pie. I reckon it'd pay if we followed him up, same as Mullins.'

'As a matter of fact, sir,' Pollard said to Major Preece-Rilby, 'I was going to put in a request for this, if it can be managed.'

'Of course it can. Put it in hand as soon as possible, Puckeridge. One thing, Stobart seems to be the sort of fellow you don't forget if you've once seen him. I suppose you'll have a direct confrontation with him soon? After all, you've got a couple of sworn statements that he was out that night when the Pendine woman said she saw lights in the field where the cars are. She sounds a queer customer. The other woman's quite normal, I hope?'

'Perfectly, sir. She's the sort who'd carry weight with a jury, if it came to that. I'm proposing to bring Stobart in here tomorrow for questioning about that midnight excursion of his. It'll be a job to get him to come, but I think he's more likely to agree to it than to letting us into his cottage. He seems to have an absolute fixation about his privacy.'

'Why not get him in tonight?'

'I think it's possible some further information about his past may come by tomorrow. At the moment we've precious little to go on. Also, if your men do get a lead on Mullins, it could virtually clear Bickley—or the reverse.'

The CC agreed, expatiating briefly on the value of thorough reconnaissance, and began to ask Superintendent Puckeridge about the negative reports which had already been received from villages on the main roads leading out of Bridgeford. As he followed these reports on a map, Pollard wondered how far, if at all, one could attach importance to them. Could any landlord remember a customer he had only seen once, over a year ago, with any accuracy, even if the chap had sported a black eye? Possibly a car owner who'd given a lift might. But unless it had been a local driver, tracking him or her down was going to be as big a problem as finding Mullins himself. It would be a tremendous step forward if only the skeleton could be positively identified with Mullins. At any rate one would know whose death one was investigating...

With only half his attention on the conversation of the others, Pollard was suddenly seized with an enormous distaste for his chosen career. Memories of physical and mental squalor and horror rose up from his subconscious. Why the hell had he chosen such a foul job, when he might have worked among normal civilized people in pleasant surroundings? With proper working hours, too, and able to get home at a reasonable hour each evening. He was visited with an appalling vision of himself pursuing types like Steve Mullins down the years ahead.

He was so immersed in gloom that he failed to register the reappearance of a constable who had already been in with a telephoned report from one of the villages. Superintendent Puckeridge took the typewritten slip and read it silently, his lips framing the words from time to time. But the studied casualness of his voice when he began to speak roused Pollard immediately.

'Looks as though Constable Rodd over to Clysthead St John could've got on to something, sir,' he remarked offhandedly, passing the paper to Major Preece-Rilby.

The latter drew himself up perceptibly as he read, and turned to Pollard with imperfectly concealed gratification.

'Landlord's wife at the local—pub called the Three Crowns—says she remembers a youth with a black eye coming in. One of the regulars bears her out, and Rodd's found some woman who says she gave a youth with a black eye a lift—silly fools, women drivers. Can't think why more of 'em don't get assaulted or murdered. Extraordinary bit of luck that all of 'em are sure it was on July 30 : fire in the village the next day, they say. Can't see what that's got to do with it, unless they think the youth was responsible.'

'I shouldn't think that's likely, sir,' Pollard told him. 'Oddly enough the fire also gave Derek Wainwright his alibi for the night of July 31. I must say I'm grateful to whoever triggered it off. And to Constable Rodd, I need hardly say, for a first-rate bit of detective work.'

Major Preece-Rilby and Superintendent Puckeridge made suitable acknowledgements of this tribute.

Pollard's depression persisted during the drive out to Clysthead St John, merely being transmuted into profound dissatisfaction with his progress in the case. He reflected that proof—or even virtual certainty—that Mullins had not returned to Twiggadon would eliminate Bickley as a likely suspect, but it would re-establish the frustrating anonymity of the skeleton. Moreover, he gloomily reminded himself, there was still no proof that he was investigating a murder. There still remained the possibility of some accident leaving no discernible traces, and the panic dumping of the victim by somebody badly frightened. Another nagging thought was that he had been attaching too much importance to the night of July 31. The lights might very well have been a figment of Sybil Pendine's overheated imagination. On the other hand, there was Nora Pearce's evidence that Henry Stobart was near the car dump on that night. Apart from the Bickley-Mullins situation, this was positively the only lead there was to work on at the moment.

Toye was tactfully silent at the wheel, and after a quick glance at him Pollard began to consider the situation geographically. They had already driven past the point where the minor road to Twiggadon branched off. If Mullins had really landed up at Clysthead St John, it meant that he would have overshot the direct route to Twiggadon by about twenty-five miles. In theory he could have made his way back there across country, but it hardly seemed likely.

Another point of interest was that he wouldn't have been heading back to London. The road they were on forked about ten miles short of Clysthead, right to London, and left to Wintlebury and beyond. Presently they came to the fork themselves, and bore left. Pollard put his conclusions to Toye, and they agreed that it looked very much as though Mullins—if he had really come this way—had been heading for Wintlebury. Traffic was now lighter, and in a comparatively short time they were running into Clysthead.

'That looks like the diligent Rodd,' Pollard remarked, as a uniformed figure came in sight, standing on the pavement with an air of expectancy. As they drew up outside the Three Crowns they received a smart salute from a youngish constable, pink-faced from a sense of occasion. He explained that the bar was full to bursting, and that Mrs Higgs, the landlord's wife, had placed her parlour at the disposal of Scotland Yard. On receiving Pollard's congratulations, he went positively scarlet.

Under the fascinated stare of a group of onlookers he escorted Pollard and Toye through a side door into a small sitting-room, and departed in search of Mrs Higgs. The muffled roar of conversation in the bar was cut off as he shut the door behind him, and silence descended.

'If that's the lady,' said Toye, studying a wedding photograph in the immediate pre-war style which hung over the mantelpiece, 'she looks the sensible sort all right. Not one of those who'll say anything to get into the papers.'

'Bouncing and competent lass,' agreed Pollard.

The next moment the unmistakable original of the portrait came briskly into the room, followed by Constable Rodd, and an elderly man with a nut-cracker face weathered to the colour and texture of old leather, a little bent but remarkably spry. Introducing him as Mr Abel Haraway, Mrs Higgs added in a loud aside that he was eighty-four, and wonderful for his age.

'An' Oi'd'ave 'ee knaw Oi b'ain't deaf,' the subject of her remark interposed. 'Long as 'ee speaks up Oi can 'ear with the best of 'em.'

'I'll do that all right, Mr Haraway,' Pollard said hastily, cutting in on Mrs Higgs's scandalized rebuke. 'I shall be very glad of anything either of you can tell me about this young man who came into the bar last summer.'

Seats were found, and Mr Haraway promptly took the floor with the utmost confidence. Unless I'm very much mistaken, Pollard thought, letting him have his head, this is the thing...

Every day of the week, the old man announced, he came into the Crowns twelve sharp for a pint afore dinner, and cleared off again at five minutes to the half-hour, dinner at his daughter's being half after twelve. That Monday, the day before Hodge's cottage went up, one of those beatniks came in, long hair like a maiden's, those tight blue trousers and a dirty old black jersey. Ripe black eye, and a mouth a bit skew-whiff, where somebody had landed him one. Pair of sandals on his feet, with his toes poking through, and carrying a pack. He'd asked for a pint of rough cider, and a coupla packets of crisps. He—Abel—could see Mrs Higgs had her eye on the chap, but Bill Higgs was hammering out the back, and would have been along in a brace of shakes. But he didn't give no trouble : just took his drink and crisps and went right over the other side, never answering a word when spoken to. Proper surly, some of these lads today.

At this point Abel Haraway cleared his throat and coughed meaningly, and Pollard took the hint; inviting the company to state their preferences and asking Toye to fetch a round of drinks.

'Is there anything you'd like to add to Mr Haraway's very clear statement, Mrs Higgs?' he asked.

'Well, sir,' she replied, giving him an amused glance,

'Granfer—that's Mr Haraway—don't miss much, as you'll have seen. It's true I didn't much like the look of the young fellow, but he paid up and didn't give me no lip, and when other customers started coming in I hardly noticed him again.'

''E went off just on twenty after the hour,' Abel Haraway stated without hesitation. 'Oi allus 'as me eye on the toime, comin' up ter dinner.'

'Did you see which way he went after leaving the pub?' Pollard asked him

'B'aint possible, zur, from wur Oi wur sittin'. Passage takes a turn, doan't 'e Missus?'

Mrs Higgs agreed. Over the drinks Pollard asked if anyone was likely to have been about in the village who might have witnessed the youth's departure. Doubt was expressed. It was right in the middle of the dinner hour, and most folks' kitchens were at the back.

Pollard considered.

'You must have had a close-up of his face when he was standing at the bar getting his cider. Would you have called him a good-looker?'

'That I wouldn't,' she replied emphatically, to the accompaniment of a shrill cackle from Abel Haraway. 'Peaky little rat-face, he had, and my, he could have done with a shave!'

'Did you notice his teeth?'

Mrs Higgs put down her glass of port, and screwed up her eyes in an effort of recollection.

'Now you come to mention it, he hadn't got a bad lot of teeth. Even, they were, and quite nice and white. Best thing about him, I'd say.'

'I know it's the devil of a long shot,' Pollard said to Rodd outside the Three Crowns, 'but I'd like you to enquire at all houses along the main road and anywhere else you think, in case anyone saw this youth leave the village. I'm particularly anxious to find out if he went back on his tracks.'

He went on to explain the Bickley-Mullins situation. Constable Rodd listened with absorbed attention, and undertook to get on to it right away.

'I'm real proud to be in on a big case like this one, sir, I can tell you. Do you think the chap at the Crowns was this Mullins, and maybe the skeleton up to Twiggadon?'

'I think it's quite possible, Rodd. However, we'd better see what this Mrs Carstairs says, who gave the lift.'

'Mrs Carstairs is a real lady,' said Rodd, in the tone of one handing out a comprehensive testimonial.

They found her attired in a canvas gardening overall with innumerable bulging pockets, feeding her chrysanthemums with liquid fertilizer. She broke off and surveyed the three men ruefully.

'I must just put in a stick to show exactly where I've left off,' she said, 'and then I'll come quietly.'

'I know you've already told Constable Rodd all this,' Pollard said to her, when the party was settled in garden chairs on the terrace outside the house, 'but I'd like to hear it again at first hand, if you don't mind, in case it suggests something fresh to me.'

Mrs Carstairs explained that she had already been ticked off by her husband for giving the young man a lift, but her son, a rugger Blue, had been with her, so it really had been quite all right. They had picked him up on the outskirts of Bridgeford, somewhere about half past eleven, and it must have been a little after twelve when they dropped him in the village.

'Did you gather where he was trying to get to?' Pollard asked her.

'He said something rather vague about jobs being easier to get in the Midlands. My son told him to make for

9

Wintlebury at the Cold Ash roundabout when he came to it, and he asked how much further it was when he got out of the car. As we drove on I happened to glance in the driving mirror, and saw him going into the Three Crowns.'

Pollard reverted to the now well-worn subject of the youth's appearance, and listened to a description which included all the items specified by previous witnesses. Mrs Carstairs' son had been driving, and she had several times turned round to make conversation with the young man who was in the back of the car.

'Did he sound like a Cockney?' he asked.

Mrs Carstairs hesitated.

'I couldn't quite place him. It's rather difficult to explain. He certainly hadn't been to Eton, but I noticed that the very rough way he spoke wasn't altogether consistent. Now and again he talked in a much more educated way. My son noticed it too, and said he expected he was revolting against a conventional upbringing, working it out of his system by living like a hobo.'

Yes, thought Pollard, thanking her, this must be the thing... Back in their car, having taken leave of Constable Rodd, the two Yard men sat and looked at each other.

'So what?' said Pollard. 'I think we've now got to accept that Mullins was here round midday on July 30. This by itself makes a return visit to score off Bickley almost out of the question, and we've got the enquiry about the roundabout as well. I'm not altogether happy about writing off all the various resemblances between him and the skeleton as pure coincidence, but as things are, I don't think we've any alternative. Let's have a final look at the map.'

At the Cold Ash roundabout the alternatives to going straight ahead to Wintlebury or returning to Bridgeford were two less used roads. One went right, and ultimately rejoined the London road, while the other led to Torcastle and the far west.

'You could get back to Twiggadon that way,' Toye pointed out. 'I drew your attention to it on the way down, if you remember, sir. But it's a tidy way, and you can't count on lifts off the main trunk roads. As Inspector Crake said, these chaps like Mullins never walk if there's a chance of a ride.'

'We'd better put our money on Wintlebury, I think. I'll get on to them when we're back at Bridgeford, although I shouldn't think there's a hope after all this time, unless he's settled down there and become a respectable citizen with an insurance card and what-have-you. Or landed himself in jail, of course. Meanwhile, let's face it: Henry Stobart is our sole remaining suspect, simply on the strength of having been out in the Twiggadon lane at midnight, at a time when the very questionable Mrs Pendine claims to have seen moving lights in the car dump field. Well, here goes. We'll go home via Twiggadon, and you can go down and tell him that he's required to help the police in their enquiries at Bridgeford police station at ten tomorrow morning. If there's no answer, push this official letter we've brought under the door.'

'Very good, sir,' replied Toye imperturbably. 'What happens if he refuses, or says he's coming, and then goes off into the blue?'

'He won't do either, take it from me. All along I've had a strong hunch that Mr Henry Stobart has somehow got us on toast, and he'll enjoy an opportunity of demonstrating the fact.'

Punctually at ten o'clock on the following morning Henry Stobart strode into the Bridgeford police station, long staff in hand and waterproof cape folded over his left shoulder. He had refused the offer of transport, and made the journey from Twiggadon on foot. Apart from his unruly shock of grey hair he was presentably, if casually dressed, and altogether appeared more normal than on his home ground, Pollard thought, although his expression was unmistakably sardonic. He nodded briefly to Superintendent Puckeridge, and sat down, apparently at ease.

Pollard went straight to the point.

'I have your statement in front of me, Mr Stobart, in which you say that you have no knowledge of the circumstances in which the body of a young man was put into the boot of a car at Twiggadon. We are giving you an opportunity to amend this statement.'

Henry Stobart returned an unqualified negative to the invitation.

'Write that down,' he added, turning to Toye who was taking notes.

'Very well,' said Pollard. 'We'll now turn to the actual night of July 31 last year. Two independent witnesses state that they saw you walking down the lane towards your cottage just after midnight. Do you deny this?'

'No. I didn't deny it when you asked me the other day, either. That had better be written down too, to put a stop to police insinuations on the subject.'

'Hardly an insinuation, Mr Stobart. I asked you a plain question, to which you have returned a plain answer. We'll go on from there. If you had merely gone out for a short stroll, you would have been seen by one of the two witnesses on your way up the lane. Therefore I conclude that you had been out for some time. What had you been doing during this time?'

Henry Stobart, sitting with folded arms, fixed his eyes on the wall above the level of Pollard's head.

'No business of yours,' he replied. 'This country isn't a police state—yet.'

'Unfortunately it is our business. You know very well that we are investigating an unexplained death, which may be a case of murder. We have some reason to suspect that the

132

body may have been put into the car during the night of July 31, just before midnight.'

Watching Stobart closely, Pollard was almost sure that he was surprised by this information, and abruptly changed. his tone.

'Did you see a light in the field where the cars are, as you came past?' he rapped out.

'No,' Henry Stobart replied categorically, for the third time.

'You admit that you walked past the field, then? That gets us a bit further, doesn't it? The gate's at the top, so anyone who came out of the field could say truthfully that he'd passed it on the way down the lane. I suggest that you were also speaking the truth when you said that you hadn't seen a light in the field. You don't see a light you're carrying yourself : you see the thing it's illuminating. A dead body, perhaps, and an open car boot.'

'You can make what suggestions you bloody well like,' replied Henry Stobart, still staring impassively at the wall. 'Why not try to convert them into facts? Tougher proposition, no doubt?'

'If they are facts, we shall establish them all right,' said Pollard. 'I expect you know that cases are never dropped for lack of evidence at the time. If they are not facts, it's up to you to disprove them, but I suppose your fixation about your privacy makes it impossible for you to see the situation objectively.'

Unexpectedly, this aspersion on his ability to think clearly touched Henry Stobart on the raw.

'What the hell do you mean?' he demanded angrily. 'I may live on my own, but that doesn't mean I'm round the bend, let me tell you. I'm a damn sight saner than people who spend their lives rat-racing and jabbering their heads off.'

'Fine,' replied Pollard. 'Let's get on with it, then, and

finish with the jabbering ourselves. Disprove my suggestion that you were coming away from the car dump that night by telling us where you actually had been. It's as simple as that.'

There was a short, tense pause.

'If you must know,' Henry Stobart said laconically, 'I was on my way home from Dincombe.'

The reaction of astonishment which followed this statement was almost tangible. Superintendent Puckeridge smothered an exclamation.

'I shouldn't have thought you were one of the sightseeing ghouls, Mr Stobart,' he remarked.

'Quite correct, Superintendent.'

'I understand,' Pollard said, trying to suppress a rising excitement, 'that it was some days before all the victims of the Dincombe flood were identified, and I remember that details were widely publicized, with appeals to people who could help to come forward. Did you go to Dincombe with the possibility of identifying someone in mind?'

'I did.'

'Who was this person who you thought you might identify?'

Inspector Crake broke the silence which followed this question.

'Excuse me, sir,' he said. 'I was sent out to Dincombe to help in the emergency, as Superintendent Puckeridge knows. By July 31 there was only one body still unidentified—a young man's.'

'I'm sorry to probe into your private life,' Pollard said, turning to Henry Stobart, 'but you'll hardly be surprised to hear that we've been making enquiries about you. We know that your wife left you in 1950, taking with her your son, a boy of about six. He would now be in his early twenties. Was there something in the description of this young man's body which led you to think that it might be this same boy, now grown up?'

'Your deductions are perfectly correct,' Henry Stobart replied.

'Had you seen your son in the interval?'

'I had not.'

'Did you really expect to recognize him beyond doubt after so many years, especially under the circumstances?'

'Since the body was subsequently identified as a near relation by someone else, it seems that I was perfectly capable of arriving at a correct decision in the matter, doesn't it?'

Pollard experienced a curious sensation ... 'as if a dam in my mind had given a tremor, and was going to collapse at any moment,' he told Jane afterwards. He realized that he must play for time.

'I think that's all for the present, then, Mr Stobart,' he said. 'May he wait somewhere, Superintendent, while we type out the statement he has just made?'

'Check up with the Dincombe records?' enquired Puckeridge, as the door closed. 'Extraordinary yarn, but if he really went there, we'll have a note of it.' He pressed a bell on his desk in response to Pollard's nod. 'Bring the complete records of the Dincombe business,' he said to a constable appearing in response to the summons.

Inspector Crake, having disposed of Henry Stobart, arrived back at the same moment as several files were brought in. Pollard watched the flicking over of the pages, longing for some fact to emerge which would make the idea at the back of his mind formulate itself.

'We put out a pretty detailed description,' Puckeridge was saying. 'Five foot ten ... red hair ... three molars filled ... old angular scar faintly visibly above left eye ... old appendix scar ... about twenty years of age.'

Henry Stobart had applied to view the body for purposes of identification at 8.10 pm on the evening of July 31. He

135

had been taken to the mortuary by Sergeant Manley of Dincombe, and after careful scrutiny, especially of the scar on the forehead, had said that he couldn't put a name to it. He had signed a statement to this effect, giving his correct name and address, and had then left.

'Well, that's a bit of luck,' Puckeridge said. 'Manley's recently been transferred in here. Find out where he is, Crake, will you, and get him along as quickly as you can? I take it that you'll want him to identify Stobart as the chap who came to Dincombe that evening?'

'Sure,' replied Pollard. 'Thanks.'

He knew that the only thing to do was to concentrate on the matter in hand. It wasn't the slightest use trying to force an idea.

'Assuming that Stobart walked home from Dincombe,' he said, 'roughly how long would it have taken him?'

Maps were produced, and Puckeridge indicated possible routes.

'If he cut across country, avoiding main roads as he probably would, three hours wouldn't be far off the mark. He looks the sort of bloke who'd cover the ground with those great long legs of his.'

'He can,' said Pollard, 'I can vouch for that. I've seen him loping along. But if he did walk all the way back, it doesn't look as though there'd have been much time for stowing another body in the car boot, does it?'

He spoke absently, and realized that Puckeridge was giving him a puzzled look as the door opened to admit Inspector Crake, with a stocky middle-aged man in tow, whom he introduced to Pollard as Sergeant Manley.

Sergeant Manley had a capacious memory, but was irritatingly long-winded. He clearly remembered the incident of a tall grey-haired gentleman attempting to identify the last remaining flood victim at Dincombe, and that he had asked if there was any place open where he could get something to eat, as he'd walked over from Twiggadon and was going to walk back. He, Sergeant Manley, had been surprised that a gentleman like that hadn't a car, and had authorized him using the emergency canteen, although rightly it was only for—

Superintendent Puckeridge cut him short, and Henry Stobart, smiling sardonically, was ushered in, promptly identified by Manley, to whom he made an ironic bow of recognition, and escorted out again.

'What I'd like to know,' said Puckeridge, glaring at the closing door, 'is just what the old bastard's laughing at. He—'

'Sergeant,' Pollard interrupted unceremoniously, 'what reason did Mr Stobart give for coming to see the body? Who did he say he had thought the young man might turn out to be?'

Manley was maddeningly slow and deliberate.

'As I recall the conversation, sir, the intervening period of time notwithstanding, the gentleman told me that he felt there was a possibility that the body might be that of a relation of his wife's.'

The idea which had been hovering on the threshold of Pollard's consciousness suddenly took shape. It was so startling that he instantly decided to keep it to himself for the moment, but its corollary was urgent.

'What about the chap who eventually did identify the body?' he asked, trying to keep all excitement out of his voice. 'Who was he?'

'Gentleman of the name of Twentyman, sir. Mr Bryce Twentyman. Very unusual names, both of them, which no doubt helped to fix them in my mind. He identified the body at once as his half-brother, Stephen Finch. Mr Twentyman is a resident of Torcastle. For your information, sir, Torcastle is a town about—'

'Never mind about Torcastle, man. What was Mr

Twentyman like? Age, and so on?'

'I should be inclined to place him in the early thirties age group, sir,' Sergeant Manley replied in an injured tone. 'A well-dressed, pleasant gentleman in a good position. The branch manager of one of the big insurance companies, he told me. Just at the moment I can't quite call to mind—'

Puckeridge and Crake, several beats ahead, were searching through one of the folders in front of them.

'Here it is,' said the Superintendent. 'A full record was kept, of course. The Galaxy. They've got a lot of business in these parts.'

Pollard suppressed an exclamation.

'The chap from the Galaxy at Torcastle,' he said.

TEN

'*Algy met a bear,*' recited the Assistant Commissioner, eyes
closed, and leaning back in his chair at an angle of nearly
ninety degrees from the vertical.

'*The bear was bulgy.*
The bulge was Algy.'

Pollard listened respectfully. He had been summoned to
report on the Twiggadon case immediately on arriving in
London by an afternoon train from Bridgeford.

'You see my line of thought,' pursued the AC. 'There
are intriguing suggestions of dual personality in this case
of yours. The skeleton could be Steve Mullins. The young
man drowned at Dincombe last year has been identified by
Twentyman as his half-brother, Stephen Finch. Your fertile
imagination is advancing a theory that he was the illegitimate son of Henry Stobart's wife, a situation which has
enabled Stobart to enjoy misleading the police without
actually telling lies. Finch could be both, of course, but if
he rather improbably turns out to be Stobart's wife's by-
blow, unrelated to Bryce Twentyman, why did the latter
make a false identification? Was it an honest mistake, aris-
ing from a fortuitous likeness? After all, the body had been
bashed about in the water, and kept in the mortuary for
some days. Or had Twentyman some sinister motive, and

if so, what? I'd like to know what you are doing to get all this cleared up.'

'First of all, sir,' replied Pollard, hoping that he sounded more confident than he felt, 'we're searching at Somerset House for the date of birth of the boy presumably registered as Henry Stobart's son, and aged about six in 1950. At the same time Sergeant Evers is at the Ministry of Defence, collecting the details of Stobart's war service. If he was overseas for any length of time it might throw light on the legitimacy question. Then we're also checking up on the Twentyman family, and trying to find out if they're connected with the Stobarts, legally or otherwise. For instance, if Mr Twentyman senior had a child by Mrs Stobart, he would be Bryce's half-brother. I thought I'd get on to the Galaxy up here about Bryce. They must have vetted him pretty thoroughly before putting him into a responsible position. And everything possible is being done to trace Mullins. The trouble is that he may have been going under an alias.'

'Quite,' said the AC dryly. 'All these steps you're taking are perfectly sound, but apart from tracking down Mullins, have they got any bearing on your case? The sole link between Stobart and the skeleton, is that he was seen near the car dump one night just after a dubious and eccentric female says she saw a light there. Aren't you accepting this light a bit too readily, and letting it focus your attention on that particular night rather exclusively? There's no evidence that the body was put into the boot then. And the only link between Twentyman and the cars is that Bickley took him to look at them some time ago, when he wanted advice about his legal responsibilities. It's all a bit thin, you know.'

'I admit that, sir,' Pollard said unhappily. 'The fact is that there's so little to go on in the case that the only thing seems to be to check up on anything in the least unusual involving the locals. They are, after all, much the most likely suspects. But Mullins, at any rate, has a definite link with Twiggadon, and there are definite points of resemblance between him and the skeleton. We're doing everything we can think of to find out if he's still alive.'

'Reverting to your idea of contacting Galaxy House about Twentyman,' the AC said after a pause. 'I can help you along there. I know Lord Lympstone, their Chairman. I'll give him a ring right away : these companies are a bit sticky when it comes to enquiries about their people. Get an appointment yourself with their Personnel Big Chief for tomorrow morning.'

'Thank you very much, sir,' said Pollard gratefully.

The AC opened an eye and looked at him quizzically.

'Press on,' he said. 'It's the hell of a case, I grant you. But keep your eye on the ball, there's a good chap.'

Back in his room, heaving a sigh of relief, Pollard fell avidly upon the first findings of the searcher at Somerset House, which had just been telephoned through to him. On August 29, 1942, Henry Stobart had married June Chadwick by special licence at a London register office. A boy, Peter, was recorded as being born to the couple on October 15, 1943, and there was no registration of his death. June Stobart had apparently reverted to her maiden name on leaving her husband, and her death from injuries received in a motor accident had taken place eighteen months ago. No children born to her after the break-up of her marriage had been traced as yet, but the search was continuing.

Apparently irrationally, Pollard felt a sudden conviction that he was moving, however blindly, in the right direction. Picking up the receiver of his desk telephone he asked the switchboard operator to connect him with Galaxy House. An appointment made for the following morning, he rang his wife to say that he was on the point of leaving for home.

'Can you take it in your delicate state of health?' Pollard asked. 'I feel it might clear my mind to give you a summary of the case in words of one syllable.'

'Not so much of the one syllable touch,' Jane Pollard replied, refilling his coffee cup. 'May I remind you that I got three highgrade 'A' levels, and my headmistress took it hard when I plumped for Art School instead of the university. Let me fetch the tiny garment I'm knitting, and then you can go ahead.'

She settled herself on a settee with her feet up, and prepared to listen. Watching her, Pollard thought that she had never looked more vital and attractive ... that colouring, and that marvellous red-gold hair ...

'Twiggadon,' he began, 'is a small hamlet ...'

'Surely the percentage of odd people and happenings is a lot above the average in this case?' Jane said thoughtfully, when the long and complicated narrative came to an end. 'There seems no end to them. The skeleton, to start with. Then rootless boys who either vanish into thin air, or get drowned and stay unclaimed for days, and an extraordinary recluse like this Henry Stobart, and a witch like the Pendine woman. You'd hardly call Derek Wainwright an ordinary, everyday type, and old Bertha and the family feud simply aren't true. Even the Bickleys seem to have something to hide. There's so much of it that one can't believe there isn't a link-up.'

'That's just what I feel. Whatever the AC says about keeping one's eye on the ball, we're not going to get anywhere simply by concentrating on that hopelessly uninformative skeleton itself. Much more chance of discovering who it is, and how it got there by investigating some of these odd goings-on.'

'That reminds me, the witch has given the *Evening Flashback* an interview about ritual murder. It's over there, by the TV.'

'Good God!' Pollard leaped to his feet and fetched the paper. 'Can the Past claim a sacrificial victim in the Present?' he read aloud. 'Mrs Sybil Pendine, well-known spiritualist and creator of miracle-working herbal remedies and aids to beauty, whose cottage, aptly styled "Watchers Way", lies but a stone's throw from the scene of tragedy ... Heavens, there's yards of it. I hope I'm not responsible.'

'What on earth do you mean?'

'I suggested to her in so many words that finding a bigger market for her products would be a healthier way of earning her living than blackmail. Think what an advertisement this will be ... You know, she really has got something. No, I'm not joking. I didn't mean to tell you about it because I felt a bit of a fool afterwards, but there was a moment when she absolutely gave me the jim-jams. Remember my asking you over the blower if you'd been hanging curtains?'

Jane looked up at him with interest.

'Yes, I meant to ask you. What was it all about?'

'It happened the first time I questioned her She suddenly went all sibylline, and gazed over my shoulder, saying she saw a pregnant woman high up, with gold on her head, and a golden river flowing from her hands. You see, I've got an awfully clear mental picture of you looking down at me from the steps, that time I came in when you were hanging these curtains. You know how a single incident will stick in one's memory. I suppose she's some kind of thought-reader and managed to intercept it.'

'How simply terrific! I'm immensely gratified to think I made such an impression. My hair, too. Definitely one of my best points, don't you think? Were you afraid she was going to cast a spell on me? Was there any more?'

'Not about you. But when we went to see her again, to see if she'd sign a statement about having seen Stobart in the lane that night last year, I made the suggestion about trying to increase her sales. She seemed genuinely grateful, I thought, and announced that she had been born under Aquarius, and had some sort of affinity with water. She went on to say that water mattered a lot to me just now.'

'Curious,' said Jane, 'with this drowned lad suddenly cropping up in the case. Perhaps you ought to focus on him a bit. I don't think one can simply write off people like the Pendine woman.'

'Actually we are following him up in quite a big way. Not because of her, of course,' Pollard added hastily.

'Naturally not. What an idea,' she replied, looking at him out of the corner of her eye.

Galaxy House was a post-war colossus of concrete, steel and glass. On entering its portals on the following morning Pollard immediately recognized the type of interior decoration which Jane called overtones of good taste. There was elegant panelling, muted colour, and much skilfully concealed lighting. As he approached the imposing reception area with Toye discreetly bringing up the rear, he realized that he was to receive an inferior grade of VIP treatment. As they departed under escort in the direction of a special lift, he heard his arrival being communicated to a higher sphere.

They were shot upwards at breath-taking speed, and decanted into the arms of a preternaturally solemn young man who led them to a door inscribed MISS M. E. FOSTER : PERSONAL ASSISTANT TO MR J. L. HIBBERD. Within, a smart middle-aged woman rose to welcome them with a nicely-adjusted blend of graciousness and efficiency.

'Mr Hibberd will be entirely at your disposal the moment he comes out of conference, Superintendent,' she informed

Pollard. 'Coffee will be sent in to you in the Visitors' Room immediately. Mr Tothill?'

The young man ushered them through a communicating door, begged them to be seated and withdrew.

'Lush,' remarked Pollard, his feet sinking into the carpet as he made for an opulent-looking armchair. He gazed round appreciatively at some excellent reproductions of domestic interiors and rural scenes by painters of the Dutch School. 'Look at these pictures,' he said. 'A touch of genius. Security and comfort—solid comfort, too, linking up in the subconscious with insurance.'

Toye looked about him with an air of disapproval, and said that it was easy to see where your premiums went.

The coffee arrived on a trolley propelled by a young woman in an immaculate white overall, and was excellent. So, too, were the accompanying sandwiches. Pollard wandered over to a side table where copies of most of the national dailies were laid out for the entertainment of Mr Hibberd's visitors. He selected some of the more lowbrow, and read the latest comment on his case with a mixture of amusement and exasperation. After an interval of about ten minutes the door opened once more.

'Mr Hibberd will see Superintendent Pollard,' announced Mr Tothill.

Miss Foster was poised in the middle of her room, and rendered a variation on the theme.

'Mr Hibberd is now free, Superintendent. Would you be good enough to follow me?'

She led the way to another communicating door, opened it, announced him, and stood aside to let them enter.

After all this ritual Pollard was relieved to find a pleasant, grey-haired man apparently unconcerned about his image and the necessity of living up to it. He came forward to shake hands, and expressed genuine interest at meeting the CID.

10

'But I mustn't waste your time,' he said, as they settled into their chairs. 'I understand that you want some information about a young branch manager of ours, Bryce Twentyman, down at Torcastle. I think I ought to begin by saying that this is just a bit disconcerting : we think most highly of him. Is it in order for me to ask if he's fallen foul of the law in any way?'

'We've nothing whatever against Mr Twentyman,' Pollard replied. 'It so happens that we're working on a case which makes it necessary for us to enquire into his family history. I'm afraid I can't be more explicit at the moment. We've a searcher on the job at Somerset House, but thought you might be willing to be used as a short cut.'

'This is rather interesting. Do smoke, won't you?' Mr Hibberd held out a silver cigarette box. 'Or would either of you prefer a cigar? No? Well, to begin with, Twentyman is illegitimate. His background was unusual enough to stick in my mind, but I have his file here for any minor details you may care to have. He was brought up in an orphanage, the Pullinger Home for Boys.'

'Somewhere in Dorset, isn't it?' asked Pollard.

'Yes.' Mr Hibberd flicked a switch on his desk. 'The address and telephone number of the Pullinger Home for Boys, please.'

'Certainly, Mr Hibberd,' said a disembodied voice, followed by a click.

'You may want to contact them. They'd had him from infancy, and he'd done extremely well, getting a grammar school place and good GCE results at both levels, and had an excellent record in all other ways. He didn't want to go on to a university—'

'Your information, Mr Hibberd,' broke in the disembodied voice. 'The former Pullinger Home for Boys is now a co-educational establishment known as the Pullinger School. The address is Upperfleet Park, Upperfleet, Dorset.

Telephone number Upperfleet 149. Over.'

'Got all that?' enquired Mr Hibberd, with a glance at Toye. 'Well, as I was saying, Twentyman didn't want to go on to the university. There were funds available, quite apart from the grants he could have got, but he was anxious to become fully independent as soon as possible. The Pullinger people are very sound and enlightened, and sent him to a vocational guidance centre. The upshot was that he applied for a job here. We interviewed him, liked him, and took him on as a trainee. We've never regretted it. He's doing remarkably well, and I think I may say—off the record, of course—that there's a future for him in Galaxy if he stays with us.'

'Thank you,' said Pollard. 'That's all most helpful. Do you happen to know if Twentyman's mother kept in touch with him?'

'When he came here for his interview,' Mr Hibberd replied, 'I was careful not to introduce the subject of his parentage, and he didn't refer to it himself. Boys from homes and orphanages are always highly sensitive about not having had a normal background, you know. But there's a letter in his file from the Pullinger headmaster, in which he mentions that the mother married, and after this contact with the boy gradually petered out.'

'How absolutely damnable,' said Pollard with sudden heat. 'I suppose the headmaster didn't happen to mention her married name, by any chance?'

'Yes, I'm sure he did. Just a moment.'

The rustle and crackle of papers being turned over was the only sound in the quiet room, high above the roar of the London traffic. Pollard stared at the tip of Toye's pen poised expectantly above his notebook.

'Yes, here it is,' Mr Hibberd said. 'He refers to Twentyman's mother as Mrs Finch.'

* * *

On leaving Galaxy House Pollard dived into the nearest telephone kiosk and rang his searcher at Somerset House. He told him that Bryce Twentyman was illegitimate, and that his mother had subsequently married a man called Finch. It was urgent to find out if there had been a legitimate son of this marriage, born about twenty-one years ago, and registered under the name of Stephen.

'That ought to speed things up,' he remarked to Toye as they walked to a bus stop. 'All the same, even if Twentyman had a bona fide half-brother, it doesn't follow automatically that he was the chap drowned at Dincombe. There's something off-beat about that identification... here's our bus.'

'Of course,' he went on, as they nosed their way into a traffic block, 'if this Stephen Finch really existed, what would clinch matters is a reliable description of what he looked like. Birth certificates give the place of birth, and we would start tracing him from there. It rather looks to me as though his parents are dead. Otherwise, why was he identified by Twentyman?'

Toye agreed.

'Anyway, sir, it would be easier to get on his trail than young Stobart's, and to find out what he looked like.'

'Yep. But there were a couple of useful scars on the drowned boy's body, remember. I think we'll get the Sallowbourne chaps to have a go at hospital records in the area.'

Pollard relapsed into silence for the rest of the crawling bus journey, anticipating possible discoveries at Somerset House, and planning related courses of action. He resolutely refused to contemplate what he would do if every lead under investigation simply petered out.

Arriving back in his room at the Yard, he fell on the report of Henry Stobart's war service which had just come in. He snatched up the typewritten sheets and began to read, automatically pulling out his chair, and sinking down at his desk. Not daring to skip he ploughed through a mass of detail, his mind racing ahead in search of the statements which his hunch at Bridgeford had led him to expect. He came on them at last, and felt a tremor of excitement. Henry Stobart had taken part in the Allied landings in North Africa in November 1942, going through the entire campaign leading up to the capture of Tunis in May 1943. Thereafter he had served with the force invading Italy, and survived the Anzio landing, but only to be captured by the Germans. He had escaped during his transfer northwards, ultimately rejoining the Allied armies...

This is it, thought Pollard, searching for the note on the birth of the boy registered as Henry Stobart's son... Peter Stobart...born October 15, 1943...Mother: June Stobart, formerly Chadwick...Father: Henry Stobart, serving in HM Armed Forces...

Lighting a cigarette, Pollard sat back with a pardonable feeling of self-congratulation. It was, however, shortlived. Gratifying as it was to have a hunch confirmed, where exactly did it lead? Was it reasonable to assume that Henry Stobart had come home in due course, and accepted the boy as his? After thinking this over, Pollard decided that it was. In the chaotic state of Italy after the Allied invasion, and because of Stobart going out of circulation as a POW, it would be easy to maintain that news of the birth during the summer had never got through to him. In any case, most men were vague as to the size of young children during the early stages, and it varied a lot, too. If June Stobart had parents or friends who knew the boy hadn't been born until October 1943, they were most unlikely to give her away to her husband. But somehow, surely, it had come out in the end, and was the reason for the sudden break-up of the marriage, and the contracting-out of Henry Stobart from the normal life of a man in his position? One of those extraordinary chance meetings perhaps, or a need for the child's birth certificate?

Pollard suddenly thought of Jane, and their unborn child, and felt a wave of sympathy towards Henry Stobart. If all these surmises were correct, it was more than enough to turn a chap anti-social.

Bringing himself back to the matter in hand, he took a sheet of paper, and began to write slowly under the heading ESTABLISHED FACTS.

1. A youth giving his name as Steve Mullins was beaten up by Reg Bickley and disappeared two days later (July 30 last year).

2. No evidence has been found that he returned to Twiggadon for purposes of revenge, although he had threatened to do so, but there are definite points of resemblance between him and the skeleton.

3. A youth of approximately the same age, but from the available evidence very different in appearance, was drowned at Dincombe during the night of July 29.

This youth's body was inspected by Henry Stobart on the evening of July 31 for identification purposes. He stated that he had thought from the official description that it might be that of a relation of his wife's, but after seeing the body, said that he could not put a name to it. Curious wording?

4. The boy born to Mrs Stobart in October 1943, and registered as Henry Stobart's son could not have been his child, as he had been out of the country for almost a year.

5. The drowned youth was subsequently identified by Bryce Twentyman as that of his half-brother, Stephen Finch.

6. Twentyman is the illegitimate son of a woman who subsequently married a man called Finch.

7. Twentyman knew of the existence of the car dump.

So what, Pollard asked himself? He mechanically lit another cigarette, his eyes on the paper in front of him. Presently he took another sheet, headed it FACTS TO BE ESTABLISHED, and started to write again.

1. Did Twentyman's mother have a son by her husband, X Finch?
2. If so, what would have been his age at the time of the Dincombe flood?
3. What did he look like?
4. What did Peter Stobart look like, and had he any distinguishing scars?

It was a relief, he thought, to have got something down on paper, but the AC's Parthian shot returned to cause him discomfort, and conjure up the gruesome photographs of the still unidentified skeleton. The sound of Toye's step in the corridor was a welcome distraction.

'I got on to the school without any difficulty, sir,' the latter reported. 'There's been a new headmaster since Twentyman's time, and he's away on holiday in Switzerland. But I spoke to the Bursar, who was very helpful. He said that if we wanted to come down and make enquiries he could get hold of a retired member of staff who would have been there in Twentyman's time, and who makes a thing of keeping in touch with former pupils.'

'Thanks,' said Pollard. 'It's difficult to decide priorities at the moment, isn't it? Take a look at these lists I've just made.'

He pushed the sheets of paper over to Toye, who sat digesting their contents, impassive as an owl behind his horn rims.

The desk telephone suddenly burred. Pollard grabbed the receiver.

'Put him through,' he said, adding 'Somerset House', in an aside to Toye. 'Superintendent Pollard here. Go ahead.'

The receiver quacked at length, and Pollard scribbled notes.

'Jolly good effort,' he said at last. 'Yes, let me have it all in writing when you get back, but I'm glad to have the gist right now. OK.'

He put down the receiver and grinned at Toye.

'Twentyman was born in 1934. His mother was a Sonia Thomas, and the father an American salesman, also called Bryce Twentyman. A year later she married Percy Finch, described as a retail ironmonger, of Colsham, Midshire. There was only one child of the marriage, a son, born in 1944 and registered as Stephen Percy.'

'So he did exist, and was Twentyman's half-brother,' said Toye thoughtfully. 'Still is, perhaps, if the Dincombe identification was phony. Where do we go from here, sir?'

'Down to Colsham,' said Pollard, suddenly coming to a decision. 'There's something static about retail iron-mongery. I can't believe it will be all that difficult to track down the Finch family. Look up trains, will you? We'd better go tonight, to save time.'

ELEVEN

COLSHAM WAS a nineteenth-century industrial sprawl, drab and unconcerned with providing amenities for visitors. Pollard and Toye spent an uncomfortable night at the Station Hotel against a background of shunting and the hollow calling of diesels. Even breakfast, usually a redeeming feature of the worst British hotel, was half-cold and served at snail's pace.

'Tell the Manager from me,' Pollard said to the girl at the reception desk as he paid the bill, 'that he'll soon be putting the Hilton out of business.'

They took their cases and walked out, leaving her staring after them with a baffled expression.

A frustrating situation awaited them at the police station. One of the town's chief stores had been raided by a gang of expert thieves during the night, and the atmosphere was one of feverish preoccupation. Pollard tactfully said that he would look in again later, and suggested to Toye that they tried a bit of research at the Public Library. Here they secured the current traders' directory, and some of its back numbers, and withdrew into a corner of the reading-room. Working backwards they found that P. Finch: Ironmonger, was regularly listed until two years previously, after which time there was no further mention of him. The address given was 76 Alma Road, which reference to a street plan showed to be in a crowded area of what looked like the poorer part of Colsham.

Armed with this information they returned to the police station, and Pollard was able to put his request for help with a conciseness which earned the gratitude of the harassed Superintendent. Within half an hour they were closeted with a startled Constable Blackett, whose beat had formerly included Alma Road. Reassured by the Yard men's friendliness and lack of starch, Blackett rapidly regained his confidence, and proved a mine of information on the subject of the Finches.

Percy Finch, he told them, had died of a stroke a couple of years back. He'd been a proper old so-and-so, begging the Superintendent's pardon, an Elder of the Strait Gate Tabernacle in Ward Street.

'What on earth's that?' asked Pollard, much intrigued.

From Blackett's description they gathered that it was a local survival of the once-popular hell-fire sects, purveying a dogma consisting mainly of the condemnation of sex, alcohol, dancing and the theatre. It claimed inside knowledge of the virtual restriction of eternal salvation to its adherents.

'What did the rest of the Finch family consist of?' asked Pollard. 'Were they Strait Gaters, too?'

According to Constable Blackett they had had no option, Percy Finch having been an old tyrant. Mrs Finch, much younger than her husband, had died before Blackett's time, but it was said she'd been a poor creature, creeping around like a shadow. The boy'd had a hunted sort of look, too. Old Finch had grudged him taking up his eleven-plus place at the secondary school, and hadn't let him stay for his 'O' Levels, making him come back to drudge in the shop. Never let him off the chain, or gave him a penny to bless himself with, from the look of him.

'Where's this boy now?'

Disappointingly, however, Blackett could not tell him, having been moved to another beat just before Percy Finch's death. But he did know that the shop had been going downhill for years, and when everything was sold up there had been a lot of debts to meet.

'There must have been a lawyer to cope with the sale,' Pollard said. 'Have you any idea who it was?'

Blackett scratched his head, and opined that like as not it was Mr Jobsall in West Street, who did a lot of work for the poorer sort of people.

'We're anxious to have a description of young Finch. What did he look like? Height, and colouring, and so on?'

In common with so many people Blackett found great difficulty in giving a recognizable description of another human being. Stephen Finch had been on the short side, certainly not tall. Not dark or fair, so that you'd notice it. Eyes? Blackett couldn't call their colour to mind at all. A thinnish lad, and looking chivvied, as he'd said just now.

'Did he have red hair?' Pollard asked casually.

'No, sir.' Here at least, Blackett was on sure ground. 'I'd swear to that, sir. They always stand out, the carroty ones. Trouble-makers, too, most of 'em.'

Pollard and Toye exchanged a quick glance of satisfaction.

'What we really want is a photograph of the chap,' Pollard pursued. 'Any suggestions? Any girl-friend you can remember who might have a snap of him?'

Blackett was not optimistic.

'If he'd ever taken up with a girl, sir, his old man would have fair brained him. I shouldn't think he'd ever had his picture taken—not ever.'

Pollard proceeded to make Blackett a friend and admirer for life by giving him an outline of what lay behind the enquiry, and he and Toye then took their leave, to go in search of Mr Jobsall.

West Street had gone down in the world. Mr Jobsall's office occupied the ground floor of a once pleasant Victorian house, the front garden of which was now an untidy car port. His clerk, a worried little man, seemed startled by Pollard's official card, and hastily vanished into the back premises. He soon reappeared to say that Mr Jobsall would see the gentlemen.

The lawyer was bald and bustling, with thick spectacles, and an air of being a man who knew his way about. He eyed Pollard and Toye shrewdly.

'What d'you want to know about my late client?' he demanded, when the purpose of their visit had been explained.

'Nothing, sir,' replied Pollard. 'We've no interest in him. But we are anxious to trace his son Stephen, in connection with a case we're engaged in at the moment, and thought you might be able to help us if you had handled his father's affairs. I may add that we've nothing against Stephen Finch.'

'Whether you've anything against him or not,' replied Mr Jobsall, leaning back in his chair, and clasping his hands over his fat paunch, 'I can't help you. I've no idea where he is. Under the terms of his late father's will, he can't touch a penny of what was left to him—and it's precious little—until his twenty-fifth birthday. He was nineteen when his old man kicked the bucket a couple of years ago. When he discovered how the land lay, he told me he was pushing off to get a job somewhere else—he was fed up with Colsham. I knew he'd been kept on a collar and chain, and offered him a spot of good advice free gratis—which I'm not in the habit of doing, by the way. I told him to keep in touch, and report back for his lolly when it fell due.'

'Has he kept in touch?'

'Nope. Come in,' Mr Jobsall called, as a knock came at the door. 'Mrs Hill? Tell her I'll be free in a brace of shakes, Smith. Anything more, gentlemen? This business of mine runs on a quick turnover and low fees, to suit my type of client.'

'Yes,' said Pollard. 'One more thing. What does Stephen Finch look like?'

Mr Jobsall seemed momentarily at a loss.

'Nothing distinctive about him. Smallish. Looked a bit pinched, if you know what I mean. Old Finch was a skinflint. A bloody old diehard, too. If he'd had the sense to modernize his business it could've been a little gold mine.'

'Colouring?' persisted Pollard.

'Not one thing or the other. Medium. The sort of chap you hardly notice.'

'Red hair, by any chance?'

'Definitely not red hair. I've told you—a vague medium sort of colouring.'

Outside in West Street, Pollard and Toye looked at each other triumphantly.

'Two independent witnesses,' said Pollard. 'Smallish and indeterminate colouring. It's inconceivable that Twentyman could have mistaken a redhead of five foot ten for Stephen Finch. I *knew* the identification stank. Where it's leading us to I haven't a clue. I wish we could lay hands on a photograph, though.'

He had hardly spoken when, on turning into the main street of Colsham, they reached the office of the Colsham *Weekly Echo*, the windows of which were full of copies of the photographs in its current number. Activated by a single thought they halted in front of a group of self-conscious youths in bathing trunks, one of whom was holding a hideous silver trophy. Underneath it was the caption COLSHAM SECONDARY SCHOOL SWIMMING TEAM TRIUMPH.

'There's a chance!' exclaimed Pollard. 'Schools have a passion for having endless combinations and permutations of themselves photographed.'

'The teachers'll mostly be on holiday,' said Toye. 'The Education Office would know if anyone's about, perhaps?'

'With any luck we'll soon unearth somebody. Back to HQ, I think.'

They hurried along, dodging through the shopping crowds. Things had calmed down at the police station, and a telephone call was put through to the headmaster's private house. He was at home, and would go straight to the school to meet the Scotland Yard officers. Transport was laid on, and Pollard and Toye were driven through the side-streets and suburbs of Colsham to a cluster of modern school buildings in spacious playing fields. As the police car drew up, a middle-aged man smoking a pipe came down the steps from the front door, and introduced himself as Charles Willis, the headmaster.

Initially on the defensive, Mr Willis thawed on learning that none of his flock was in trouble in a big way. Pollard gave him a modicum of confidential information, a tactic which worked admirably. Records were speedily produced, Stephen Finch's dates established, and the iniquities of Finch Senior in cutting short his son's education enlarged upon. An immense, elongated photograph of the whole school, taken in the boy's last year, was uncoiled and weighted down for examination. Finally Mr Willis pointed to a face.

'That's Finch,' he said. 'A bit small to be much use, I'm afraid.'

'I expect we could get it blown up,' Pollard said, as he and Toye studied the photograph eagerly. He covered the neighbouring faces with his hands in an attempt to make Stephen Finch's stand out. 'I suppose he wasn't in any team which might have been taken separately?'

The headmaster glanced round the walls of his study, which were covered with framed photographs of groups in various types of games kit, together with their equipment.

'He certainly wasn't outstanding as a younger boy,' he said, 'and left so young, as I was telling you. I'll have a look through the games records, all the same.'

Pollard wandered round the room, and discovered to his delight that the school motto was actually *Mens sana in corpore sano.*

'That was a lucky shot of yours, Superintendent Pollard,' Mr Willis said suddenly. 'Finch was twelfth man for the Third Cricket Eleven in his last term. It's coming back to me now. His wretched old father bellyached like anything about the boy playing in Saturday afternoon matches. I believe that's why he took the boy away, so that he could work in the shop. Yes, here's the team photograph. Taken more from the point of view of morale than because of any athletic achievement, of course.'

He unhooked a framed group, blew the dust from its top edge, and brought it across to his desk.

'Here you are,' he said. 'This is Finch, poor chap. Not much to look at, is he? Eyes too close together for my liking. A bit rat-faced, too.'

As there was no reply he glanced up. Pollard and Toye were looking not at the photograph but at each other.

Later that day several people in Bridgeford unhesitatingly picked out Stephen Finch from the photograph of the Colsham Secondary School Third Cricket Eleven, and identified him as Steven Mullins.

'That's Mullins right enough,' said Mr Stentiford. 'Younger, o' course, an' wearin' 'is 'air short. Bit thinner, too, an' not so sure of 'imself in those days.'

Mrs Stentiford, interviewed separately, was equally decisive.

Mrs Cupple, located in the Red Lion just on closing time, burst into tears on arriving home and being shown the photograph.

'Thas 'im,' she said, experiencing some difficulty with her consonants and prodding with a fleshy finger. 'Thas Steve Mullins, pore boy. Done b'a gang. Shameful. Wash the perlish doin'?'

Trevor Cupple stared at the photograph open-mouthed.

'Woy,' he remarked at last, ''e said 'e'd been ter the Grammar.'

'Mr Cupple,' Toye said patiently, 'do you recognize anybody in this group?'

'Course I do. That's 'im.'

'That's who?'

'Blimey, Steve Mullins. Ain't I tellin' yer?'

'Cuh!' exclaimed Moyra Fox, who was hanging over his shoulder. 'Fancy pickin' up with a guy with a dial like that!'

Her prospective mother-in-law looked at her venomously.

Practising self-restraint, Pollard had not accompanied Toye, but remained at the police station to study the various reports which had come in. From Sallowbourne he learnt that no one had yet claimed to have any clear recollection of the Stobarts. There were some vague memories of a tall, funny-tempered husband, a young wife, and a little boy with red hair. The family had lived in a road of small houses where constant changes of population seemed to be the order of the day. A local newsagent remembered that the Stobarts had gone off suddenly, and there'd been talk about the furniture being sold as well as the house. The idea of enquiries at the hospitals of the district had, however, turned out a trump card. Patient research in the records of one of them had shown that a child called Peter Stobart, son of a Mr and Mrs Henry Stobart, of 5 Mellow

Way, Sallowbourne, had been admitted as an accident case at the age of three. He had fallen on the sharp edge of an open coal bunker, receiving two converging cuts above the left eye which required eight stitches. Two years later he had been in the hospital again, for the removal of his appendix.

There's no reasonable doubt that the Dincombe boy was Peter Stobart, Pollard thought. Surely Twentyman and Stobart must have been in cahoots. How could Twentyman have been sure that someone wouldn't turn up after all, and declare that the chap must have been a relation of theirs, and bring forward proof that whoever it was had been at Dincombe? Someone who'd been abroad or in hospital at the time of the flood. It would have been a mad risk to take, whatever the motive behind it...

Frowning, he turned to the result of the enquiry into possible local contacts of Henry Stobart, initiated by Major Preece-Rilby.

Henry Stobart appeared to be a quite familiar figure to the police within walking distance of Dincombe, but none of them had ever seen him call at a house, or meet up with anybody. If he went into a pub for a beer, he'd down it quickly, and push off again, without a word to his fellow drinkers. He was known to spend a good deal of time bird-watching in the remoter parts of the moor.

Pollard stared unseeingly at an out-of-date calendar hanging on the wall facing him. Twentyman would obviously have a car. Surely it would have been possible for them to have met in remote country lanes? But this didn't get round the difficulty of understanding how they were in touch at all. There was no family relationship, and no apparent link in the past. Besides, Stobart had been living a hermit's life at Twiggadon for the past fifteen years, while Twentyman couldn't have been branch manager at Torcastle for long, in view of his age

11

His thoughts straying to Toye and the photograph, Pollard was seized with impatience to know what progress he was making. Suppose he came back and said that Finch had been positively identified with Steve Mullins? Or that he hadn't, and they were back to Square One... Square One...

It was no good going on like this. He shook himself, and read a report on the mail received by Henry Stobart. A regular monthly registered letter from a bank in London... perhaps he'd sunk everything in an annuity? Letters with the name of some Nature magazine on the envelope. That would be the articles on birds which he was known to write. Rural District Council communications and a few circulars. Never anything looking like a private personal letter. And there was no phone at the cottage: Pollard had made a point of looking for wires.

Mullins. There was a brief report from Wintlebury, to say that they had nothing to report, but that enquiries were continuing.

Pollard stifled a huge yawn, and realized that he was desperately tired. No, he wouldn't ring Jane. It would only bother her, and you could never fool her by saying you were feeling fine.

Mullins—Finch—Twentyman—Stobart, and at the end of the line a skeleton which would always defy physical identification...

Afterwards, he realized that he must have dropped off for a few moments, as Toye was coming in at the door, a flat brown paper parcel under his arm, and the nearest approach to excitement on his solemn face that Pollard had ever seen.

'Finch is Mullins, all right,' he said almost breathlessly 'All of 'em picked him out and said he was Mullins almost before I could ask 'em.'

'So the skeleton can be Finch, Bryce Twentyman's half

brother,' Pollard said slowly, with the feeling of struggling out of the misty fluid world of anaesthesia into reality at last. 'And Twentyman—well, what are the odds that he's a murderer, with or without Stobart as an accessory?'

Toye, still holding the parcel, stared at him, transfixed.

'But what has all that business of the fake identification to do with it? It doesn't seem to make sense.'

'Doesn't it?' An indescribable expression came over Pollard's face as he sat with his hands gripping the edge of the desk. 'Remember what the kid said? Young Wainwright. He stuck to it that alias and alibi were the same thing. He said something to the effect that pretending to be somebody else was an alibi for the person who was really you. In this case, I rather think the idea was to scotch any suggestion that the skeleton in the boot could be Stephen Finch. In other words, the murderer tried to provide an alibi for the corpse.'

TWELVE

POLLARD WOKE irrevocably at six o'clock on the following morning. After a few minutes he decided to get up and go for a walk before breakfast : the weather looked promising, and he felt badly in need of fresh air and exercise. Dressing quickly he went downstairs, startling the night porter, who emerged from the back premises swallowing hastily, a bleary-eyed figure in shirtsleeves.

'OK,' Pollard reassured him, 'this isn't a flit.'

It was pleasant to step out of the enclosed stuffiness of the sleeping hotel into the crisp early morning, with the sun coming up in a clear sky, and a feeling of anticipation in the air. As if the curtain's on the point of going up, he thought, passing reticent windows. A black cat dropped soundlessly from a high wall like a spoonful of dark treacle, and melted under a gate. A car shot past the end of the road, the snarl of its engine quickly swallowed up in the silence. Turning left, he made for the sea front, which ran the mile length of Bridgeford Bay to the headland at the far end.

It was low tide, and Pollard went down a slipway to the beach. The sand was firm enough to walk on with comfort, and apart from a few dog-walkers he had the whole clean-washed shore to himself. He set off briskly for the headland under the impersonal scrutiny of the ranks of herring gulls lined up on the sea wall. At first he resolutely banished the case and all its attendant problems from his mind, surrendering to the sheer pleasure of space, silence and a peerless summer morning. But soon he realized that he wanted to get to grips with it again, and became absorbed in thought.

His moment of illumination the night before had been exhilarating, bringing for the first time the problems of the skeleton's identity and the bogus identification at Dincombe into a credible relationship. But, of course, there was not so far one single atom of proof that Bryce Twentyman had murdered Stephen Finch, or even that the skeleton *was* Finch. Moreover, it was never going to be possible to establish this latter fact through the physical characteristics of the skeleton. Therefore, the only possible approach was through an investigation of motive and opportunity where Twentyman was concerned.

On arriving at the headland Pollard stood absently watching the breakers creaming over the end of the long reef marking its former extension seawards. Obviously, he thought, turning for home, the next move was a visit to Torcastle to get all possible information from the local police about Twentyman ... It was an odd experience to suspect a man of murder whom one had never set eyes on ... They'd go over this morning. But above all, he mustn't rush things. It was vital that Twentyman shouldn't realize anything at this stage.

Then there was the problem of Henry Stobart's part in it all. His behaviour had been suspicious, to say the least of it. First, he'd declined to identify the body at Dincombe, and subsequently allowed Twentyman's statement that it was Stephen Finch to pass unchallenged. Did this imply collusion for some criminal purpose, or not? Could it be explained in terms of Stobart's warped outlook on life?

165

After further thought Pollard found that he thought it could. He decided that he had not given enough attention to the motive behind Henry Stobart's visit to Dincombe, an action so out of character in a man who had done everything possible to cut himself off from the rest of the human race. Hardly plain curiosity. Could it imply that Stobart had regretted the break-up of his marriage, and retained affection for the boy whom he'd believed to be his son? His sheer pig-headedness could quite well have prevented him from admitting this, even to himself. But the death of another person has a sharply clarifying effect on one's real feelings towards him ... Perhaps, when the description of the body with its distinctive scar was circulated, Stobart's long-repressed feelings came uppermost, and he felt that he had to know ...

Pollard decided not to tackle Henry Stobart at the moment : there were other more urgent lines of enquiry to follow up. As he reached the outskirts of Bridgeford, his thoughts shifted in the direction of the sojourn there of Stephen Finch, alias Steve Mullins. A significant point was the timing of his departure. If this had been with the intention of tracking down his half-brother, did it mean that he had only just discovered that the latter was at Torcastle? If he had already known this, wouldn't he have gone to Torcastle in the first place, instead of spending a month on a not particularly attractive job in Bridgeford, and living with the Cupples? Mrs Cupple had stated that he had come back on the Friday afternoon later than usual, and seemed to have made up his mind about something. Waiting at traffic lights, Pollard tried to imagine what this could have been.

Through one of life's more startling coincidences he was to find the answer on the opposite side of the road. As he walked across his eye was caught by the large gilded sign over the Galaxy Offices, and he paused to inspect the display window. Its central feature was a large map of the county, indicating the towns where the Company was represented. Each of these was shown by an illuminated circle, and Bridgeford itself, which contained the Area Office, by a larger one which attracted attention by flashing on and off. From each town a scarlet ribbon ran to a notice giving the address, and the name of the branch manager.

Pollard drew a sharp breath as he read.

TORCASTLE
24 High Street
Branch Manager: Mr Bryce Twentyman
At Your Service

This could explain it, he thought. Finch could have strolled around after his morning's work, and spotted the name. Surely he would have known his half-brother's name, and it's a pretty unusual one.

Cheered by what seemed an omen of success, he hurried back to his hotel, and returned to his room to make a more leisurely toilet. Then he descended to the dining-room and embarked on a hearty breakfast. He was well into this when an apologetic Sergeant Toye appeared.

'Sit down, and stoke up,' Pollard told him. 'There's quite a day ahead of us. I woke early, and thought I'd have a stroll along the beach, and do some thinking. This, roughly, is the upshot of it . . .'

Toye listened absorbed while doing full justice to the breakfast menu.

'Torcastle, then, sir,' he said with controlled enthusiasm, as Pollard's narrative came to an end. 'Reckon you threw that six we wanted last night.'

Before leaving for Torcastle Pollard called in at the police station to collect a photograph of Stephen Finch blown up from the one he had borrowed from the school.

'We'll go by way of Clysthead St John,' he said to Toye, as he rejoined him in the car. 'I'd like to try the photographs on those two women. Then we'll go on to Torcastle by way of the roundabout. That's the way Finch would have gone, assuming that he was the chap who got the lift and went to the Clysthead pub.'

Both Mrs Carstairs and Mrs Higgs were at home, and identified the photographs as the boy they had seen on July 30 of the previous year.

'He's quite a bit younger in these,' observed Mrs Higgs, 'and I'll say he hasn't improved with age, what's more. He's a misery here, but the time I saw him he'd got to look more crafty, like. You'll remember I told you I didn't care for the look of him. Would you be wanting Abel Haraway to see the pictures, sir?'

Pollard hastily disclaimed any such wish, and after thanking Mrs Higgs they took to the road again.

There was not a great deal of traffic on the Torcastle road, but Toye pointed out that it was early yet.

Pollard agreed.

'I think it's safe to assume that Finch could have thumbed a lift, and got to Torcastle that afternoon or evening.'

'Do you think he'd have gone to the Galaxy office when he arrived?'

'No, I don't. I think he was probably sharp enough to realize that he wasn't dressed for the part of the manager's brother, and would have tried to find out his private address. From the telephone directory, perhaps. We'll get it from the police. To save time, I thought you might go along and see what sort of place Twentyman lives in while I'm pumping the Super about him.'

Toye, who enjoyed sleuthing on his own, agreed with alacrity. They had left the hilly country behind them now, and were running through farmland in which rose-red soil set off the vivid green of grassland and the ripe gold of barley and wheat. In a surprisingly short time they were on the outskirts of Torcastle, and found the police station close to the centre of the town.

Here they were received with some surprise and keen interest by Superintendent Maggs of the County Constabulary. Over cups of coffee Pollard summarized the various developments in the Twiggadon case, and explained that he had come to ask for help.

'I'd like you to tell me everything you know about Bryce Twentyman, Super,' he said. 'Remember, I've never to my knowledge set eyes on the chap. And I needn't say how grateful I'd be for your personal opinion of him. Then, there's another thing. If Twentyman did kill his half-brother, it seems quite probable that it happened here. It's certain that Finch had left Bridgeford, and got himself as far as Clysthead St John, so it's unlikely that he returned there. And even if by a fantastic coincidence he thumbed a lift here from Twentyman, and was slugged in the car, the body might very well have been brought back here to be hidden temporarily. So while you're telling me about Twentyman, I thought it wouldn't be a bad idea if Sergeant Toye scouted round where he lives, if you'll give him the address.'

'I can do that easily enough,' Superintendent Maggs replied. 'I drive past the place every day; it's on my way home. You passed the entrance to the road as you came in, on your right. It's called Myrtle Avenue, and the house is Highmead. It was divided into two after the war, and Twentyman's got number two. And as you'll see, Sergeant, a damn good place it would be for a bit of dirty work. It's well off the road, sheltered by a shrubbery affair, and in a very quiet part, too. If I might put in a suggestion, the people who were there before him were called Raymond. Young couple with small kids. He was in the Inland

Revenue, and got moved to Wintlebury. If you run into anybody it might be handy to say they were friends of yours, and you thought they were still living there.'

'A jolly good scheme,' said Pollard. 'Thanks very much. Right, Toye. You push along, see what you can pick up, and I'll be around here until you get back, if Super-. intendent Maggs doesn't mind.'

Superintendent Maggs made it plain that, far from mind-ing, he was greatly enjoying this unexpected contact with a senior officer of the Yard. He was a big-featured man, with an impassive face, grizzled hair and keen eyes in which Pollard thought he detected an expression which intrigued him.

When Toye had departed they settled down to talk over cigarettes.

It transpired that the Torcastle branch of the Galaxy Assurance Company was quite an important one, catering for a large rural area as well as for the town itself. When Bryce Twentyman had been appointed manager three years ago some people had thought him too young. It soon be-came clear, however, that he was well on top of his job. He'd set about some sensible reorganization in a tactful way, and showed himself to be a real worker. Nothing was too much trouble, and he had soon begun to attract new business. People of all sorts liked him. He wasn't too grand to give proper attention to small clients, and managed to get on well with big ones, too.

'What about the social side?' asked Pollard. 'I should think that's quite important in a smallish place like this.'

Here, too, it seemed that Bryce Twentyman had gone down well. He was a good tennis player, to begin with, and was soon playing in the club first team. Good darts player, and ready to give anyone a game in a pub. Ready to wire in when it was a case of a local effort in aid of something or other. He wasn't a film star, but average decent-looking, anyway, and always spruce without being a cissy. And had the girls fallen for him—he could have had his pick of the marriage market, but hadn't been in any hurry, and careful not to get himself talked about. And now he'd done damn well for himself, getting engaged to Susan Bennett, whose old man owned the Torcastle Arms, the only decent hotel in the place, not to mention his other interests. And Susan was his only child, too.

'Why do you dislike Twentyman, Super?' Pollard asked him bluntly.

Superintendent Maggs looked slightly taken aback.

'Sticks out all that much, does it?' he asked with a rueful grin. 'Thought I was being completely objective. Well, it's not an easy question to answer. He's got plenty of good points, I'll grant you that, but I can't get rid of the feeling that every blessed thing the chap does is part of a planned operation to further his own ends. Putting it briefly, I don't feel he's genuine, and I'd never trust him. I don't mean over my insurance : you'd be safe there, because of his professional reputation. But over more personal matters, say.'

'What do you think his ends are?' Pollard asked thoughtfully.

'First and foremost to be a success. Rise in his firm, and hoist himself up into a higher social circle. Have the security of plenty of lolly behind him, and so on.'

'Do you suppose that he's told Mr Bennett that he's illegitimate, and was brought up in an orphanage?'

Maggs uttered an astounded oath, and looked really startled.

'I should have thought he'd've been out of the door on the toe of Jim Bennett's boot. And yet, I dunno. Susan's always had her own way, and Jim's a wily chap. He'd realize he couldn't stop it—she's of age, and you know what girls are these days. No, on second thoughts he'd make the best of it. Tie up Susan's money like grim death, and boost Twentyman for all he was worth. After all, he's got a lot of Jim's own qualities—drive and energy, and so on.'

'You think Twentyman wouldn't have tried to hush up his origins?'

'Not him. Much too canny. He'd know Jim would be on to it like a knife if everything wasn't out in the open. He'd play the honest straightforward bloke.'

'Being illegitimate is one thing,' said Pollard, 'especially if you've risen above it, and are getting on in the world. But the sudden appearance of a scruffy half-brother from a very different social level, and quite possibly on the run, is rather different, don't you think? Suppose Stephen Finch turned up that night, with a suggestion that as long as regular payments were made he'd keep out of the lime-light? He'd soon see by looking round the place that Twentyman was very much on the way up. I expect there's a studio portrait of the girl on the mantelpiece, don't you?'

'If Finch tried any little game of that sort,' Maggs said grimly, 'or even if he just turned up, I don't think it would be long before the idea of liquidating him struck Bryce Twentyman. Plain ruthless under his party manners, to my mind.'

While Pollard was closeted with Superintendent Maggs, Toye had driven to the neighbourhood of Bryce Twenty-man's house, parked in a side street a little distance away, and set off to prospect on foot. The drive gate of Highmead was open, and carried a board inscribed HIGHMEAD ONE and HIGHMEAD TWO. The drive itself was rather weedy, and flanked with a dense growth of laurels and other shrubs. Some trees met overhead, and the overall impression was that of a rather gloomy green tunnel.

Toye advanced quietly. Round a bend in the drive he

came on the house, medium-sized, square and solid, once a prosperous family house with a staff of servants. Just short of it the drive forked, one branch bearing right past a door marked TWO. Toye followed this branch round to the back of the house, and found that it led to a garage with a communicating door into the house itself, and a turning space outside. After listening intently he tried the door, and found it was locked.

He came out of the garage again, and stood looking about him, agreeing with Superintendent Maggs that the layout was ideally suited for funny business. Of course, much would depend on the sort of people who lived in the other half of the house, but anyone could come and go unobserved on foot as far as Twentyman's part was concerned. And although a car might be heard, there was only one window from which the inmates of HIGHMEAD ONE could see it.

As Toye considered these points he heard a door open, and walked round briskly to the front of the house. An elderly, bearded man was carefully depositing a suitcase on the step of HIGHMEAD ONE, and looked up.

'Do excuse me troubling you, sir,' Toye said politely, 'but I'm trying to find some people I met on holiday some years ago. They said they lived in Torcastle, and invited me to look them up if I happened to be this way. Raymond was the name. It is next door, isn't it? I can't get an answer.'

'Dear me! I'm afraid they don't live here any longer. What a disappointment for you,' said the old gentleman sympathetically. 'It was three years ago that they left, wasn't it, my dear?' He turned to address a white-haired old lady who had come out, walking slowly with a stick.

'Yes, three years ago last June,' she told Toye. 'They were such delightful neighbours, even if the children were a little noisy sometimes. So good to us in so many ways.'

'Neighbours make a lot of difference,' Toye agreed, seizing the opening. 'I hope you've been fortunate in the Raymonds' successors?'

'Indeed we have,' they replied in chorus. 'Most fortunate,' went on the old gentleman. 'A young insurance manager called Mr Twentyman. A bachelor, but he's just got engaged to a charming girl, and we're so afraid they may not stay here long.'

'Won't you come in and join us in a cup of tea?' suggested his wife. 'We can give you news of the Raymonds : we had a letter quite recently ... No, it would be a pleasure—we have so few visitors these days. You won't mind the house being in rather a muddle, will you? We're going off on our holiday in just an hour's time—our son's fetching us by car. Our name's Follett, by the way. And yours?'

'Tedburn,' improvised Toye. 'Gregory Tedburn.'

Hardly able to believe his luck Toye was soon seated at the Folletts' kitchen table, partaking of tea and biscuits. Thanks to Superintendent Maggs he was able to ask the right questions about the Raymonds, but the old couple needed very little prompting. They poured forth a steady stream of information in the manner of the elderly who have few social contacts.

It was not difficult to guide the conversation in the direction of Brycè Twentyman, and Toye listened to a positive litany of his virtues and endless kindnesses, the latter ranging from mending fuses and putting out the refuse bins to taking the Folletts for drives in his car.

'And do you know, Mr Tedburn,' Mrs Follett told him, 'Mr Twentyman gave me such a wonderful present last summer. Really, I was so touched I hardly knew what to say. It was a lovely new wheel chair. You see, I can't walk very far now because of my tiresome arthritis, and little outings are such a treat. We had one already, but it was the heavy, old-fashioned sort, and getting rather too much for my husband to manage. Neither of us are getting any younger, I'm afraid ... Dear Bryce must have noticed this, and the new one is as light as a feather. Made of aluminium, you know. It's made all the difference in the world.'

Toye experienced the mental equivalent of a severe electric shock, but managed to show nothing beyond polite interest. He remarked that an aunt of his had a chair of that type, and found it most useful, especially as it could be folded up and put into the car.

'I expect yours is going on holiday with you?' he asked casually.

'Actually no, as my son's neighbour very kindly lends one. So we are leaving mine here, in Twentyman's garage, next door. He very kindly lets us keep it there, as our garage is let. We don't keep a car, you see. Yes, it was this time last year when we came back from our holiday that we found the chair waiting for us—such a lovely surprise.'

Toye asked if they usually went on holiday at this time.

It transpired that they did. Their son and daughter-in-law took their own holiday earlier, now that the children were grown up, and so they were all ready for the old folk towards the end of July. Actually they were a little later than usual this year, as their son had had workmen in the house. This time last year they were just about coming home again ...

Wisely Toye did not enquire more closely into dates. Saying that he must not take up any more of the Folletts' time as they were going away so soon, he thanked them again for their hospitality and the news of the Raymonds, and took his leave. He resisted the temptation to pay a second visit to Bryce Twentyman's garage, and returned to the police station. He sent in a message to say that he had arrived, and within a few minutes Pollard joined him in the car.

'What have you been up to?' he demanded, as he got in. 'You look like a cat that's just put back a saucer of cream.'

'I've found the chair, sir,' Toye told him with a pardonable touch of self-satisfaction.

'Chair? Come again.'

'That first time we went over to Twiggadon, and took a look at the cars. You said that if an outsider'd brought the body by car, he'd have parked in the layby at the top, and run it down in one of those folding invalid chairs, all nice and quiet. Well, there's just the job in Twentyman's garage. I got on to it this way...'

'Good God!' Pollard exclaimed, as the story of the visit to Highmead came to an end. 'What absolutely staggering luck! Not that luck's much help unless you keep your head. It's one of the neatest bits of work you've ever pulled off, old son. The next thing is having a look at that chair.'

'You don't expect to get anything from it after all this time?' Toye asked, not very hopefully.

'I don't know. It's amazing what the backroom boys can do. Any mud the chair has collected round here would be this red stuff. If it was used up at Twiggadon, especially after a lot of heavy rain, the mud would be quite different. It's jolly difficult to get the underneath part of wheeled contraptions absolutely clean. Anyway, it's worth having a look. But if possible, I'd like to make sure that Twentyman's safely out of the way before we go up there. Look here, you go and ring the Galaxy office, and say you want an appointment. If he's going to be available this afternoon, be a bit vague about times, and say you'll look in on chance, which you won't do, of course. If they say he'll be out, try to pump them about when and where. I'll hang on here.'

Alone in the car, Pollard lit a cigarette, and began to chew over the morning's findings. Superintendent Maggs's opinion of Twentyman wasn't evidence, but it did suggest a possible motive for the murder of Finch. If you'd been deprived from birth, and fought your own way up, inch by inch, to the status and security others had as a birth-right, and had just pulled off a masterstroke by getting engaged to Susan Bennett . . . Then, completely out of the blue, Stephen Finch turns up, perhaps with every intention of cashing in on the situation, and becoming a perpetual menace hanging over you . . .

Pollard's thoughts turned to the lay-out of Highmead, as described by Toye, and the business of the chair. He wondered if it would be possible to trace the date of pur-chase. Had it been bought quite genuinely as a present for Mrs Follett, and simply come in handy? Or had it been bought after Stephen Finch's arrival, with the disposal of his body in mind?

After consideration, Pollard came to the conclusion that the chair must have been bought with the perfectly genuine idea of giving it to Mrs Follett when she returned from her holiday. Finch could not have arrived at Highmead until late on Monday, July 30. When had Twentyman identified the body of Peter Stobart as Finch? Searching through the case file, Pollard found that this had been done on Thurs-day, August 2. Surely Twentyman, in his role of zealous competent Galaxy manager, must have been quite abnor-mally busy during the early part of that week? The floods had by no means been confined to Dincombe. Rising rivers had led to widespread losses of stock and crops over the area, and claims must have come pouring into the office. If, into the bargain, Twentyman had murdered his half-brother, and had to evolve a plan for the disposal of the body, he'd hardly have had time to buy a present for an old lady. Anyway, it would have seemed a most curious thing for him to be doing at that particular time : quite out of keeping with his carefully-cultivated professional image.

At this juncture Toye reappeared. He had been informed that Mr Twentyman would unfortunately be away from

12

the office during the afternoon, as he had to visit a client some distance from Torcastle. He would, however, be available to see enquirers at any time on the following morning.

'Come on, then,' Pollard said, 'we'll go and have something to eat. I've had some interesting gen from the Super, by the way.'

At two o'clock Pollard decided that it was safe to go up to Highmead. Toye took the precaution of choosing a different parking place, but they found Myrtle Avenue deserted, and entered the drive unobserved. A reconnaissance showed that the Folletts had departed, and a ring at the door of Twentyman's house remained unanswered.

The wheeled chair was found without difficulty, covered with a tarpaulin, and leaning against the wall in a corner of the garage.

'Light isn't good enough in here,' said Pollard. 'Let's get it outside.'

They set up the chair in the bright sunlight, and examined it carefully. It was well made, of aluminium, as Mrs Follett had said, and was in good condition, obviously having been cleaned from time to time, but there were traces of red mud round the hubs of the wheels. They turned it upside down, and as Pollard had expected, an appreciable amount of dirt had adhered to its under surfaces, and in particular to those of the footrest.

'There's mud of a different colour caked round that left screw, sir,' Toye said, peering through a lens. 'Lightish brown.'

Pollard grunted, as he scrutinized the screw himself.

'Knife from the case,' he said, 'and a couple of pill boxes.'

With extreme care he removed a sample of the caked mud, and labelled the pill box to which he transferred it. The same procedure was followed with the red mud from several parts of the chair. They were just replacing the latter when he suddenly raised his hand in a warning gesture. The next moment there were unmistakable footsteps on gravel.

'May have to bluff,' Pollard breathed into Toye's ear.

They stood immobile, listening intently. There was the sound of a latchkey being inserted, and what appeared to be the front door of the house opening. The footsteps went briskly past the door leading from the garage into the house, but did not stop. Pollard jerked up his head, and they crept towards the exit into the garden. With a swift movement he retrieved his case, which he had left lying on the ground. There came the sound of windows being thrown open, the steps passed the inner door again, and were followed by the rushing of water down a wastepipe, and the familiar clatter of washing-up.

'Daily woman?' mouthed Toye.

Pollard nodded with a wry grin, and led the way quietly and swiftly across the open space outside the garage into the cover of the shrubbery.

'Damn careless of me leaving that case outside,' he said, as they wormed their way through the bushes. 'Lucky, too, that Mrs Mop doesn't let herself into the house from that door in the garage.'

They emerged cautiously into the drive near the gate, and after brushing themselves down walked out into the road.

'Back to the station?' asked Toye.

'Yes. We'll get these samples posted off to Wintlebury right away, and I'll see if I can get hold of Alan Pulman. With a bit of wire-pulling we might get a preliminary report phoned through to us tomorrow. We don't want a detailed chemical analysis at this stage : just an idea of the sort of area the brown mud has come from, if the boys can find out.'

This programme was duly carried out. Dr Alan Pulman of the Forensic Laboratory greeted Pollard like an old friend, and undertook to have the samples of mud dealt with as promptly as possible.

'Provided you come along when it's all over, plus the shouting, and tell me how you did it,' he stipulated. 'It's a peach of a case from the onlooker's point of view.'

'You're in for a long wait,' Pollard told him.

Alan Pulman uttered a disbelieving snort.

'What's the betting that the Yard's youngest Super will be hitting the headlines again in a week or two? I'm on! Be seeing you.'

He rang off, and Pollard came out into the passage, almost colliding with Superintendent Maggs, who was obviously in a state of barely suppressed curiosity.

'Got a few minutes to spare?' Pollard asked tactfully.

Returning with the Super to his office, he briefly described the discovery of the wheeled chair, the part he thought it could have played in the crime, and the steps he had taken about the samples of mud.

Maggs listened with rapt attention.

'Blimey!' he exclaimed. 'That Sergeant of yours is a smart chap. Head screwed on, too.' Pollard emphatically agreed.

'All the same,' he said, 'we're not within a hundred miles of making an arrest at the moment. There isn't a shred of evidence so far that Twentyman was anywhere near Twiggadon on the nights of July 30 or 31, or possibly August 1, and it's going to be damn difficult to get anything definite after all this time.'

'Of course you could charge him with making a false statement to the Dincombe police,' Maggs said, 'but he'd be granted bail, and might slip through your fingers. I tell you what. We'll look up the reports of our chaps on the beat those nights—beats including the Galaxy office and Highmead. There might possibly be something about a car coming in very late. Worth trying. Care for a cuppa while we're waiting?'

But to the Super's chagrin no information of any interest came to light.

'Mind you,' he said, 'it's a very quiet part all round Highmead, and a fairly big beat up there. The chances are that a car could have come and gone without our man seeing it. We'll do a bit of discreet ferreting for you.'

Pollard thanked him.

'We'll be along early tomorrow,' he said. 'I've asked Wintlebury to ring me here about those samples, by the way. Meanwhile, I've got to decide on the most convincing pretext for calling on Twentyman. I feel I can't take the enquiry any further without forming a personal opinion of him. But I don't want to put the wind up him if I can help it.'

After they had driven a few miles Toye glanced at Pollard, who was deep in thought, and asked if they should branch off on to the hilly minor road which would take them back to Bridgeford through Wilkaton, and past the Twiggadon lane.

'Main road all the way, I think,' Pollard replied, rousing himself. 'Sooner or later Henry Stobart will have to be tackled, but I'd rather concentrate on the best way to approach Twentyman just now.'

They drove on in silence. As they came up to the roundabout they joined the tail of a small queue of waiting cars. The Riley immediately ahead of them was indicating that it, too, was about to bear right. Pollard idly watched the light flicking on and off. Suddenly he was back again on the pavement outside the Galaxy office in Bridgeford, where he had stood that morning, and the map he had seen there rose up in his mind with photographic accuracy. As the car moved slowly forward he caught his breath sharply. He had been so absorbed in the information given about the Torcastle office, that he had disregarded the lines linking every branch office with Bridgeford. Mightn't it be worth while contacting the area manager? It was just possible that there would be some record of urgent claims investigated by Twentyman immediately after the disaster at Dincombe. If one could only get on to some of his movements during those days, perhaps it would lead to others . . .

'Stop at the first telephone kiosk we come to,' he told Toye.

It was almost half past five, but he just caught Mr Andrew Nicholl, the area manager, as the latter was leaving for home. Sounding slightly puzzled, he suggested that Superintendent Pollard should call at his private house that evening, when he would be glad to be of any assistance he could.

Caginess? Pollard wondered, walking back to the car, or just professional reticence? At best it was likely to be a tricky interview.

Mr Nicholl's house proved to be a pleasant modern one on the outskirts of the town, with a well-kept garden, and a general air of prosperity. He came out to greet Pollard and Toye as they drew up at the front door, and within a few minutes they had been ushered into a small study and provided with drinks and cigarettes. The area manager was somewhere in his early fifties, Pollard adjudged. He had a long, narrow, rather humorous face, probably a professional asset. There was unmistakable hardheadedness behind it.

'You're on the Twiggadon case, aren't you, Superintendent?' he enquired pleasantly. 'I must say I'm intrigued by this visit of yours. I've been racking my brains to discover how I can possibly come into it.'

'You don't, in any personal capacity, sir,' Pollard told him. 'If I may, I should like to start off by asking you a very general question. What, roughly speaking, is the degree of liaison between the Company's branch offices and their district headquarters, like yours here? For instance, are the branch managers allowed to make their own decisions on such matters as claims, or do they have to be ratified by you?'

'That, of course, depends on the amount of the claim and the circumstances. If it's a case of a lady dropping a lighted cigarette on a new frock, a branch manager would deal with it. But if a considerable sum of money was involved, say as the result of a fire, or if he had any hunch that there was something fishy he'd bring us in from the start.'

'I suppose you have general working principles in regard to claims?'

'Oh, certainly. We try to have a consistent standard throughout the country. For that reason, each area has regular monthly meetings at its area office. Any cases of interest are discussed, and branch managers have the opportunity of hearing the official point of view.'

Pollard felt a small stab of excitement.

'In the case of a disaster affecting the territory of several branches, would you then hold an emergency meeting? I'm thinking of a situation like that of the floods at the time of the catastrophe in Dincombe.'

'Would we not,' replied Mr Nicholl with feeling. 'My God, I shan't forget that week in a hurry! In answer to your question, I called an emergency meeting for the branch managers concerned—there were four of them, poor devils. I knew they were having the hell of a time, but it was obvious that very large claims were going to come in, and in any case I'd had my own orders from Head Office in London. Superintendent, just what is this in aid of?'

Pollard watched his glass being refilled.

'Thanks,' he said. 'Mr Nicholl,' he went on, 'I realize that this is most irritating to a man like yourself, but I've got to ask you to take this all on trust at the moment. I'm simply not in a position to be explicit. I expect it's one you're only too familiar with yourself in your profession.'

To his relief, Mr Nicholl gave him a friendly grin.

'OK,' he said. 'I'll stifle my natural curiosity, and be a model citizen, going all out to help the police. I realize you wouldn't be along here if it wasn't a serious matter.'

'I appreciate that,' Pollard replied. 'Now, I want you to tell me everything you can remember about that emergency meeting. Never mind how trivial it seems. Sergeant Toye will take it all down, so that we have your information to refer to. Will you start off with the actual calling of the meeting?'

Mr Nicholl leant back in his chair, frowned in concentration, and finally embarked on a careful and considered statement.

The violent thunderstorm which, after days of heavy rain, had led to the disastrous floods of the previous summer, had taken place during the night of July 29-30. Early on the 30th it was clear that catastrophic damage had been done, and Mr Nicholl had telephoned the London office. He had subsequently rung each of his branch managers in the worst affected areas, and an emergency meeting was arranged, to take place at Bridgeford on the following evening at eight p.m. It was felt that by then they would be able to give a fairly comprehensive picture of the situation in their respective areas. Realizing that they would have been under great pressure, Mr Nicholl had arranged for a working dinner at the Grand Hotel, after which the party had gone to the office to finish their business.

'Do you want the names of these chaps?' he asked Pollard.

'We may as well, while we're about it,' Pollard replied, hoping that his reply was no clue to the state of his feelings.

'Well, there was Mr Waring from Cranworthy—his beat includes Dincombe itself. He had already been over the day before, as obviously his area was the worst hit. Mr French came from Lutton, and Mr Hartland from Mardle. Then Mr Twentyman came over from Torcastle. He takes in quite a large rural area, and there'd been considerable damage to some of the low-lying farms.'

'I'd rather like to know,' Pollard said, judiciously selecting a red herring, 'the names of any really substantial claimants whose cases were discussed that night.'

'I'll have to refer to records for names and addresses, but I could let you have them tomorrow. Would that do?'

'Thank you. That would be most helpful. Could you send them down to the police station?'

Mr Nicholl replied that this would be done as soon as the office opened in the morning, and reverted to the subject of the emergency meeting. It had ended at about half past ten, after which the four branch managers had gone off thankfully in their cars, and he himself had staggered home after a fifteen hour day.

'Don't I know those days,' said Pollard. 'And I expect you won't be sorry to knock off now, seeing that it's Friday night. You do a Saturday morning session at the office, then?'

The conversation moved easily on to more general topics, and presently he rose to leave.

'I'm most grateful for your co-operation, Mr Nicholl,' he said, 'and I'll look out for that list tomorrow morning. No week-ends for us when we're on a case, worse luck. I'd like to see more of the country round here.'

'It takes a lot of beating,' Mr Nicholl agreed, as he escorted them to the car.

As they drove out of the gates Toye permitted himself a

low whistle.

'It's been quite a day,' remarked Pollard. 'First the chair, and now the emergency meeting which didn't break up till about half past ten. Honours easy, don't you think? How about dropping into a pub somewhere?'

THIRTEEN

HALF AN hour later Pollard and Toye returned to the Bridgeford police station, to be greeted by Superintendent Puckeridge with the announcement that the Chief Constable wanted a further conference on the Twiggadon case.

'Sorry, but tomorrow morning just isn't on,' Pollard told him. 'As it's Saturday, it's my only chance of dropping in on Twentyman at his office before the week-end shut-down. Listen : this is roughly the position.'

Puckeridge listened, impassively absorbed.

'Reckon the Major'll have to miss his afternoon round of golf,' he said. 'Why, you might have come to the point of wanting a warrant for Twentyman.'

'Unlikely. You realize that we haven't an eye-witness for a single thing connected with Finch's murder or the disposal of his body—if he was murdered, that is? We still can't prove the skeleton's Finch. It's all circumstantial evidence, and looks like staying that way for the moment. Will you fix up tomorrow afternoon, then? We ought to be back here by lunch time.'

Toye had vanished to type out the notes of the interview with Mr Nicholl. Pollard went back to their temporary office, sat down at the desk, lit a cigarette, and began to consider what the area manager had told them.

If Finch's objective had been Torcastle, it seemed reasonable to assume that he would have got himself there by the evening of Monday, July 30, going on from Clysthead St John. Since the emergency meeting had been arranged on the morning of that day, Twentyman already knew that he would have a legitimate reason for travelling to and from Bridgeford late on Tuesday night. A choice of routes was open to him : either the main road all the way, or the short cut which went over the moor and past the Twiggadon lane. Struck by a sudden idea Pollard unfolded the large-scale map of the district, and was poring over it when Toye came in.

'Just run through the names of those other branch managers, and where they're based,' he said, without looking up.

Toye consulted his typescript.

'Besides Twentyman himself, there was a Mr Waring from Cranworthy, a Mr French from Lutton, and a Mr Hartland from Mardle.'

'Come and take a look. Waring and French would have gone out of the town in the opposite direction, but Twentyman and Hartland would at any rate have started off on the same road. Here's Mardle. You turn off from the London road about four miles beyond the fork on the way to Clysthead and the roundabout. What's the betting that Twentyman stuck to Mardle like glue as far as the fork?'

'Making it look as though he was going home by the roundabout and the main road?'

'Yea. Then he'd turn back on his tracks when he'd shaken off Hartland, and take the minor road up to Twiggadon, going on home that way when he'd done the job.'

'Looks as though you're on to something there, sir.' Toye, an experienced driver, had an excellent bump of locality, and was studying the map with interest. 'Of course, he could have doubled back to Twiggadon from the roundabout-Torcastle bit of the road, but that'd take much longer. How does the other fit for timing?'

'This is it. If the Pendine was speaking the truth, she saw a light in the field "at midnight", and it went out shortly afterwards, whereupon she fell to the ground. Remember? Nora Pearce says she saw Stobart going down the lane "just after midnight". There's a certain amount of give in both these times, of course, but according to our reconstruction, Stobart must either have seen a car parked at the turning, or met it coming away. We'll have to tackle him again tomorrow, although it may be bashing our heads against a brick wall as before. However, let's go back to the timing question. How long would anyone take to get a body out of the boot of a car—and rigor might not have gone off completely—get it securely fastened into that folding chair, wheel the contraption down the lane and across the field to the dump, choose the most suitable boot and stow it inside. All this by moonlight and presumably with an electric torch.'

Toye sat deep in thought.

'I'd say not less than twenty minutes, and then he'd have to get back to his car and push off. It hardly seems possible that Twentyman could've gone out to vet the cars earlier on the 31st, so he'd have to do a bit of looking around. And be careful not to make a row falling over bits of junk.'

'That's more or less my estimate,' Pollard said. 'Now let's see how it works out. Mr Nicholl said that the meeting finished about half past ten, and Twentyman would have cleared out of the field by just after twelve, unless he collided head-on with Stobart, who flatly denies this ... Of course, if he heard Stobart coming and lurked in the field, according to us Stobart must have seen the car up at the top, blast him ... If my idea about Twentyman and

Hartland is sound, how long would it have taken Twenty-man to get up to Twiggadon after he'd shaken Hartland off?'

They returned to the map, measured distances and calculated.

'I reckon about fifty minutes for the whole trip,' Toye said, 'not allowing for a lot of hanging around when they came away from the meeting.'

'They may not have been able to park bang outside the Galaxy office. Say Twentyman drove off at 10.40. That would get him up to the turning at about 11.30 on our reckoning. Quite neat, isn't it? A pity it's all based on pure surmise.'

'What about going over the ground ourselves before breakfast tomorrow?' suggested Toye.

'Quite a good scheme. Anyway, it gives one the illusion of doing something. Come on, we'll just go over the Twentyman bits of the file again, and then we'll turn in.'

It was half past eleven when Pollard and Toye returned to their hotel. The night porter straightened up briskly from the evening paper, and asked if he could get the gentlemen anything.

'Nothing tonight, thanks,' said Pollard, 'but we'd like an early call tomorrow. Six o'clock. Could you rustle up some tea at that hour?'

'Just leave it to me, sir,' replied the porter in a conspiratorial tone. 'Your room numbers, gentlemen?'

They told him and went towards the lift under his speculative gaze.

Long experience had taught Pollard that nothing was more calculated to encourage insomnia than struggling to banish a problem from one's mind. Instead he would let his thoughts range freely over the case he was engaged on, without attempting to systematize them. On this occasion he switched off the bedside lamp, found a comfortable relaxed position and put his tried technique into practice.

As always after a day in which he had travelled some distance by car, hedges began to flow silently past his closed eyes. The bedclothes about him contributed to the enclosed sensation of being in a car ... It was curious how cars kept coming into the case. A picture formed in his mind of two figures standing by derelict cars. One of them was Reg Bickley, shirtsleeved and vociferous with indignation towards old Daggs and the public generally. The other, spruce but faceless, was listening attentively, registering the situation and offering shrewd advice ...

Two small fair-headed figures were clambering about in the car dump now, and wrestling with the handle of a boot. Through their joint efforts they were hoisting up the cover ...

A sharp distress roused Pollard to full consciousness again. He turned over, rearranged the pillows and relaxed once more. This time his thoughts drifted to Highmead. Suppose Finch had arrived there in the late afternoon of July 30. Unable to get into the house, he would probably have made himself as comfortable as he could in the garage, to await his half-brother's return. He would have been picked up by Twentyman's headlights as the latter drove in later than usual after an abnormally heavy day ... a slouching scruffy figure in the shadows. Had Twentyman recognized him at once, or had he established his identity through producing information about the family?

Pollard visualized the pair going through the door into the house. Would the garage doors have been left open? Later on they could have been closed quietly. Nothing would have been seen or heard from outside once they were shut. In a flash Pollard saw a possible answer to one of the problems presented by the case. The Folletts were away. No one would have heard a car engine running. Under a show of friendliness Twentyman could have suggested drinks. In the course of conversation Finch would begin to show his hand, his caution possibly diminished as a result of alcohol on an empty stomach. Twentyman, playing for time, would produce more drinks, laced with aspirin, perhaps, or sleeping pills. So many people had sleeping pills these days... With Finch flat out there would be time to think, to assess the situation, to weigh up risks and finally come to a decision. So easy to drag a doped Finch into the garage, and dump him on the floor close to the exhaust pipe. Then start up the engine. There would be no signs of injury, if only the finding of the body could be delayed long enough. A gamble, of course, but the stakes were high : a life ambition. After an hour or so, switch off the engine, strip the clothes from the body, and heave it into the boot. Lock the boot. The face must be made unrecognizable, of course, but not here. There might be—traces. The light from the house falling on the folding chair bought for Mrs Follett, the catalyst of the elaborate plan for the disposal of the corpse of Stephen Finch...

Hell, thought Pollard, how can we ever prove it? He broke into a sweat, and flung back the bedclothes. Presently the hedges began to stream past again, and the road unwound endlessly ahead. Would a dead weight in the boot affect the steering? Going round corners, for instance? Funny, there didn't seem to be—any—corners—

Just before half past six on the following morning the police car slipped quietly out of the hotel drive. The experimental timing trip was carried through without incident, and took forty-eight minutes.

'Time enough for the job, all right,' remarked Toye in a tone of suppressed triumph, putting away his notebook.

By prearrangement Toye took the initiative when they

arrived at the Galaxy office in Torcastle.

'Morning, Miss,' he said, advancing towards a personable young woman behind a typewriter. 'Happen your manager's free now? I rang you yesterday, and said I'd be looking in on chance.'

'That's right,' she said brightly, getting to her feet, 'I remember your call. He's got an appointment for eleven, but he's disengaged at the moment. Would you and your friend take a seat, please—What name shall I say?'

'Toye. Gregory Toye.'

She vanished up a staircase at the rear of the office. Toye cocked an eyebrow at Pollard, who nodded. They sat down on chairs grouped round a low table, on which a scatter of pamphlets about the Company flanked an ashtray and a bowl of marigolds. Voices were audible overhead, but words were indistinguishable. Pollard wondered why Bryce Twentyman was so persistently faceless to him. Usually his imagination conjured up a vivid mental picture of a person whom he was about to meet for the first time.

The young woman came tripping down the stairs.

'Would you come up, Mr Toye, please? Mr Twentyman will see you right away.'

Like the office below the manager's room was bright and business-like, but there were status touches appropriate to its rank in the Galaxy hierarchy: a square of haircord carpet, curtained windows and a couple of armchairs drawn up in front of the desk.

As Bryce Twentyman came forward smiling, with hand outstretched, Pollard's reaction was startled recognition. Then he understood his odd premonition of facelessness. This was the archetypal young executive, stepping confidently out of the photographs of a thousand advertisements, energetic, clean-limbed and fresh-faced. The eyes were alert, the hair impeccably sleeked, the whole turn-out immaculate, yet manly. The entire vigorous personality was focused on the impending interview, business acumen nicely blended with understanding of the client's particular problem and appreciation of his social standing . . .

He's wanted to become this sort of chap so much that he actually has, Pollard thought. His ordinary plain humanity and real self have gone under. This was what Maggs meant : everything's subordinated to maintaining this success-image . . .

They were settling into the chairs, and Twentyman was holding out his cigarette case.

'I don't think we've met before, Mr Toye,' he was saying. 'Are you from these parts, or planning to move this way, perhaps?'

'Actually, I'm the caller, Mr Twentyman,' Pollard said, taking his official card from his wallet. 'We didn't want to alarm the young lady downstairs.'

He held it out, watching professional caution flash into the other's face, followed by the descent of a blank mask. The thumbnail of the hand holding the card reddened from the pressure of the grip. After only fractionally too long a pause Twentyman looked up, smiling.

'Superintendent Pollard of New Scotland Yard? Why, aren't you investigating that extraordinary case at Twiggadon?'

'I am.' Pollard matched the easy pleasant tone. 'You must be wondering why we're paying you a call. Mr Toye is Sergeant Toye, also of the Yard, by the way. He's working with me. Well, we're here in the hope that you may be able to help us, of course.'

'I'll be only too pleased if I can, but I can't imagine how. This is most interesting.'

As if to intimate that normal business was being properly laid aside, Twentyman pushed his chair back a little, and rested his right elbow on the desk.

'First of all, do you know Twiggadon?' Pollard asked.

'Quite well. We have a client over there : Mr Bickley of Twiggadon Farm. He's a character. Have you met him?'

'I have. As you say, a character. I'm asking you if you know the place because we're interested in contacting any-one who was near it late on the night of July 31 last year.'

Just for a split second, Pollard thought, the resemblance to Stephen Finch was more marked : to the chivvied-looking Stephen Finch of the school photograph. Twenty-man flicked the ash from his cigarette with a certain deliberation.

'What makes you think I'm in that category, Super-intendent?' he asked.

'Because your area manager, Mr Nicholl, gave me a list of those attending an emergency meeting at Bridgeford that night, and your name was on it. Do you remember going over for it?'

'Remember? My God, I should think I do !' Twentyman replied with vigour, an unmistakable note of relief in his voice. 'None of us is likely to forget it. It was just about the last straw on top of two of the most ghastly days—Of course, you probably wouldn't realize that it was the time of the Dincombe disaster and the floods over half the county.'

'It certainly must have been a gruelling time for the insurance world,' agreed Pollard. 'Well, to return to the purpose of this call on you, we studied the map, and wondered if by any chance you came back here by the minor road over the moor which passes the turning down to Twiggadon?'

'Afraid not.' Twentyman, completely composed again, shook his head and smiled. 'It's shorter in mileage, but you can't get up any speed on it by night. Too many sharp bends. I stuck to the main road, and came round.'

'I suppose none of the others at the meeting would have come that way?'

'No, none of them. There were only four of us there besides Mr Nicholl, and two come from the other side of Bridgeford. Bill Hartland lives at Mardle, but that's off the London road. He was on my tail, actually, till he turned off.'

Pollard gave a small shrug indicative of resignation.

'Oh, well. Another possible lead gone west.'

'Surely,' Twentyman asked, with an air of intelligent interest, 'it's almost impossible to get reliable details of people's movements after so long?'

'Almost, but not entirely,' Pollard replied. 'If you happen to ask the right questions it's surprising how much people do remember. A chance encounter, for instance, which they've never thought of from that day to this. Still, I'll grant you that enquiries of this sort are difficult to the point of being frustrating. However, all jobs are at times, I suppose. That flood period must have been pretty tough going for you, for instance.'

'You're telling me!' As if grasping at the diversion, Twentyman elaborated.

Pollard watched him with interest as he listened to a competent account of the catastrophe, shot through with proper sympathy for the victims, yet ever subtly slanted to Galaxy's interests. This is where he feels secure, he thought, in this professional personality he's built up so successfully out of the anonymity of the orphanage. At a suitable moment he cut into the narrative.

'I believe you were personally involved in the disaster, too, weren't you?' he asked.

Twentyman nodded, looking down for a moment as he stubbed out his cigarette with slightly exaggerated thoroughness.

'It still doesn't seem quite real,' he said. 'You know—the sort of thing that happens to other people, and you read about in the papers. A young man the police couldn't get identified turned out to be my half-brother.'

'Did you know he was down at Dincombe?' Pollard asked conversationally, offering his own cigarette case.

'Thanks.' He hesitated, as he lit up, and then went on. 'I hadn't a clue. I really hardly knew him. I wasn't *persona grata* at my stepfather's house. It's an ancient chapter of family history which I won't inflict on you. But the awful part was that I didn't cotton on to the possibility that the unidentified lad might be Stephen for so long, and all the time he was being hawked round to everyone who turned up. We were simply swamped with claims pouring in, and I didn't look at a paper or switch on the telly for days.'

There was a brief pause.

'Entirely understandable,' said Pollard. 'In any case, surely it wasn't solely your responsibility? Weren't there other relatives?'

'I wouldn't know,' Twentyman replied tersely. 'I'd been out of the picture more or less from birth until the day of my mother's funeral. Apparently she'd expressed a wish on her deathbed that I should be contacted. I was an early lapse of hers, conveniently handed over to an orphanage. The funeral was the first time I'd met Stephen Finch and his father, and there didn't seem to be any other relatives there. Anyway, no one came forward. Afterwards I checked up on old Finch, and found he'd died.'

For a brief moment smouldering bitterness showed through the carefully cultivated mask of the successful young executive.

'A remarkable story,' Pollard said easily. 'It shows how loosely integrated society's become, doesn't it? A couple of generations back families hung together much more closely. Well, we mustn't take up any more of your time, Mr Twentyman.'

He got to his feet, Toye following suit.

'Sorry I haven't been able to help you,' Twentyman said, escorting them to the door. 'Naturally I'm interested in the case, knowing the place and Reg Bickley. He must have taken it hard—the car dump's like a red rag to a bull to him.'

'It's certainly an eyesore,' Pollard agreed as they shook hands.

On leaving the Galaxy office they walked towards the police station, silent for a few moments.

'It struck me as very significant,' Pollard remarked presently, 'that he sheered right off the question of the date. Ninety-nine people out of hundred would have asked automatically why we were interested in it, even if they knew we shouldn't give anything away.'

Toye concurred.

'Going into all those explanations about his past history, too, which wasn't any concern of ours on the face of it. Think we've rattled him, sir?'

'Not seriously, I think. He knows we can't identify the skeleton, and that we can't have proof that he was at Twiggadon that night. I'm not sure that we mayn't come to rattling him deliberately, in the hope that he might lose his nerve and do something incriminating, though I can't imagine what. My God, this is a bloody awful case, Toye.'

'Meaning so near yet so far?'

'Yea.'

They both relapsed into a gloomy taciturnity, and on arriving at the station found the news that the report on the mud samples had just been telephoned through from Wintlebury, a welcome relief.

The forensic laboratory stated that slides had been made, showing that the two samples were of different composition. Sample A, from the wheels and underside of the chair's footrest, was recent, comparatively moist, and consisted basically of red clay and grains of red sand. Geologically speaking it was typical of an area of Permian or Triassic rocks, such as that around Torcastle. Sample B, caked on to the screws on the underside of the footrest, was an older dried out deposit, consisting basically of coarse grains of a different type of sand, traces of a whitish clay and of peaty matter. It could be taken as representative of a granitic area.

'Here a little, and there a little,' said Pollard, putting down the paper, 'but unfortunately all circumstantial. However, it's no use just bellyaching. After we've put the CC and Puckeridge in the picture this afternoon, we'll go over to Twiggadon and have another go at the old bastard Henry Stobart. If he can't—or won't—talk, we'll run up to Town by a late train, and I'll put it to the AC about pulling Twentyman in on the charge of giving false information to the police. But you know, I shouldn't be surprised if he managed to wriggle out of it. Family history, and all that. And unless we could prove that it's linked with the murder, the false identification would have been so pointless that a mistake would seem the only possible explanation. He'd have quite a promising defence, and the Press would go to town on us.'

Initially Pollard had felt exasperated by Major Preece-Rilby's demand for another conference on the case, but as he set out the complicated unravelling of facts so far achieved, he realized that he was clearing his own mind and beginning to feel more cheerful. After all, quite a bit had been done from a virtually hopeless beginning . . .

'So you see, sir,' he concluded, 'I still have hopes of getting something out of Henry Stobart. Nora Pearce is a reliable witness, who says that she saw Stobart go down the lane just after midnight, and Mrs Pendine come up it soon afterwards. If there really had been a light in the field connected with the dumping of Finch's body, I don't see how Stobart could have failed to see a car, either parked near the turning or coming away. And we know that Twentyman could have been there at that time.'

'God!' exploded Major Preece-Rilby. 'Imagine driving round all day with a corpse in your car boot. The man's a hardened criminal! We've got to get him.'

Pollard reminded him once again of the total absence of proof, and was outlining his scheme of possibly returning to consult the Assistant Commissioner when there was a knock at the door.

'Come in,' called the Chief Constable impatiently.

A uniformed constable entered and saluted.

'Superintendent Pollard wanted on the telephone, sir. A Mr Wainwright of Twiggadon.'

'What on earth can he want?' exclaimed Pollard, uneasily startled. 'Excuse me a moment, sir.'

Derek Wainwright was hesitant and apologetic.

'I hope I'm not being a complete fool,' he said, 'but the kids came in with rather an odd story at lunchtime. After talking it over, Rachel and I thought perhaps you ought to hear it. Of course I know children romance, but one can usually tell ... anyway, it was a bit tame for an invention, if you know what I mean. Perhaps I'd better not go into details over the phone. Shall I run them over to see you?'

'No, don't do that,' Pollard said. 'I'm just coming out as it happens. And thanks for ringing me. What ...? Not at all, they're often first-rate witnesses at their age. We'll be along. Good-bye.'

He put down the receiver, and stood for a moment trying to analyse his sense of urgency.

FOURTEEN

A croquet set had been unearthed at Moor View, and the twins were being instructed in the game. On catching sight of Pollard, however, they downed mallets and came running. He was aware of irrational relief at seeing them safe and sound.

'Hullo!' he said. 'I hear you've got a report to put in.'

'This is it,' Philip told him excitedly. 'We had simply terrific luck being there just then.' He glanced round and lowered his voice. 'Someone's on H.S's trail. It can't be one of our people—they'd know all about him from N.P.'

Derek and Rachel advanced with slightly embarrassed expressions.

'I hope you don't think we're round the bend,' Derek said, 'but the chap the children met this morning—'

'Daddy!' they squealed in anguished chorus. 'It's *our* report! Please let *us* tell the Super!'

'I think you'd better have a private interview,' Rachel suggested, catching Pollard's eye. 'Then, if Superintendent Pollard's got time, we'll have drinks all together, and talk about it. I'm afraid the house is in a bit of a mess,' she added. 'We're beginning to collect up the china and glass and what-have-you that we're keeping.'

'We've actually sold the place,' Derek told him. 'At least

those people you saw here the other day have paid the deposit on it. They want to get in before the winter, so we've got to get cracking over the furniture.'

Pollard was congratulatory. It was extraordinary, he thought, how relief from tension seemed to add inches to a man's stature.

'I don't want to hold you up,' he said, aware that the twins were hopping with impatience. 'Perhaps Philip and Clare could report out here, and then we won't be in the way in the house?'

As soon as he and Toye were seated in a couple of garden chairs the two children flung themselves down on the grass, their hands clasped round their knees and their eyes eagerly expectant.

'Ladies first,' said Pollard. 'You begin, Clare. Look, Sergeant Toye's got his notebook out.'

'We were up in our secret observation post,' she said, bright pink with pleasure and shyness. 'With the b'noculars, and a car came down the lane and stopped outside the farm.'

'Dark blue Cortina,' Philip cut in, struggling to extract a small dog-eared notebook from the pocket of his shorts. 'I've got the number, S23Y48. A man got out and went in. To the farm, I mean. Time : twenty past twelve.'

'Was he there long?' asked Pollard, returning the ball to Clare.

'It seemed ages. We thought we were going to be late for dinner, so we came down, and went along to the bridge. Then he came out, and all of a sudden stood still and stared and stared. Not at us. Behind us.'

'So we turned round, and there,' said Philip, with a nice sense of the dramatic, 'just coming through the gap, was H.S., looking like a bl—'

'You mustn't say that word,' admonished his sister. 'Mummy said so.'

'We'll take it as said,' suggested Pollard, earning an appreciative man-to-man glance from Philip. 'Carry on.'

'Well, H.S. went into his cottage. Then, when the man noticed us coming up to the car, he asked who H.S. was. It was a bit difficult, not knowing whose side he was on, so I said we didn't know. And then Mrs Bickley came running out with a case the man had left behind, and bust everything.'

'You mean she told him Mr Stobart's name?'

'Yes, and lots more. All about him. How he lived there all by himself, and hated anyone going to the cottage, and went off bird-watching first thing in the morning, so he wouldn't meet people. She talks an awful lot. Mrs Steer who helps N.P. says she's a proper clacker.'

'What happened then?'

'Clare was tugging at me and saying we'd be late, so we went on and left them, but we heard the farm gate slam, and when we looked back the man hadn't got into his car. He was walking up the path.'

'Did he go to Mr Stobart's cottage?'

'No. We thought he would, and watched, but he went past it, and through the gap. We didn't think we'd see him again, but we did.'

'Where?'

'Up on top of Buttertwist. We saw somebody moving about on the flat bit when we got back here. Dinner wasn't ready after all, so we had a look through the glasses, and it was him.'

'Are you quite sure?'

Both children nodded vigorously.

'He had a light sort of suit on,' said Clare. 'It was awfully tidy for down here. Best shoes, too.'

'Collar and tie,' explained Philip. 'One of the long floppy kind.'

'What did the man look like?' asked Pollard. 'His face,

203

I mean?'

'Oh, nothing special.' Philip wrinkled his freckled brow. 'His hair was brown—I remember that. Not really long : he was too old for that, or a beard or anything.'

'Tall?'

'Just ordinary,' they said. 'About like Daddy.'

'Well,' said Pollard, 'this might turn out to be a very useful report, you know. You're a pair of helpers worth having, aren't they, Sergeant? Do you think your father would let us use your telephone?'

'What'll you bet?' he asked Toye, when the twins had run off excitedly.

'Looks a cert to me, sir. What the heck does it add up to, though?'

'That's what we've got to find out. Pronto, too.'

The Moor View telephone was in the breakfast-room. As he waited for his call to go through Pollard thought how quickly the house was losing its sleek stuffy opulence. Pictures had been taken down, leaving faded rectangles on the walls. There were bare dusty surfaces, and tables crowded with bric-à-brac and odds and ends. The end of an era, in fact . . .

The receiver suddenly came to life.

'Torcastle Police Station?' he said. 'Superintendent Pollard here, speaking from Twiggadon. Can you tell me if a dark blue Cortina, registration number S23Y48, is owned by a Torcastle resident?'

'Would you hold the line, sir? Happens a traffic warden's just come in.'

Pollard waited, tapping gently with his right foot.

'Superintendent Pollard, sir?'

'Go ahead.'

'The car in question belongs to a Mr Bryce Twentyman, sir. He's the manager of the local branch of the Galaxy

Insurance Company, in the High Street.'

'Thanks very much. Is Superintendent Maggs on the premises?'

'Yes, sir. Shall I put you through?'

'Please do, if he's free.'

'It may be a mare's nest,' Pollard told Maggs a few moments later, 'but it's just possible I may want some help later on this evening. I'd rather not say any more at the moment. I'm speaking from Twiggadon, by the way.'

He could hear heavy breathing, and sensed intense interest.

'OK,' came the would-be laconic reply. 'I'll be around here. Just give us a ring.'

'That's fine,' said Pollard. 'Thanks.' He rang off.

As they contemplated the precipitous face of Buttertwist from the track, Pollard pointed out a ledge about six feet below the toothy rocks of the summit.

'That's the flat bit the kids meant all right,' agreed Toye. 'I suppose there's a way up from the back.'

On going round to the far side of the tor they found that the ascent was an easy scramble. Above a mass of clitter forming a scree, tilted slabs of granite provided a natural staircase on a giant scale, leading up to the ledge. This was about four feet wide at the point of entry, narrowing to nothing in the direction of the cottage. The latter was not visible, owing to a projecting buttress running down the steep face of Buttertwist and causing the track to make a slight bend. The ledge was smooth bare rock, only slightly dissected by cracks. A solitary chunk of granite rested on it near the narrow end, about twelve inches by eight, forming a rough cube.

Pollard glanced upwards.

'I don't believe that could have fallen from the top,' he said. 'Surely it would have bounced off, for one thing?

Sorry, I'm proceeding on my stomach from this point. I've no head for heights—it's my secret shame. I could never coax down a roof squatter.'

He crawled along the ledge, and examined the chunk of rock carefully, tilting it on its side.

'It's damp underneath, and there are traces of what looks to me like soil. We'll get the gear and take a sample presently. You see what my mind's running on, no doubt... Now then, let's face looking over.'

Toye, also tactfully on his stomach, joined him, and they peered down at the track. Presently Pollard gave a grunt, and went into reverse.

'Let's sit down and think,' he said, his back against the rock wall and his legs out in front of him. 'Well, this is how I can see it. If I'd recognized Stobart as the rum-looking chap I'd met as I drove away from Twiggadon on the night of July 31, last year, and if I'd had a call from two Scotland Yard blokes saying how interested they were in that night, and had I come home that way, I'd feel that shutting the chap's mouth was a top priority. And when I heard that he was in the habit of setting out alone at first light along a track which ran under a handy precipice, really it would almost look as if it were meant, wouldn't it?'

'Accidental death from a rock fall,' said Toye thoughtfully. 'And the place littered with bits of rock. It mightn't even be possible to fix on the one that hit him. Sunday morning, too.'

'Yes. Bickley hasn't a big dairy herd, and probably takes an extra hour in bed on a Sunday, and holidaymakers aren't very likely to arrive out here at crack of dawn. Plenty of time to make a getaway, cutting across the moor to some lay-by where you'd left the car. Nothing unusual about camping out in a lay-by at this time of year. Risky, of course, but suppose the police get on to questioning the rum-looking chap?'

Pollard stared across to Skiddlebag, half-consciously identifying the twins' secret observation post.

'I think the next step is to see if Stobart will play,' he said. 'Do you know, I believe the idea might appeal to him. After all, he is an escaped POW, isn't he? I'd better tackle him alone, while you take a sample of the muck under that bit of rock. Then go down and wait for me in the car. We may want to call on the Bickleys.'

Although tall and well-built, Pollard had the gift of moving almost soundlessly. He arrived at the cottage door unnoticed. It was half open, and he put his foot over the threshold before knocking. Within there was hasty movement and an angry exclamation. The next moment Henry Stobart strode forward.

'Joke over,' remarked Pollard conversationally.

'What the hell d'you mean?' came the automatic response, faintly tinged with astonishment.

'Exactly what I say. We all have our idea of humour, haven't we? Blocking a murder investigation by witholding information, for instance. Don't, please, pretend you don't understand, Mr Stobart. It's such a bloody waste of time.'

'Why the hell can't you get on with your own job, and leave me alone? You're supposed to be finding out who put that stiff in the car boot, aren't you? My private affairs have nothing to do with it. I should have thought you could hardly have spared the time to come up here trying to be clever.'

'Actually, I am doing my job, which is basically the protection of the public. I have reason to believe that an attempt will be made on your life quite shortly, probably early tomorrow morning.'

There was silence. Pollard watched Henry Stobart's expression change slowly from incredulity to blank incomprehension.

'I'm perfectly serious, you know,' he said. 'I think you'd be well advised to let me come in, and listen to what I've got to tell you.'

To his astonished relief, Stobart turned back into the room with a gesture of ungracious acquiescence. He stepped inside, wondering if he were the first visitor to cross the threshold since the departure of Constable Haycraft's moving men from Epsom, fifteen years previously.

His impression was one of order and comfort. Defensive comfort, somehow, he told Jane afterwards. A stage set for a play about a man who knew he was going to be the only survivor of an atomic catastrophe. The feel of a dugout. Ample stores, neatly arranged on shelves at one end of the room. Books, and more books. A radio. A good chair, deep and comfortable. Realizing that he must at all costs retain the initiative, he went straight into action.

'You were very fond of your wife's son, weren't you?' he said. 'Even the discovery that he wasn't yours didn't kill your affection for him, did it?'

He watched the impact of this first spoken reference to the tragedy after long years of silence. It seemed to him that Stobart was finding the situation so incredible that he was temporarily beyond resentment.

There was no reply, and Pollard went on.

'That's what I find so difficult to understand,' he said. 'I mean, how, feeling as you did about the boy, you could have allowed his dead body to be used to cover up a crime.'

Henry Stobart reacted with a sudden violent movement of his whole body. His chair gave a protesting crack.

'What the hell are you talking about? Obviously the other chap made a mistake. What was the point of stirring up a lot of mud?'

'Of course I realize that the thought of the publicity there'd be if you came forward with the truth would be almost intolerable to you, but you were guilty of at least a technical offence in allowing Mr Twentyman's false identification to stand.'

Henry Stobart made it abundantly clear that this was a matter of complete indifference to him.

'Anyway, how can you prove that the chap did it deliberately?' he demanded.

'Quite easily, if we could have a light,' Pollard replied, picking up his brief-case.

Without speaking Stobart got up, struck a match and lit a petrol lamp. In sudden strong light he looked haggard and wild.

'These,' said Pollard, 'are enlargements of a photograph of Mr Twentyman's half-brother, Stephen Finch. I think they're a sufficient answer to your question.'

Henry Stobart took the photographs with a hand which was not quite steady, and examined them one by one. He flung them abruptly on to the table, and wheeled round, his eyes blazing.

'You said it was done to cover a crime. What crime?'

'According to our theory, murder.'

'Whose murder? That little rat's?' He indicated the table contemptuously.

'According to our theory, yes.'

Stobart stared at him, dumbfounded.

'My God!' he shouted. 'You don't mean that the skeleton in the car up there was this chap in the photograph?'

'That's the line we're working on.'

'And that swine Twentyman hit on the idea of identifying Peter as him?'

'It looks very like it to us. Neat, don't you think? A new technique for solving the corpse problem. You provide an alibi for your victim's body. Now, perhaps, Mr Stobart, you'll be prepared to answer questions about the night of July 31 last year in the spirit rather than the letter of the truth. I'm asking you if you saw anything that could have

14

been even remotely connected with a body being put in one of the cars in that field.'

Stobart sat down.

'There was a car,' he said briefly.

'Where?'

'On the main road. As I came up the last hill the head-light beams were coming over the crest. As I got to the top it was about a hundred yards away. I remember thinking it was making rather heavy weather of the gradient. Then it picked up, and shot past me. I was half-blinded by the lights, and didn't see what it was like, or who was in it.'

Pollard considered.

'Did you hear it starting up before you saw the headlight beams?'

'You couldn't hear a thing. It was blowing half a gale... Where's all this leading?'

'To the point that although you couldn't see the driver, he saw you all right, against the sky as you came over the top. You're a distinctive figure, you know, Mr Stobart, with your height, and those long arms and legs of yours. Not to mention your staff. And he seems to have recognized you again this morning, as you came home to lunch through the gap between the tors out there.'

As he watched, Pollard saw grim but pleasurable antici-pation appear in Henry Stobart's face.

'So you think he's going to try a bash at me, do you?'

'Don't get me wrong, Mr Stobart,' he said. 'This is a police job. You didn't let civilians take part in military actions in North Africa, did you? There's going to be a stand-in for you. Where you come in is over briefing us about your early morning routine. I'll be back with my sergeant when I've done a spot of urgent telephoning.'

Sitting beside Toye in the police car Pollard pointed out

that it would be impossible to be around all night without being discovered by Reg Bickley.

'Especially if a couple of extra chaps come over from Bridgeford,' he added. 'So we'd better risk letting him in on things up to a point, and hope we'll get the use of his telephone.'

As he locked the car, Toye remarked that if Stobart had been persuaded to play, anybody might.

The call at the farm began inauspiciously. As they opened the gate a posse of dogs streaked round from the back regions barking and growling furiously. Ruby Bickley appeared in the doorway, and on recognizing the visitors clapped a hand to her mouth. Simultaneously her husband thrust his head out of the kitchen window, and roared at the dogs. A sudden silence descended which he broke with a bellow which would have done credit to a bull.

'You ain't puttin' a foot inside my 'ouse without you've gotta warrant,' he informed them. 'Shut that door, Ruby, and bolt'n.'

The heavy front door thudded, and a bolt shot home.

'Good evening, Mr Bickley,' Pollard said equably. 'We can talk to you from here if you'd rather.'

Reg Bickley stated forcibly that he had no intention of conversing with him under any conditions, and made to shut the window.

'Just a minute, please,' Pollard said authoritatively. 'You may have got hold of the wrong end of the stick. A lot has happened since we were last here. For one thing, we're no longer interested in you in connection with our case.'

Bickley digested this remark.

'T'ain't good enough. Not by a long chalk. Think there 'asn't been talk? Long as you 'aven't copped the chap as did it, talk there'll be. About me. An' you in an' out won't 'elp matters.'

'There's a chance of copping the chap, as you put it,

tomorrow morning, round about dawn. If I can get local co-operation, that is. I need a telephone urgently. Are you prepared to let me come in and use yours?'

'This some ruddy perlice trick?'

'Come on, Sergeant.' Pollard turned away abruptly. 'We can't waste any more time here. We'll go up to Mr Wainwright.'

''Ere, I never said I wasn't lettin' you in,' shouted Bickley as they started walking to the gate. 'Open up, Rube.'

He withdrew his head as the door groaned on its hinges, and feet pattered hurriedly away over stone flags.

'Wife's upset, an' no wonder,' Bickley remarked, meeting them in the passage. ''Phone's in there.' He jerked his head in the direction of the kitchen. 'It's all yours.' He strode out into the back garden.

'Short, sharp and successful,' said Pollard, as Toye carefully closed the door behind them, and went to inspect another leading to a further room. 'Now for Torcastle, to begin with.'

In the intervals of his conversations, first with Torcastle, then with Bridgeford, and finally with Torcastle once more, Pollard was sharply aware of his surroundings. There was something suggestive of a fortress about the farm kitchen with its immensely thick walls and huge oak beams. Something timeless too, in the deep silence notched implacably by the steady tick of the grandfather clock as the little ship ploughed its way through the waves on its endless voyage . . . He felt unbelievably remote, isolated from the complex supporting machinery of the Yard, none of which could help him at this juncture. He'd got to go it alone, pitting mind against mind, and perhaps brawn against brawn in the last resort . . . As usual, he was finding the stage of closing in exhilarating, but shot through with panic. Suppose he was wrong about Twentyman from start to finish? Suppose the arrangements he'd just put in train ended in the utter bathos of nothing happening at all?

At this moment Superintendent Maggs came on the line again. Plans were checked once more before he rang off. Pollard put down the receiver.

'Got all that down?' he asked Toye. 'They've rung High-mead on the wrong number tack. Twentyman was there. His car's still in the garage: they've got a chap hidden in the shrubbery. If Twentyman makes a move, he'll ring us here from a kiosk at the corner of Myrtle Avenue.'

Reg Bickley was leaning against the back door, smoking a cigarette. As Pollard and Toye emerged from the kitchen he straightened up and came towards them.

'Thanks for the use of the phone,' said Pollard. 'There could be a call back anytime. May I sit in a corner some-where to wait for it? The rest of us can wait in the car.'

Bickley gaped.

'Rest o' you? 'Ow many'll you be?'

'Five, counting Mr Stobart.'

' 'Ere, what's bloody well 'appening? 'Tis my land, when all's said an' done.'

'We're expecting an attempted murder by the same chap. That's all I can tell you at present.'

Bickley slowly digested the information.

'What's wrong with our kitchen for the 'ole lot o' you?' he demanded at last, in the tone of a man whose hospitality had been put in question. 'The wife'll lay on a bit o' grub. Better'n outside. There's a smell o' rain. Reckon it'll let down b'dawn.'

'Decent of you,' said Pollard. 'Thanks very much.'

At a later hour Pollard was momentarily amused by the cloak-and-dagger appearance of the kitchen. Reg Bickley, unconsciously enjoying the role of host to the conspirators, sat at the table demonstrating local topography with assorted cutlery. His audience consisted of Toye, Inspector Crake, who had come over from Bridgeford with a constable, and, incredibly, Henry Stobart, whose re-entry into community life seemed to have passed unnoticed. In the background Ruby Bickley was playing the woman who keeps up a steady supply of food and drink. The constable sat at a small table dealing with a heaped plate, looking slightly dazed under the barrage of her conversation.

Ten miles away an unfortunate was keeping watch under decidedly less comfortable conditions ... Pollard was seized with fresh qualms. The chunk of granite could have perfectly well been taken up to the ledge for a giggle by hooligans hoping to frighten people passing on the track below. Or did Twentyman take it up to act out a wish-fulfilment, born of a sudden terror on seeing Henry Stobart again? Or had he really thought of killing him at first, but subsequently changed his mind, trusting that his luck would hold? All these possibilities could lead to one thing only—a ghastly deflating anticlimax.

In an attempt to exorcize these tormenting doubts Pollard walked across to the party at the table, and put them into words.

'What price our chap's thought better of it?' he asked.

They looked up at him with a surprise which was hardly reassuring.

'He'll hardly come till it's starting to get light,' said Inspector Crake. 'He's got to pick his way over the moor: no one would be fool enough to come down the lane past the houses and risk setting off the dogs here.'

Reg Bickley pointed out that this meant another couple of hours, and suggested they could all do with a bit of shut-eye. Ruby vanished upstairs, saying she'd be down before the telephone stopped ringing. The rest of them settled down in chairs. Pollard dragged his close to the telephone, and tried to relax. The electric light had been switched off, and a couple of candles left burning on the table. He tilted his head back and watched the faint animation of the shadows on the ceiling as the candle flames flickered in imperceptible draughts ... When he got home he'd take Jane out to dinner. They would go to that little Italian restaurant where you dined by candlelight ... He tried to picture the moment when the telephone would ring, keeping at bay the dread that it might keep obstinately silent until the moment when they rang from Torcastle to say there was nothing doing. He did not exactly fall asleep, but hung poised in a timelessness, from which he was jerked by someone giving an explosive snore. The fraction of a second later the telephone bell rang stridently; and he found himself grabbing the receiver ...

'It's on,' he said half incredulously, to a room suddenly full of bright light and people.

Outside, once his eyes were acclimatized, it seemed surprisingly easy to find one's way about. A faint sound indicated the opening of the cottage door, and he followed in the wake of Toye and Henry Stobart.

'Shut the door,' said the latter. 'I've blacked the place out.'

They synchronized their watches.

'Remember to slam the door like hell when you come out,' Pollard said to Toye, 'and make as much row as you can tramping along the path. Use the staff. And for God's sake jump for it when I yell.'

'I've got it all taped, sir,' Toye assured him.

'And take over that gun Mr Stobart's got in his hip pocket, and stop him from behaving like a bloody fool.'

'Very good, sir.'

Henry Stobart handed over a service revolver with a reluctant grin. 'Aren't our police wonderful?' he remarked.

'Be seeing you,' said Pollard, and went out.

He paused once again to let his eyes adjust themselves, and went quietly down the path, over the little rise and round the black forbidding mass of Buttertwist. Picking his way carefully over the clitter, he reached the foot of the rock staircase, and checked his cover behind a large boulder. Then he climbed up, suddenly feeling excited, and sat on the topmost step, facing away from the track and in the direction of the road as it curved towards Wilkaton.

A light drizzle was falling, and he shivered a little, but knew it was from tension rather than physical cold. Tiny sounds were magnified in the enveloping silence : the running of the stream, small stealthy movements, the stirring of a sleepy bird, and once a small, pitiful squeak, but his whole being was focused on the road which lay invisible beyond the intervening sea of darkness. Once he glanced eastwards, and fancied he could detect a pallor at the world's rim. When the first faint light came from the quarter where the road lay, his heart gave a humiliating bound. Then the light intensified and resolved itself unmistakably into the beams of a car's headlights. It slowed down, stopped, and suddenly disappeared.

Pollard gave a low whistle which was answered twice, climbed down, and went to ground. It was damp and uncomfortable, and he was glad of the sacks provided by Reg Bickley. Setting himself as best he could, he switched over to his sense of hearing.

It seemed an eternity before there were sounds of someone approaching. Then they became obvious enough to suggest a state of complete confidence. Feet squelched on a patch of boggy ground, there was a slight stumble and the rattle of a stone dislodged among the clitter. Then an unnerving nearness, when harsh breathing was audible. Faint noises came from the region of the stone slabs. Finally all was silent once more.

Pollard realized that he was holding his breath painfully, and released it in a long sigh. A glance at the luminous dial of his watch told him that it was ten minutes past four.

Ten past three by sun time, he thought. In half an hour Toye and Stobart would begin to move. He looked around and saw that form was tentatively emerging from the void of the dark. He watched the process gain momentum, and waited for the first trace of colour to manifest itself, all the while straining to catch the first sound of activity from the cottage.

It proved to be the screech of a window being thrown up. A good move, he thought. It'll alert Twentyman, and keep him from coming down and wandering around. Presently a door was noisily unlocked and flung back, so that it hit a wall. The throb of a small engine started up, pumping the water from the well behind the cottage. It struck Pollard in the midst of his preoccupations that Henry Stobart had really dug himself in very comfortably. Another longish interval followed, indicating that breakfast was being prepared and eaten. Finally the motor was switched off, the window slammed down, and a moment later a door was shut with such force that the impact echoed between the two tors.

Pollard was half-way up the granite slabs in a flash. He discovered that they were unpleasantly slippery from the light rain, and narrowly avoided a fall. Creeping upwards he heard the latch of the cottage gate click, and heavy purposeful footsteps on the track, punctuated by the jab of a walking stick on hard ground.

Hoisting himself noiselessly to the level of the terrace, he saw a figure lying towards the narrow end, slightly raised on its left elbow, and looking intently downwards and to the left. Its right hand steadied the lump of rock, now precariously poised on the edge.

As the footsteps drew nearer there came the prearranged burst of coughing from Toye, under cover of which Pollard advanced further. Then, as the figure's right hand moved, he gave a tremendous shout. A splintering crash below was followed by a yell of 'OK!'. For the fraction of a second he stood looking down into Bryce Twentyman's face, so contorted with frustration and rage as to seem hardly human. The next moment he was down beside him, desperately struggling to prevent him from flinging himself over the edge.

A torrent of obscene abuse flowed from Twentyman as he wrestled and fought like a madman, now intent on dragging Pollard over with him. With the feeling of being caught up in a nightmare, Pollard put out every ounce of his strength as they slipped perilously on the greasy wet rock of the narrow ledge. He shouted for help, wondering as he did so if it could possibly come in time. As he made a supreme effort to drag Twentyman back, pulling him on top of his own body, while trying to keep the clutching hands from his throat, he was at last seized and securely held.

There was a confusion of voices. He saw that Twentyman had gone limp, and was lying with trickles of saliva coming from the corners of his mouth... The stuffing's running out of him, he thought, still slightly bemused... As if he wasn't a real person...

'No, I'm perfectly all right, thanks,' he said, surfacing. 'Get him down off this bloody deathtrap, and into the car, and I'll charge him.'

FIFTEEN

'YOUR REPORT fascinates me, Pollard,' said the Assistant Commissioner, opening an eye. 'The entire investigation based on a half-baked woman's claim to have seen spectral lights on Lammas Eve ... What's happened to her, by the way? Is she still giving the Press interviews on the case?'

'Not that I know of, sir. She seems to be launching out commercially. There's an arty-crafty sign outside the bungalow announcing THE HOME OF HEDGEROW HERBALS. And I hear she's been asked to broadcast on local folklore.'

'Good God! Well, the least you can do is to become a regular customer.'

'I admit it was a bit unorthodox, sir. But as the chap Bickley had beaten up had vanished into thin air, and Derek Wainwright petered out as a suspect, there simply wasn't another lead to work on. Not that I'm satisfied with my handling of the case.'

'Why, what's biting you?'

'Chiefly the feeling that I ought to have pulled Twentyman in sooner. It was pure chance that the Wainwright children saw him around that morning. If they hadn't, Henry Stobart would almost certainly have been killed.'

'He'd only have had himself to thank,' said the AC unfeelingly. 'He ought to be charged with deliberate obstruction. No, I don't think I agree with you about pulling in Twentyman. A clever Counsel might very well have persuaded a jury that the identification business was simply a mistake. After all, on his own showing Twentyman had only seen Finch once. And with that disposed of, the murder charge wouldn't have stood up. The evidence was almost entirely circumstantial. Even the attempted murder of Stobart is, up to a point, although it pulls your case together. Still, as Twentyman's certain to be pronounced unfit to plead, it's all of academic interest now. The thing that matters is that a killer like him won't be in circulation. In my opinion you've done a good job, Pollard.'

'Don't eat too much of that cake,' said Jane Pollard. 'I've got something rather special for supper, to celebrate ... As I said before, you do land out-of-the-run interesting cases, don't you?'

'This one's all right in retrospect,' her husband said indistinctly. 'It was hell to work on, though. All the elusive dead ends, and that grinning unidentifiable skeleton as a sort of backcloth all the time.'

'Interesting people on the whole, though. Some of them likeable, too, from what you say.'

'Not the Pendine,' said Pollard with unusual vehemence. 'Even now the idea of her intercepting my private thoughts about you gives me the willies. And Twentyman was a spine-chiller.'

'I suppose something must simply have snapped when he realized that you'd caught up?'

'It felt like a pathetically small-scale version of the Faust theme,' he said. 'Just as if he'd bartered his soul long ago for status, and then it was suddenly settlement day.'

'The thing that strikes me as so odd was his going to Twiggadon that Saturday. I mean, there wasn't any business reason for it, was there?'

'None whatever. I asked Ruby Bickley if he'd given any reason for calling at the farm, and she said she'd wondered at the time why he'd troubled to come out on a Saturday morning about some insurance scheme against foot and mouth, which wasn't in the least urgent.'

'But do murderers really revisit the scene of the crime?' Jane asked. 'I thought that idea'd been exploded.'

'Not altogether. You see, I think all murderers are paranoiac to some extent, and certain that they can get away with it. Deliberate murderers, I mean. Then the shock of discovering that the police seem to be uncovering their trail completely unnerves some of them, and they get the feeling that they must go over the ground and check up, however pointless this is. I'd underestimated the amount we'd rattled Twentyman.'

'What's the latest report on him?'

'Apparently he's still completely inert. He doesn't take anything in, or show the slightest initiative. And dribbles. Horrible!'

'Here, have some more tea, and try to get him out of your system. Tell me what's happening to Henry Stobart.'

'Thanks, I think I will.' He gave her his cup. 'Old Henry's definitely coming up to breathe. Lending Reg Bickley a hand, and so on. So perhaps the whole beastly affair has done some good, over and above removing Twentyman from the scene.'

'It certainly has in the Wainwright circle. You know, I could never have married you if I'd thought you were the sort of man who needed constant psychological nursing. Your robust appearance and unflappability weighed with me a lot. Perhaps I'm subconsciously the clinging type.'

'Can't say I've seen any sign of it so far,' he told her between gulps of tea. 'I'm encouraged, though. Sometimes I wonder if you're finding me a very humdrum bloke. And reverting to Derek Wainwright and his financial inadequacy complex, I should have done a lot better in terms of £.s.d. in Big Business.'

'Haven't you grasped by now that I don't hanker after mink and luxury cruises? But I'm awfully glad about the Wainwright money. She must have had a tough time. I'd like to meet them. They sound our sort of people.'

'As a matter of fact,' said her husband, a tinge of self-consciousness in his voice, 'in a weak moment I told the twins I might be able to show them my room at the Yard when they came up to Town.'

He glanced up to find Jane looking at him quizzically.

'You sure fell for those twins in a big way, didn't you?' she said. 'What a relief!'

Pollard sat up abruptly, and seized her hand.

'Darling, you don't mean . . . ? Not really?'

She nodded, her eyes dancing.

'Isn't it absolutely super? No possible doubt whatever. I've had an X-ray!'

Best-selling fiction in Tandem editions

Edith Pargeter's memorable trilogy
of medieval England and Wales

The Heaven Tree 60p
The Green Branch 55p
The Scarlet Seed 55p

Romance and history combine in a swift-moving story of border warfare, power politics and private feuds on the Welsh border in the reign of King John.

'A highly dramatic and intense story, beautifully written'
Glasgow Evening Times

Elizabeth Lemarchand

Death of an Old Girl 45p
The Affacombe Affair 45p

Two first-class detective stories featuring Chief Detective-Inspector Tom Pollard of Scotland Yard, and sure to appeal to anyone who enjoys Agatha Christie.

'A superbly told tale or blackmail and terror'
Manchester Evening News

'A real genuine police detection story . . . a hundred per cent winner'
Sunday Times

Catherine Cookson

Hannah Massey 45p
The Garment 45p
Slinky Jane 45p

Compelling and moving novels, set in the North Country which Catherine Cookson has made famous.

'In an age when so much rubbish is published and writers are two a penny, Mrs Cookson comes as a boon and a blessing. She tells a good story. Her characters live'
Yorkshire Post

Name ....

Address ....

Titles required ....

....

....

....

....

....

....

- - - - - - - - - - - - - - - - - - - -

The publishers hope that you enjoyed this book and invite you to write for the full list of Tandem titles.

If you find any difficulty in obtaining these books from your usual retailer we shall be pleased to supply the titles of your choice upon receipt of your remittance.

Packing and postage charges are as follows:

U.K. One book 18p plus 8p per copy for each additional book ordered to a maximum charge of 66p.

B.F.P.O. and Eire 18p for the first book plus 8p per copy for the next 6 books, thereafter 3p per book.

WRITE NOW TO:
Tandem Publishing Ltd.,
14 Gloucester Road,
London SW7 4RD

A Howard & Wyndham Company